I0773996

Lethal Lettuce

Terry R Cooper

Visit our website at www.terryrcooper.com for more information.

Printed in the United States of America.

ISBN 979-8-9879139-8-7

1 2 3 4 5 6 7 8 9 10

CHAPTER 1

Thursday, April 27

I pulled to the curb and stopped, dropping the scooter's kickstand into a couple inches of rain runoff. It was still drizzling, but I didn't have to look for the house address. I'd been delivering an eighth-ounce of weed to the Chesters every Thursday for nearly a year.

After collecting their order from my scooter cargo bin, I headed across the driveway and up two creaky wooden steps to the front door. Their knockoff doorbell camera winked its red light, letting me know I was being recorded. I rang the doorbell, glad to be under their stoop and out of the fading drizzle for a few minutes.

I flipped up my helmet visor and waited. Ray and Kay Chester were in their sixties, always friendly, and glad to chat. I'd rather have been on my way to my next delivery so I could get home and dry, but tips were my livelihood and chatting increased my financial gain.

They were always a little slow to answer my ring, but after a minute, I rang the doorbell again. I could hear the ding-dong sound inside the house. And there was a cat meowing just inside the front door. I remembered they had two cats.

Thinking they hadn't heard the bell for some reason, I rapped on the door and called out, "Delivery." The cat continued to meow. I noticed it pawing at the bottom of the door sidelight. It looked sick. Thin. Not something I wanted to pet.

The Oregon delivery laws of cannabis prevented me from just leaving the order by the door. I had to hand it to a human who matched their ID and collect the payment. This stop was taking way too much time. I thought about dropping the order back into my bin and moving on, but the Chesters were nice, friendly people. I wanted to go the extra mile for them. They were the kind who rewarded for that.

I cupped my hand to the sidelight glass. The cat stood on its hind legs, pawing at the glass, and meowing pitifully. From the window, I could see a big swath of the living room. No lights, no TV, no people. Down the hall, I could see a sliver of kitchen. A light was on in there, but I couldn't see anything else but cabinets and tile floor.

As I started to turn away, movement caught my eye. There was something moving on the floor. I slid to the edge of the sidelight for a better viewing angle. It was an insect flying around near the floor. Several of them. Big flies. And they were landing on something on the floor, but I couldn't see enough to figure out what it was.

The cat pawed at the sidelight again. I glanced at it, then back to the kitchen. It was the face of the other cat on the floor. The flies were swarming in and out of its mouth.

Fire shot through my brain. The cat on the floor was dead. Had been for a while. Which meant the Chesters could be dead, too. Or gone. But they wouldn't leave the cats alone, and they didn't seem the type to hire a pet sitter. Their old Toyota pickup sat in the driveway.

I took another glance at the cat with the flies. Definitely dead. And there was something dried on the floor next to it. My stomach lurched. I turned and barfed into the boxwood flanking the steps. A rookie move, but it was my first real crime scene. And real dead bodies. Not like the labs in my college criminology classes with dummies, fake blood, and contrived situations.

My brain, along with some of my training, kicked in. I needed to call this in. To the police.

I stuffed the order into my coat pocket and dug out my phone. I'd never called 911 before. My sudden nausea had calmed down after I barfed, but my heart pounded in my chest. I took a couple of deep breaths. Then I punched 9-1-1.

CHAPTER 2

The woman on 911 wanted me to stay on the line, but I had things to do. I called Gage, my store manager, and told him the situation. He asked for the address and said someone would be by to pick up the other orders and complete my deliveries.

There was something creepy about this whole situation. The hair on my neck was doing a dance and my palms were sweating. I knew my adrenaline rush was causing that, but still, my brain wasn't clicking quite right. If the Chesters were like the cat on the kitchen floor, I was gonna be questioned for days by the police. A gem of information from my criminology classes popped into my head—my memory of events, like the memories of every witness, would become faded, confused, and inaccurate over time. I needed to document everything.

I hustled out to the street and took several pictures of my scooter with plenty of background so it was clear where it was parked. Given the hubbub I anticipated, I decided to get it out of the street. I wheeled it up over the curb and parked it in the driveway behind Mr. Chester's truck. I noticed his license plate expired this month. Maybe today was his birthday. I took a picture of his license plate with my scooter in the foreground. I opened my delivery bin and took a picture of each of the remaining nine items to be delivered. Then I took pictures of the Chester house, the front door, the cat now lying on its side by the sidelight, and finally zoomed in as best I could to get a picture of the dead cat on the kitchen floor. I thought about going around the house and looking in the kitchen window, but I was afraid of what I might see. Still, I wanted to document all of this…just in case. I didn't know in case of what. But something told me I was going to need the information, particularly if this was a homicide. You could never have too much detail in a homicide.

I dashed around the house, squishing in the wet grass, and pulled myself over the old wooden fence. The kitchen had one of those stuck-on greenhouse windows. It was three-sided, had a sloped upper panel, and protruded from the house by eighteen inches. I slid between a couple of bushes that framed it. I didn't want to look inside. I didn't want to see anything. But I took a dozen pictures with the phone held to the glass, trying to guess where to point and frame so I got pictures of as much as possible, without looking.

A siren wailed in the distance. I retraced my steps, climbed over the fence, and brushed some leaves off my jeans. By the time I got back to the end of the driveway, a police car squealed to a stop. There was a big number twenty-seven painted on its roof. The guy from the passenger side climbed out and said, "You the one who called 911?"

I nodded.

His partner walked up and stood six feet to the left. He took out a pad and pen. "Name?"

"Buck Buchanan."

He started scribbling. He asked for more of my information—address, phone number, etc.

The cop said, "Why are you smiling?"

"You guys have body cams and audio recording. But you still take notes on paper."

"So?"

"Nothing. Sorry." I didn't want to piss these guys off, but really, they had full audio and video recording of our conversation, and some guy was taking notes, too? Seemed like a colossal waste of time to me. I thought they'd feel the urgency I did to get into the house.

The cop writing the notes, whose badge had the name Copeland, held out his hand. "Driver's license, please."

I fished it out and handed it to him.

"What's your name again?"

"Buck Buchanan."

"Not what this says."

I grimaced. "Legal name is Cody Buchanan, but I go by Buck."

"Why?"

I shrugged. "Cody never fit."

He looked at me for a moment, glancing back and forth between my ID and me. "Next time a cop asks your name you tell him your legal name, not some handle of the day." He pulled out a phone and snapped a picture of my ID, then handed it back. "Feel better?"

I glanced at the passenger door guy. His badge said Gonzalez. He said, "Tell us why you called, Mr. Buchanan."

I recounted my story about trying to make my cannabis delivery and the meowing cat at the side panel glass. When I told them about the flies and the other cat on the kitchen floor, they seemed to perk up.

Officer Gonzalez said, "Did you try to open the door?"

"No."

"Didn't touch the handle. Just rang the doorbell?"

"Yes. Probably some handprints and maybe nose prints on the glass where I looked through."

He glanced at my sneakers. "Okay. Would you mind sitting in the back of our cruiser while we have a look in the house?"

"Why?" I didn't want to be locked up in their car. From my training, I knew a witness was unreliable, particularly one who calls 911 and is hyped on adrenalin. But I didn't want to get wrapped up in their investigation any more than necessary, and I needed to steer clear of becoming a suspect. If they put me in the car, it was a sure sign they didn't trust me, and the thought of being put in the back of a police car at a crime scene scared the crap out of me.

"It would be safer and quicker for us. Otherwise, we have to call a backup squad in and that could take time. If there's someone in there who needs help, I'd like to get in there as quickly as possible."

"I can just wait here. I won't run off." I glanced at their car. My stomach gave another twitch.

Gonzalez sighed. "Let's say there's a murderer with a gun in there, kid. He comes out blasting everything and everybody. We need to protect you 'cause you're our only witness. If you sit in the cruiser, he won't see you or shoot you." His eyes opened wide, and he leaned towards me.

I knew this was intimidation, but it had the desired effect. My stomach objected again, and I farted, hopefully silently.

I did not want to be locked up in the back of his cruiser. Still, I saw his point. It made sense. I shrugged. "Okay."

Gonzalez took my arm and led me towards their car. "That your scooter?"

"Yeah."

"What's in the bin on the back?"

"Deliveries."

"How many?"

"Nine."

A fire engine pulled up in the street, red lights flashing. Like ants, a stream of firemen exited and began moving towards the house.

"Where's the delivery package for this address?" He opened the back door of the car.

I pulled it out of my pocket and showed it to him.

"Keep it for now. Duck your head and climb in. Regardless of what we find, we won't be gone long." He shut the door and walked away.

I'd never been in the backseat of a police car before, but I knew the door was locked. Still, I tried it.

My phone buzzed. It was the shop. I didn't want to talk to Gage right now.

The police radio chattered with conversations between units and the dispatcher. I stared out the window, watching the two policemen walk up the sidewalk with a line of firemen behind them. As they got to the front steps, the radio chatter caught my ear. "Unit twenty-seven, hold for further instructions." Both policemen stopped. Gonzalez reached to his shoulder mic. I could hear him on the radio. "Roger. Holding." They stood there for a minute or so, almost back-to-back, one watching the house front door and the other watching the street and the line of firemen.

Two black Chevy Suburbans pulled up. One parked in front of the police car and the other behind. A pair of black-suited people got out of each vehicle. One of each pair stayed at the curb by their vehicle while the other two paired up and approached Gonzales and Copeland.

The people in the suits, a man and a woman, showed black wallets that I presumed was their ID. They chatted briefly, then Gonzalez and Copeland walked back to their car. Gonzalez looked angry. He opened my door. "Get out, kid. These guys are taking over."

I climbed out, Gonzales slammed the door, and climbed into the front seat. They pulled out, did a U-turn, and disappeared around the corner. The firemen marched to their fire truck and disappeared inside. Their lights went out, and they drove off down the street.

The woman walked up to me and showed her badge. It didn't have a name on it. There was an ID above the badge with her picture, but she didn't leave it open long enough to read.

"I'm Marshal Massey. You called 911?"

"Yes. I was trying to deliver an order and no one answered. I looked…"

She held up a hand. "Save it. Stay here. And stay off your phone." She waved a hand towards a Suburban. "They'll stay with you."

She turned on her heel and she and the man from the other Suburban walked up the driveway to the porch. The woman, Marshal Massey, pulled a key ring from her coat pocket and unlocked the door. That surprised me. Marshals. Federal. I tried to remember which agency had marshals. Not FBI. Not CIA. Then I remembered: Department of Justice. U.S. Marshals. Why would the marshals have a key to the Chesters' door?

The cat, lying by the door staggered out between Massey's legs. They ignored it, pulled on gloves and masks that covered their nose and mouth, then disappeared inside.

I glanced at my two chaperones. They were watching the cat. It was weaving down the driveway like it was drunk. Its mouth kept opening like it was mewing, but it wasn't making any sound. When it got to the sidewalk, it looked both ways like it was crossing a street and checking for traffic. After a moment, it walked across the sidewalk and flopped down in the grass directly in front of me. The guy to my right was talking quietly, I guess into a microphone in his sleeve or hand. He had an earpiece, so I presumed he was talking to the other agents. Or marshals. Whatever they were.

I heard the Suburban door open on the other side. The agent there was leaning inside the passenger door and pulled something out. It was a milk carton. I almost laughed. Could this be a dream and I was making all these characters up? What adult drank milk these days?

The milk guy was tall with darker skin and wore a white turban. I thought of him as a genie, like the one from *Aladdin*. But his perpetual scowl said he might be the evil twin brother version. Still, he walked over to the cat and squatted. A knife appeared in his hand, and he sliced off the upper half of the carton then held it out to the cat.

The cat raised its head and sniffed. Its whiskers twitched. The agent slid a hand under the cat and helped it stand. He held the carton in his other hand while the cat began lapping the milk.

I dug my fingernails into the palm of my hand, trying to make myself wake up. But it didn't work. It just left white nail marks on my hand.

Another black Suburban pulled up and parked where the police car had been. The agents who had gone into the house came out and got into the back seat of the new Suburban and closed the doors. I noticed that all three Suburbans were still running.

It was starting to get crowded on the street. I was sure the neighbors had been standing at their windows craning their necks to see if a TV crime drama was unfolding. A knot of four or five now stood together at the foot of the neighbor's driveway.

This felt eerily like a TV cop show. When Gage pulled up in his beat-up white Mazda, I half expected someone to yell, "Cut!"

As Gage walked towards me, he called, "Dude, what's going on?"

Marshal Massey stepped out of the Suburban and cut him off. "Who are you?"

"I'm Gage."

"Why are you here?"

He pointed towards me. "Buck called me. I'm the shop manager. I came to get the other deliveries. We're gonna be late now and the customers will be unhappy."

She pointed at the house. "The Chesters won't mind. If your customers complain, you can blame them."

Gage looked from her to the house and back. "They dead?"

She waved her hand towards my scooter. "Get your stuff and get out of here. And keep your mouth shut until we know what's going on. No social media posts, no sharing. Or we'll be knocking on your door. Understood?"

Gage swallowed. "Sure."

The woman got back into the Suburban as a brown UPS truck pulled up. Oddly, no one got out. It just sat there, the engine running.

Gage walked towards me. "You okay?"

"I don't know. These Suburbans showed up and chased the police away. They've got me just standing here. One of them said they were U.S. Marshals."

Gage's dilated eyes grew big. "Man, what have you gotten into?"

I felt the same way. I was the one who called 911. The police responded, but the Chesters must have been important or the marshals wouldn't be here.

"I don't think they're going to let me finish my deliveries. That's why I called. Take the orders back to the shop and call Jimmy. Maybe he can come in early."

He looked at me, then at my scooter. "I don't have a latch in my car for the CannaBin."

CannaBin was the bin on my scooter where I stored the deliveries. It was specifically made to transport cannabis products and included a camera system to record anyone accessing the bin and a twelve-hour battery to operate the monitoring electronics. The bin latched on to my scooter or my car via a special welded-in cradle, so it was more of a vault connected to the vehicle than it was just a safe. But it was detachable via a separate electronic keypad lock like the one that opened the bin lid.

"Take the whole thing back to the shop. Cradle it there and you can get the deliveries out."

Gage nodded thoughtfully.

He walked over to my scooter, keyed in his code, and detached the bin. It began to beep and would continue to do so until it was cradled again. He carried it to his car and slid it into the back seat. "What about the order for this house?"

"I still have it." I pulled it out of my pocket and held it out.

"If the spooks don't take it, bring it back to the shop."

Spooks. Yes, they were spooky. But Gage meant like the intelligence kind, CIA, or NSA. Spies. That kind of spook. I had no reason to believe these guys weren't run-of-the-mill marshals. But, on this topic, I had no training. I wouldn't know a CIA agent from a mall rent-a-cop. I'd only barely heard of U.S. Marshals.

Gage did a mock salute and left. The UPS truck pulled forward so Gage could pull out easily.

I jumped when the cat rubbed against my leg.

The evil genie guy who fed him milk said, "He likes you."

"You fed him. He should like you."

"That is not how animals work. You should take him home with you when you are released."

That felt like a command from him. The cat was purring against my leg. "No, I don't like cats. I don't have pets. Don't want any."

"Perhaps he will grow on you."

"I feel bad for him. I guess he was locked in there for a long while. No food or water."

"Yes, it does appear that way."

I squatted down and scratched the cat's head behind his ear. He leaned into my hand. "Think he needs water?"

"Probably. I do not have any with me, though."

"I've got a bottle on my scooter. Okay if I get it?"

"Yes. You may use this milk carton."

I poured some water into the half-carton and the cat came right over and started lapping. I noticed it had a collar, and as it drank, I started gently sliding it around the cat's neck to see if there was any ID, name, or phone number on it. Nothing. Except there was a small black cube attached to it. I was puzzled at first, then realized it was a camera. There was a micro SD card slot on the back. The card was still in the slot.

The side door on the UPS truck slid open and two guys in brown uniforms got out. They nodded to the two agents standing by the Suburbans, then headed towards the house. All the while, I'm thinking about the cat's SD card and what might be on it. For some reason, I didn't want these Suburban guys to have it. These guys didn't ask me enough questions. They weren't here to investigate; they were here to bury the Chesters and whatever happened to them. If the Chesters were dead, and I was sure they were, the criminals should be brought to justice. I liked the Chesters. They deserved answers. It felt like any evidence would be lost in a black abyss of Suburban hell.

While everyone, including the cluster of driveway people, was watching the UPS guys, I used my thumbnail to push on the SD card. It popped out and I slid it into my shoe. I could feel my hands starting to sweat but said, "Hey! The cat's got a camera on its collar."

The guy with the turban who gave me the milk carton came over and looked at it, turning it over a couple of times. Then he rose and walked away. I could see he was talking into his sleeve, but I couldn't hear what he said.

Marshal Massey and her partner climbed out of the middle Suburban. She came over to the cat and examined the camera. Then she and her partner went into the house where the UPS guys had disappeared.

The two UPS guys came out and opened the back of their truck. They unloaded a big hand truck and two rolling boxes that looked like a cross between toolchests and janitor cabinets. Three handles, like those on mops or brooms, stuck up out of one of the rolling toolboxes. They rolled both inside.

A moment later, the two marshals came out. Massey walked directly to me. "May I see your ID, please?"

I pulled out my DL, she took pictures front and back, then handed it back. "We'll be in touch. Get your scooter and head out."

I stood there for a moment, dumbfounded, wondering why they didn't want to question me. It was completely bizarre.

Massey stared at me. "What? You can go."

"You didn't even question me."

"Should we?"

"I don't know."

"You asked. You must think so. But most people in your shoes would have already high-tailed it out of here." She cocked her head. "Is there something you want to tell me."

I felt like I had stepped into quicksand. I was getting sucked in and I needed to get out before I really got into trouble. "No. No, I'm just surprised."

"Did you have anything to do with what went on inside this house?"

I shook my head. "Just making a delivery."

"Then what information do you have that would be useful in my investigation?"

It was time to bolt out of here. She left the door open, so I took it. "Nothing. Nothing at all." I turned and started toward my scooter. The cat got up and followed me, meowing loud enough to be heard. I turned and he rubbed against my leg. I looked back at Massey.

"What's going to happen to him?"

She jerked a thumb over her shoulder towards the genie agent who fed him milk. "He'll probably take it to a shelter."

I hated what I was about to say. Cats and I don't get along. They make me sneeze and they usually hiss at me. But this one was different.

"Okay if I take him?"

She smiled for the first time. "Be my guest. If I need to question the cat, I'll know where to find him, too." She turned on her heel and headed back into the house.

I scooped up the cat, unzipped my jacket, and tucked him inside. I should probably take him to a vet for a checkup, but that wouldn't be cheap and it wasn't my cat. This was only temporary. But I did pick up some cat food on the way home.

CHAPTER 3

When I returned the Chesters' delivery to the shop, Gage wasn't there. I loaded my Vespa onto my car rack and headed home. The cat seemed content curled up in the passenger seat of my old Honda Element. I don't think he moved while I was inside the market. When I set the groceries in the back seat, he lifted his head. His whiskers twitched a couple of times, and he put his head back down.

As I pulled into the driveway, he raised his head. By the time I had parked, he was standing. I scooped him up with one hand and grabbed the grocery bag with the other. As I turned, the front door of my house opened.

My uncle Tony pointed to the cat. "What's that, Buck?"

"A cat."

"Why are you carrying it?"

"I don't want it to run away."

He stood in the doorway, blocking my entry. "You think it's coming in here?"

"Yeah. Is that alright?"

"I don't like cats."

"Me, neither."

"Then why's it here?"

I lowered my voice. "I think it might have witnessed a murder."

He looked at me a moment longer, then stepped aside.

I carried the cat and grocery bag to the kitchen island. When I set the cat on the floor, he stood looking around, his whiskers twitching.

While I put the groceries away, the cat stood in the middle of the kitchen and watched. My uncle watched both of us from the doorway, arms crossed over his chest.

I popped open a can of tuna cat food and set it on the floor. The cat knew what to do and started eating immediately. I set the eco-friendly cat litter box by the back slider door and dumped some cat litter into it. The cat took a break from eating and came over to see what I was doing. He sniffed a few times, then went back to eating.

My uncle sat down in his worn black recliner. "Gonna fill me in?"

I grabbed a bottle of water from the fridge and sat down across from him in a somewhat newer beige recliner. They were the only two chairs in the living room and flanked an older sofa, all of which faced the outer wall, windows, and slider door. A flat panel TV sat on a stand between the windows. A pair of small end tables and a coffee table crowded the space between our recliners and the sofa.

I told him what had happened at the Chesters', ending with my quick trip to the market for cat supplies.

He ran a hand through his thinning hair and shifted in his chair. "WITSEC."

"What?"

"Federal program. Witness Protection Program. Run by U.S. Marshals."

"Guess whoever they testified against, found them."

"Maybe. Maybe not."

"What do you mean?"

"Lots of other people in WITSEC. Retired CIA operatives. Defectors from other countries. Anyone Uncle Sam wants to hide."

"I wonder who the Chesters really were?"

My uncle Tony is a retired Treasury agent from a bureau called Financial Crimes Enforcement Network—FinCEN for short. He carries a gun, but he's a tech nerd and does all his work from a computer. He spent his whole career working there. Or at least that's what he's told me.

I've lived with him since my parents died ten years ago. That's when he semi-retired, and we moved from Maryland to Portland, Oregon. He still does occasional "contract work," as he calls it, from his office upstairs next to his bedroom. It's loaded with computers and electronics. The last time I was in there, I counted nine computer screens. For all I know, though, he could be playing online games.

"Where did they live?" Uncle Tony asked me.

I knew what he was going to do. He'd find the Chesters and print several inches of paper background on them. A twinge of guilt made me pause. They were customers. Dead customers, though.

The cat meowed from the slider. Apparently, it was house broken and maybe I didn't need the litter box. I got up and let it out, hoping it would come back.

I stood at the door watching him. He peed for a minute and then seemed to try to poop. But that was unsuccessful. Then he came straight back to the door and sat down. He began grooming his face with his paws.

I opened the door, and he shot inside. "I guess we should name him."

"What for? He staying long?"

I shrugged. "How about Chester?" I picked him up and scratched his head. He began to purr. "You like Chester?" I asked him.

He continued to purr. I noticed his collar and remembered the SD card I'd removed. I put the cat down and sat in the recliner. I pulled off my shoe, dug out the SD card, and held it up for Tony to see. "This might tell us what happened to the Chesters."

"Where'd you get that?"

"The cat, Chester, has a vid camera on its collar."

He stood up. "Do the feds know you stole evidence from a crime scene?"

I swallowed. I knew enough about police procedures to know he was right. My butt puckered. "I don't think so. But they didn't seem to much care about the cat. I pointed out the camera to them.

They looked at it and shrugged. Said they were going to take Chester to a shelter."

"But you'd already snagged the memory card?"

"Yeah."

He shook his head. "Tampering with evidence at a homicide scene. You know how serious this is. You could be charged and convicted." He pointed at me. "What's the max punishment?"

"Umm…third degree felony. Max five years plus fine."

"Worth it?"

"Not when you put it that way."

"What other way is there?"

His face was flushed. I could see he wanted to yell at me but was trying to remain calm. "I'm sorry. I shouldn't have taken it."

"The judge who tries your case won't care that you're sorry." He sat back down and rubbed his face with both hands. I thought he was trying to slow his breathing and calm down.

We sat there in silence for a few minutes. Although Tony was right, I just didn't see how anyone would ever know I took the video card. It was a crime, yes. But unless it was discovered, was it really a crime? I knew the answer. I was thinking like a kid who just wanted his way and ignored or bent the rules and logic. Time to grow up, Buck. It was wrong. I could go to jail. I could use the excuse that stress of the moment had affected my judgment—and I would, if ever prosecuted—but I knew the rules well. Not just right and wrong from Tony, but I'd graduate in a couple of weeks with a Criminology degree. Of all people, I should know when I'm committing a crime.

Tony held out his hand. "Gimme."

"Why?"

"You can't take it back. So let's see what's on in."

"That would implicate you, Tony. No sense following one bad decision with another one."

"I have immunity."

I stared at him. "No, you don't. How would that work? No, you can't have immunity."

"I'm just snooping to see what my nephew, criminal that he is, has been up to. It's a parenting move, like checking your texts."

Did he just admit to monitoring my phone texts?

"Do I get to see what's on it, too?"

"You want to? Think about your nightmares and double that. It might be on that card."

"I don't care. I feel…connected to the Chesters. Almost responsible. They were my customers. I want to know what happened to them."

"I'm not sure you know what you're getting into. Those school criminology labs are all neat and tidy. Fake blood washes easily. The real world is a lot more gruesome and doesn't always wash away. He looked at me for a minute, then stood up. "Come, let's go see what's on it."

We trudged up the stairs. Chester followed. The office door had a thumbprint lock. When we moved to Portland, we stayed in an apartment for the first year while this seven-unit complex was being built for Tony. His office was unfinished when we moved in. He completed it himself with reinforced walls, floor, and ceiling so it was a kind of panic room. Plus, it was encased in a wire mesh faraday cage so no electronic signals could get in or out.

Our two-story owner's unit at the back had no common walls with any of the other six bungalow-style apartments that flanked both sides of the parking lot.

Tony fingered the lock, and the heavy metal door swung inward. I handed him the card and he plugged it into a slot in a laptop. He typed on a keyboard for a moment and a list of files appeared on the forty-inch screen on the wall. There were twenty-eight files, each named with numbers.

Tony pointed at the screen. "One file per day. Smart little camera." He pointed at the last file. "That's last Sunday. Probably ran out of battery."

He opened that file, and a dark video began to play. It flickered.

"Low frame rate. Black and white. Allows the card to store more days."

There really wasn't much to see. It looked like some floor and the baseboard of a wall.

"Cat's probably asleep. Let's skip to some motion."

He clicked a few buttons and after a few moments, the video stopped. There was a red square in the upper left corner of the last frame.

Tony pointed at the square, "Yep. Ran out of battery." He closed the playback. "When was your last delivery?"

"Last Thursday."

"Let's see what the cat saw that day." He opened the file with last Thursday's date.

Again, it started dark with some floor and baseboard. Tony skipped ahead to motion when the cat got up. He continued to play the video at fast speed. Most of it was views of another cat, table legs, and the shoes of Mr. and Mrs. Chester. You could tell them apart. Mr. Chester had black leather walking shoes and Mrs. Chester had white shoes that looked like Vessi's. They moved around the kitchen where the cat seemed to spend most of its time.

At one point, the cat seemed to jump up and start running behind Mrs. Chester's walking feet. The front door came into view. It opened and Mrs. Chester shuffled around, pushed the cat back with her foot a couple of times, and then the door closed.

"Stop," I said. "Can you back up and look at the shoes outside the door.?"

Tony played with some keys and the video backed up to where the door opened, then rolled forward in slow motion.

"Stop. Those are my shoes. You can read the 'Hoka' name on the side." I looked down at my feet. I was wearing the same shoes as I had last Thursday. My delivery shoes.

"So, we know the Chesters were fine when you made your last delivery."

"Yeah. Let's see what happens after that."

Not long afterward, the cat apparently hopped up on a countertop. We had a full view of the kitchen. The Chesters sat next to each other at the kitchen table. They opened my order, broke up a bud, and began filling the bowl of a water bong. In a minute, Mr. Chester flicked on a lighter and they began smoking, passing the bong back and forth.

The other cat jumped up on the table and sat down. Mr. Chester blew smoke rings at it. The cat had clearly done this before.

He just sat there, letting smoke blow over him. He almost seemed to have a grin on his face.

After ten minutes, they stopped. The cat jumped off the table.

Tony said, "Look at that. Is he sick or just high?"

The cat landed on the floor with a splat. That adage about cats always landing on their feet didn't hold true at the Chesters' that day.

"He's not moving." I thought about what I had seen from the front door side glass and how the kitchen was laid out. "He was still there when I got to their house today. I could just see his face from the front door."

Tony said, "Look at the woman. She looks frightened and she's shouting at the man."

Mr. Chester pulled out a cellphone and began to tap buttons. Mrs. Chester slumped onto the table.

"She's passed out. And the guy is struggling. His vision must be going. He keeps wiping his eyes."

I watched as Mr. Chester continued to try to type on the phone. Then he collapsed and fell off the chair below the table.

Nothing else happened for ten minutes. Then the cat hopped down from the counter. It went over to the other cat. You could see blood drooling from its mouth. The cat went around the blood and moved toward Mrs. Chester's chair.

Tony pointed. "She's pissed herself. See the urine dripping from the chair."

The cat seemed to back away. Mr. Chester lay on his side beyond Mrs. Chester's chair. His back was to us, but his pants seemed to be wet as well.

"Whatever it was," said Tony, "it was fast-acting. Ten minutes and they were dead."

"You think it was the weed I delivered?" If the feds think it was the weed, they'll haul me into interrogation for a month.

"Maybe. Could have been in the bong. Or in the bong water. But your cannabis is the most likely source. Otherwise, someone would have had to break into their house and lace the bong."

"It was in the smoke. It killed the cat, too."

"Right. But still, it could have been the bong or the bong water. You have to keep in mind all options until you can eliminate them. Don't jump to the obvious."

At first, I thought we might be selling poisoned weed to everyone, but I made other weed deliveries today and last week, and those customers were fine. It's just the Chesters. So the Chesters were definitely targeted.

"You think we're going to see anything else of interest on the vids?" I asked.

"That clip pretty much shows what happened. I think the rest will be a lot of the cat searching for food and water."

"I have some pictures."

"Of what?"

"Through the kitchen window. I took them today."

"You what? Why would you do that? They find your footprints in the grass or the planter bed, they're going to be paying you a visit, Buck."

I hung my head. I knew he was right. "I couldn't help myself. Something just compelled me to take a quick look. Besides, I wanted my own documentation of how things were…in case someone decided I was involved."

He folded his arms across his chest. "What is wrong with you?"

"I'm just protecting myself. Making sure no one decides some of this is on me. Besides, these aren't some fictional TV druggies or lab dummies. They're real people who I know. Or knew. Nice people. We talked. Mrs. Chester gave me cookies. Veggies from her garden. She was nice to me."

"Why aren't cops allowed to investigate crimes involving relatives or people they know personally?"

"Because they're biased. But I'm not investigating, I'm just documenting everything for my own protection."

He nodded. After a moment, he said, "What did you see in the window?"

"I didn't look."

"What do you mean?"

"I took the pictures with my eyes closed. I didn't want to look. I didn't want to see the Chesters dead."

"Give me your phone."

I handed it over and Tony plugged a cable into it.

"Don't you need my password?"

He just glanced at me.

A moment later he opened my camera roll on the screen. There were nine pictures taken through the Chesters' kitchen window. The first one was mostly obscured by my finger over the lens. There was little to see on the others. Mrs. Chester was slumped onto the table. You could just see the shoulder of Mr. Chester on the floor. The bong and phone sat on the table. There was nothing gruesome about the pictures.

"I wonder who he tried to call?" I asked.

"Probably his WITSEC emergency number."

I thought about that. If he had an emergency number, would he memorize it, or would it be on speed dial somehow? A favorite. Maybe he needed to protect it somehow so if someone got to his phone, they couldn't get the number.

"Tony, do you think he had the number protected some way so anyone who got his phone couldn't find it? Or did he just memorize the number?"

"It wouldn't have been a regular phone number. He'd have keyed a code, like those hidden codes all phones have. Probably started with star or star hash, then some numbers. That would have automatically dialed a phone number, but the number wouldn't show on his phone."

I had a vague knowledge of secret dial codes on phones. There was a lot of Internet folklore around it, and the characters in my video games often used special codes on their phones. I wondered if the gamers got that idea from the government, or vice versa.

"Do you think he got the code in? Did he make the call?"

"I doubt it. They've been dead a week. If he'd made the call, someone would have found them a lot sooner."

"Unless those were the people who killed them."

"Now you're thinking like a detective. Don't rule out any options. Excellent."

"How could we get the number, if Mr. Chester called it?"

"Buck, why are you so interested in this? It's a homicide. Clearly, the feds know that and are investigating. Leave it alone. You'll only get into trouble poking around."

He was right. There was absolutely no reason for me to get involved. These people were dead and there was nothing I could do for them. The authorities knew about it and were doing their job. I needed to trust in the system to do what it does.

My phone vibrated. It was a text from Gage.

2 guys in a black Suburban were here. They wanted to see your delivery schedule for the last two weeks.

Did you show it to them?

Gave them the corporate number. They sat outside for a while, then drove off. Made customers and employees nervous.

Thanks 4 update.

CHAPTER 4

As I approached our table at Insomnia, Gretchen looked up and her head stopped swaying to her ear bud music.

"Hey," I said. "What are you listening to?"

"'Bubbly.' Colbie Caillat. You know her?"

"No. What kind of music?"

She scrunched up one eye, which told me she was thinking. "Pop. Pop rock. Maybe folk pop. Is that a genre? She released a new single last week. 'Worth It.' Made me want to listen to some of her older stuff."

I put my backpack on the table and sat down, unsure how to begin.

She sneezed. "This must be serious, Buck. Couldn't tell me on the phone and all that. You know how to amp my curiosity."

I nodded. "Sorry. Just wanted to be careful."

"About what?"

"It's complicated. Probably risky. Definitely dumb."

She just stared at me, her eyes a little wider. Gretchen was half Filipino, half Chinese. She had a vague Asian look to her face and stood six feet tall. Last semester I'd learned that she hated when guys said she looked "exotic." It was, in her view, like calling her a freak and confirming her half-breed outcast status with both sides of her extended families.

"Something happened today. To a couple of my regular customers." I stared at my hands for a moment, wondering if I was crazy for even thinking of this, let alone sharing it with her.

She sneezed again. "Tell me."

"The Chesters. My customers. They were murdered."

"No shit." She lowered her voice and leaned in. "Buck, you didn't…"

"No! I had nothing to do with it. I was the one who found them." I retold the story including the video Tony had pulled from the cat camera.

"That, at least, explains why I'm sneezing. I'm allergic to cats."

"Sorry. I'd have changed clothes if I knew."

She waved her hand. "I'll live with it. But why are you telling me all of this?"

"I want to go back to their house and look around."

"Look around? You mean go inside, look for clues, shit like that? Breaking and entering. Contaminating a crime scene. Maybe implicating yourself in the investigation, if not becoming a suspect. Are you crazy?"

"Maybe. But I feel responsible, somehow, Gretchen. The Chesters didn't have anybody. They were a sweet couple. Apparently, they were in WITSEC, but they were still so nice to me. And those U.S. Marshals were…off. They barely questioned me. Called a wagon to haul off the bodies. They'll probably clean up the crime scene and end of story. Either they didn't care who killed them, or…"

Her eyes widened. "Or what?"

"The feds were in on it." I shivered. Crooked feds? I needed to stay out of this. But if that was the case, no one would ever be held accountable for the Chesters' murders.

"And you called me because?"

I sighed. This was a dumb idea. I knew it. Gretchen knew it. There were so many risks. I might never be able to get a job in law enforcement if I ended up with a record, particularly if I ended up in jail. I knew she was right. "I guess I wanted to know if you thought this was a dumb idea and…if you'd go with me. As my partner."

She leaned across the table, only a foot from my face. "This is the dumbest idea I've ever heard from you, Buck. It is so filled with risks and strong possibilities of bad outcomes. Criminal record, fines, jail—no possibility of a law enforcement career." She leaned back and stared at the ceiling for a moment. "Did you run this by your uncle?"

"No. I know what he'd say."

"And you didn't expect the same thing from me?"

It felt a lot like what I expected Tony would say. But I thought she might see how much this was tempting me. It would be a chance to investigate a real crime scene instead of those staged labs where they purposely tried to trick and mislead us. And I did care about the Chesters.

"I guess so."

"Now I see why you didn't want to talk about it over the phone. You never know who's listening when you talk about committing a crime. At least that was a good choice."

"Thanks." I felt embarrassed and stupid. It was a dumb idea. This was something my teenager self might have done, but I should be more mature and rational now. I was about to graduate. I was an adult.

She drummed her fingers on the table for a few moments as she gazed past me out the window. Then she drained her coffee cup and set it on the table with a bang. "Buck, you need to go shower and change clothes."

"Why?"

"I can't be sneezing while we're in the Chesters' house."

* * *

During our CSI lab, we had to wear stretchy black coveralls, head coverings, and shoe coverings. Gretchen reminded me that those would be appropriate tonight. She picked me up a half-hour after we left Insomnia.

As soon as I got into her car, she grabbed my arm. "Buck, could all the weed from your shop be poisoned?"

"I thought of that. The delivery that killed the Chesters was a week ago. I had other weed customers who were fine today. Others would have been reported dead if that was the case."

"Then there must be someone in the shop that's in on this. Someone who put the laced weed in your deliveries."

"Yeah. Thought of that, too. They're just a bunch of budtenders about our age. Someone may have paid one to slip the package in, but no one there is behind this."

"I'm not convinced, but let's assume you're right. What are we looking for at the Chesters' house?"

"I don't know, Gretchen. Let's just see what pops out."

"The bodies will be gone, right? I don't want to deal with any week-old cadavers and the sea of fluids they release."

"I'm sure the bodies are gone. And all the related stuff within their reach. The kitchen was really the crime scene, if you want to call it that." I told her about the UPS truck and the guys who seemed like regular UPS guys who went into the house. I was sure that was a clean-up crew.

Her deep blue MINI Cooper was practically black at night, but the top was white and easily seen on dark streets. I had never ridden with her before. She drove like a maniac, but as we got within a few blocks, she slowed. By the time we got to the Chesters' block, she was rolling along slowly.

I knew there was an alley behind the Chesters' house, so we parked there. One side of the alley was a wall of arborvitae trees. The other was a solid wooden fence six or seven feet tall that bounded the Chesters' back yard. It was hard to tell how tall it was because it sat on top of a three-foot rock wall. There didn't seem to be any gates in the fence.

"Over the fence?" whispered Gretchen.

I shrugged, then nodded.

She backed up a couple of steps, then ran towards the fence, skipped onto the top edge of the rock wall, sprang into the air, and with both hands on the top of the fence, swung over and disappeared on the other side.

I stared at the fence for a moment, reminded again of how much I didn't know about her. Apparently, she was a gymnast or something like that. She made that look easy. But I had no such gymnastic skills, so I stepped up onto the edge of the rock wall, grabbed the top of the fence with both hands, pulled myself up until I could hook a foot on the top, and scrambled over. I felt like an uncoordinated dork compared to her with her graceful vault. Still, we had a job to do, a potentially dangerous one, and I couldn't afford to be distracted. I shook it off.

We squatted together on the ground and listened for a full minute. My mind drifted and I wanted to ask about that move over the fence but tucked it away for later. There was no noise or movement. We put on our shoe covers, hoods, and latex gloves. We'd discussed this, trying to figure out the right time to put on the gear. We didn't want to be spotted on the street like this because we'd look like obvious burglars. But we wanted them on as soon as possible so we didn't leave any evidence like hair or fingerprints. We figured the shoe covers would help mask our shoe prints, if we left any.

As planned, I walked over to the kitchen window and shined my flashlight inside. It was completely empty. No bodies, no table, nothing on the counters. Completely bare. If they'd left the bodies, we were going back the way we came.

When I'd been here earlier in the day at the kitchen window, I'd noticed two presumably-bedroom windows further back along the wall. As I recalled, they were the flimsy kind that had two panes, one of which slid open horizontally. Unless the Chesters had blocked them with a dowel or something, their latch would be easy to open with a credit card.

I flashed my light at Gretchen, and she joined me as I moved to the bedroom window. Shining my flashlight through the window, we looked for any alarm sensors. We didn't see any. Nothing at the bottom blocking the window, either. I slid a credit card in against the latch and wiggled the window. The latch released and I pushed the window back.

Gretchen whispered, "Where did you learn that?"

"Long story. Another time."

"It sure wasn't Portland State."

We stood there for another minute listening. It was silent, but it also felt creepy, knowing there had been dead bodies here a few hours ago.

Gretchen shined her flashlight inside, then slid through the window on her belly. Once inside, she whispered, "I'm officially a criminal now. Breaking and entering."

"Not if we don't get caught."

"Technicality."

While I crawled in, she steadied a lamp on a desk that was pushed against the wall under the window. I closed the window, and we stood listening again in the darkness. I could hear Gretchen exhaling forcibly through her nose. The cats. She was going to start sneezing. I grabbed her hand and whispered into her ear.

"They had two cats here. You gonna be alright?"

She pulled a white facemask out of her pocket and hooked it over her ears. There was a time when this might have been weird, but after Covid you saw facemasks everywhere and thought nothing of it. This one was an N95 model. We stood there another minute and then she tapped my shoulder.

"I'm good."

I flicked my flashlight back on and led us down the short hallway to the kitchen. The smell of disinfectant filled my nose. I hoped that would help Gretchen deal with her cat allergy.

The kitchen had been wiped out. Literally. The table, chairs, and everything on any surface was gone. The floor was shiny-clean with no trace of any fluids.

I jumped when a fly buzzed by and thumped into the kitchen window. It sputtered there for a few seconds, then went quiet. I wondered if they had sprayed an insect killer to ferret out the flies that must have spread throughout the house.

Gretchen touched my arm and pointed her light to the floor where the cabinets made a right angle. Several black flies lay there, one or two twitching a leg.

"Insecticide," she whispered.

We worked our way from one side of the kitchen to the other, looking inside every drawer and opening every cabinet. It would have been easier in daylight, but that wasn't an option. We moved slowly, carefully, looking over each other's shoulders and making sure we didn't miss anything. Apparently, only the surface had been cleaned. Everything still seemed to be inside the drawers and cabinets.

We found nothing of interest. Silverware, dishes, glasses, pots, pans, and baking dishes. The stuff in everyone's kitchen. Near the hallway, we found their junk drawer. Matches, packing tape, scissors, screwdrivers, string, etc. The only thing of interest was a key ring with four keys. One was a Toyota key, presumably for the rusty truck sitting in the driveway.

We moved through the living room and came up equally empty. The garage door was off the entry hallway. After scanning it for alarm sensors, I thumbed open the deadbolt and opened the door. Now we knew why the truck wasn't in the garage. It was filled with cardboard boxes stacked seven feet high. There was a workbench against the wall to our immediate left. Some tools, a hammer, screwdriver, and power drill lay about randomly. A power lawnmower hugged the wall just beyond the workbench. You could walk along the workbench and mower to get to the main garage door. Otherwise, the whole space was crowded with boxes. Each had a label, presumably indicating the contents of the box. The labels were centered on the box, and all faced outward.

"Gretchen, do people really label each box this carefully?"

"It's like they were moved here together, but never opened."

"Stuff from before they were in WITSEC?"

"Or part of the WITSEC props. This stuff could have been moved in to convince the neighbors. The Chesters probably didn't bring anything from their old life so they couldn't be traced."

She shined her light around the rafters of the garage. "Something's off."

I followed her light. Other than cobwebs, all I saw was an array of roofing nails protruding through the sheeting between the trusses.

After a minute, she shined her light on the floor at the base of the boxes and walked along them slowly. She stopped at the far side. "Look here."

I shined my light on the floor around me and found a lone red brick sitting next to the doorframe. I used it to prop open the door, something I bet the Chesters did too because there were several marks on the bottom of the door right at brick height. Like us, they had reason to make sure the door didn't inadvertently close and lock them in. I wondered what Gretchen saw, and walked over to her and looked at the floor she was illuminating. It seemed to be scuffed a bit more than the rest of the floor.

She said, "They've moved these boxes. Several times."

"Something they needed?"

"No. I think there's something back there. Beyond the boxes in the back of the garage."

My heart leaped. "What do you mean, 'something?'"

"Not like that. This garage isn't as deep as it should be. It's only sixteen feet. Needs to be at least eighteen but should be twenty." She shined her light over the top of the boxes towards the back wall of the garage. "There's something behind that wall."

"Master bedroom."

"No, there's a space between the garage and the master. Help me move this box."

The boxes in question were banker boxes stacked seven high. Gretchen stuck her hand into the hand hole of the bottom box and pulled. The whole column of boxes slid out as well as the column between it and the wall. The two columns were attached, somehow, and were set up to be easily pulled aside.

She shined her light into the opening. "Shit, shit, shit. What have you gotten me into, Buck?"

I craned my head into the opening and shined my light around. A makeshift tunnel led to the back wall. It was four feet wide and nearly six feet tall. One row of boxes was stacked over the tunnel. They were level with the top of the other boxes so you could never tell the tunnel was there unless you moved the boxes in front of it.

The makeshift roof over the tunnel was nailed together with two-by-fours and plywood, just eight feet deep. We both shined our lights around the back wall looking for something to explain this. We didn't see it at first, but after I crouched a little, I could walk into the tunnel. On the right side of the back wall there was a hand-sized rectangle about waist high. On closer examination, the rectangle had been cut out of the plywood, then put back in place to fill the opening. I pushed and pulled on the rectangle until it popped out, revealing a recessed lock like you sometimes see on file cabinets.

I felt Gretchen lean into me from behind. "They went to a lot of trouble to hide this, but not very well. I mean, we walked right in here and figured it out. I'm wondering if it could be some kind of trap."

We both stepped out of the tunnel and turned out our lights, listening for any sound. A car drove by on the street. A siren sounded in the distance. No sounds came from within the house.

I turned on my flashlight and looked at a couple of labels on the nearby boxes. Each had hand-written contents on the label. Things like "Good Dishes," "Spare Towels," and "Tax Records." All the kind of stuff you'd see in storage. But when I looked closely at "Spare Towels," the label also had printed information. "Cochran-P34-1006." The hand-written part had been written on the label with black marker. The printed part was small and would be ignored if you didn't pay close attention. Hidden, but not very well. Why?

The dust in the garage was tickling my throat. I whispered to Gretchen, "You have a spare mask? The dust in here is getting to me."

She pulled one out of her pocket and handed it to me. I put it on.

"Shine your light on this box," I said. I pulled the Spare Towels box off the column and set it on the floor. I pulled out my boxcutter and slit the tape. Inside, we found paperback books, mostly from the 1950's. Not towels. I pulled down another box, slit it open, and looked inside. Three vases wrapped in newspaper. Not "Summer Tops."

I stood up on tiptoe and looked at the top boxes behind where I'd pulled these two. The labels were visible, but nothing was written on them. I checked a couple more places and confirmed: only the outside boxes had hand-written labels. The rest were all labeled Cochran-P34 with a different extension number. Probably sequence numbers for the boxes.

"Gretchen, whoever wrote the labels on the boxes had no idea what was inside."

"Yeah. This is just cover for the tunnel and what's behind the wall."

"Casual cover. Convincing, but not intended to hold up to scrutiny. Why?"

"Maybe they knew it was only good for a casual look. The WITSEC marshals or someone else would tear the place apart, even if it was super well hidden."

"Or maybe they just wanted someone to think there was a secret hidden here. And it's really elsewhere."

"That's a lot more clever."

"You game to open that door?"

"Sure. You have the key?"

"No, but I think I know where to find it. Can you get pictures of a couple of these labels? I have a hunch this isn't even the Chesters' stuff."

"Grab some tape. We need to put these open boxes back."

I walked back to the kitchen junk drawer and fished out the key ring with the Toyota car key. There was a small silver key on the ring I guessed might fit that lock. I grabbed the tape, too.

When I got back to the garage, Gretchen taped the opened box flaps shut and re-stacked the boxes. I moved into the tunnel. Gretchen hung back, staying clear of the opening—in case the door blew up, I guessed.

As I expected, the little silver key fit. I turned it and the whole end of the tunnel turned out to be a door that swung inward. Inside was a four-foot space between the fake garage wall and the actual wall of the master bedroom. There were banker boxes stacked here, too, but they weren't labeled. Nine of them stacked in three columns.

I flashed my light back into the garage, and Gretchen joined me.

She shined her light across the floor inside the secret room. "You can't see footprints, but you can see where someone has walked and scuffed up the dust."

She was right. The scuff marks led behind the now-open door. We squeezed inside and shut the door. I lifted a box lid. It was filled with folders full of papers that seemed to be very detailed engineering information about electronics. Stuff I didn't understand.

Gretchen looked at it, too, but she couldn't make sense of it either. She was a better snoop than me, though. She shined her light across the tops of the boxes. "Look. The dust is swept away from the end one."

I flipped up the lid on that box. More folders and papers, but only half full. There was empty space in the front of the box. We almost missed it, but I slid my hand along the inside of the box's front panel. My hand bumped something in the corner. I shined my light inside. A ring of four keys and an electronic key fob hung there from an adhesive Command hook attached to the inside panel.

I pulled it out and looked it over. There were no car brand markings on the fob. I held it up and said, "I think it's for a car, right?"

"Looks like it to me. What else uses key fobs?"

"It only has four buttons. None have markings. Maybe it's an after-market fob?"

"So if found, you can't tell what car it goes with. Or what the keys fit."

"That makes sense." I put the key ring in a plastic bag and slipped it into my pocket. Without a word, we put the boxes back in place and turned to study the wall where the scuff marks ended.

There was a silver metal door set right at floor level. It was a two-foot square with a handle on the right side. A can of WD40 sat on the floor next to the door.

Gretchen played her light on the hinged side. A piano style hinge went from top to bottom.

I said, "I'm betting the WD40 is used to keep the hinges from squeaking. Sprays it each time someone goes in or out. There's a little puddle of oil on the floor under it."

She picked up the can and sprayed the hinge from top to bottom. "Why would he be concerned about the squeak?"

She grabbed the door handle and twisted. The door swung outward with only a slight moan. She sprayed the hinges again while the door was fully open.

"It goes through the outside wall of the house. Neighbors are close. Maybe he doesn't want them to get curious?"

The smell of something rotting rolled in from the open door. Outside was a four-foot-square plywood box sat atop a man-sized hole in the ground. I shined my light into the hole. More plywood lined the six-foot deep hole. A ladder leaned against the far side. At the bottom of the hole there was a black opening of another tunnel leading to the right.

Gretchen said, "I hope there's nothing dead down there."

"This plywood box would look odd outside. Neighbors might get curious. They'd have to disguise it somehow. Given the smell, I'm guessing it's part of a compost bin."

"Rotting eggshells, coffee grounds, and grass clippings. Full of worms. That supposed to make me feel better?"

"Probably no maggots."

Gretchen sighed and crawled in, climbed down the ladder, then disappeared into the tunnel. I made sure the door latch worked from our side before I shut it. Then I followed her.

About three feet into the tunnel, it sloped steeply downward. I could see Gretchen's bouncing light ahead. And then it stopped moving.

When I caught up with her, she was lying on her back. Shining my light over her head, all I could see was blackness.

I tapped her boot. "Why'd you stop."

"The tunnel ends. It's a storm drain. There's a ladder to the left that looks like it leads up to a manhole. Probably in the alley."

"Is there room for me to get by you?"

"Not in the storm drain. Has to be here in the tunnel. You crouch on all fours, and I'll slide under you."

I didn't think that would work. I thought it would have been better to go side-by-side. But she slithered right under me in a few seconds, and I climbed into the storm drain. The ladder was just a set of iron rungs set in the concrete. A few steps up and I was at the metal manhole cover. There didn't seem to be any latches, so I stepped up one more rung and set my shoulder against it and pushed. One side tipped up an inch or two to reveal flashing blue lights. I peeked out the crack and saw a police car ten feet away. It was parked next to Gretchen's MINI Cooper.

I eased the manhole cover back down and scrambled down the ladder.

Gretchen said, "What's wrong? Did you get it open?"

"It's a police car. Next to your car. We gotta go. Back through the house, *fast.*"

"Let me turn around."

She pretzeled herself around and dove back into the tunnel. I followed along on all fours. By the time I'd retraced my steps, Gretchen was already standing by the boxes in the garage. She shoved them back into place, hiding the tunnel again.

I said, "Hang on. I gotta find a gas can." There had to be one here for the lawn mower. I found it quickly on the floor at the end of the bench. It looked surprisingly new and had maybe a quart of gasoline in it.

"Let's go. We ran out of gas. Walked to a gas station and got this."

As we rushed through the house, Gretchen started towards the bedroom through which we entered.

"No, out the front door. We can't go out the back." I yanked the door open, then shut it. "Wait. Dump the coveralls." We stripped them, the shoe covers, and head covers, and left them on the foyer floor.

We hustled around the street corner, then slowed to a brisk walk. I hoped the flashing lights didn't draw enough attention for anyone to spot us leaving the Chesters' house. But it was too late now, and we had a bigger problem.

The cop was standing with his back to us, writing on a pad. Probably writing a parking ticket. I didn't want to startle him, so I called out. "Hello, Officer."

He wheeled towards us, dropping his pad, and shifting his hand to the top of his gun holster. We stopped. "Sorry. Didn't mean to startle you."

"Who are you?" He looked us up and down.

"That's her car." I hefted the gas can. "Ran out of gas."

"Why are you wearing masks?"

My hand shot to my face. We'd dumped the coveralls but forgot we still had the N95 masks on. Before I could react, Gretchen said. "Covid. We both tested positive."

"Where'd you get the gas?"

My familiarity with the neighborhood came in handy. I figured this would be a question, so I had the answer ready. "Arco. On Allen Boulevard." I pointed back across Denny Road. "Up Lombard."

"They sell you the can?"

"No. Loaned it. We gotta take it back."

He looked towards Gretchen. "What's your name?"

"Gretchen Kho."

"You have some ID?"

She pulled out a small wallet from her shorts and slid out her driver's license. The officer reached for it.

"Sure you want to touch it? Covid and all."

The cop hesitated, then pulled a flashlight and shined it on Gretchen's license. He studied it for a moment, then said, "Okay. Get your gas in there and get going. I'll wait."

Gretchen popped the gas cap, and I poured the gas from the can into her car. We climbed in and Gretchen started the car and did a sharp U-turn in the alley. The cop backed out onto Denny to let us pass. We drove down Denny Road, then right on Lombard.

Gretchen said, "I hope that gas doesn't ruin my car."

"It'll be fine. Even if it has some ethanol in it, we're not adding enough to make a difference when it mixes up. You'll never notice."

"The cop is following us. Is there really a gas station this way?"

"I think there's one on the right just after Allen. But I don't know if they're open."

It was open. When she pulled into the station, the cop turned right on Allen and disappeared down the street. We went into the gas station anyhow. The cop might check up later.

The guy in the plexiglass booth had a dirty Trailblazer cap on backwards. A toothpick twitched between his lips.

I raised the gas can so he could see it. "We had to make up a story for a cop about running out of gas. Told him we got the can and gas from here. You can have the can. For the next person who needs it."

He smiled. "You in the Fanno Creek parking lot? They chase horny kids out of there all time."

I tried to sort out what he said. Fanno Creek was a park nearby, just off Denny. I'd seen the sign a few times driving by. That was a good cover story. The rest, about horny kids, implied we were sneaking in there to have sex.

Gretchen said, "Yeah, guess we'll have to find someplace else." She took the can from my hand, set it on the ground, and waved to the guy. Then she took my hand and led me back to the car.

As soon as she was inside, she fired up the engine and said, "Where to?"

Maybe it was me coming down from the adrenaline or my wacky sense of humor, but I said, "I was thinking the Fanno Creek parking lot."

She backhanded me in the chest. "Think again."

CHAPTER 5

We ended up back at Insomnia at our usual table. I got us coffees while Gretchen fired up her laptop. It was just after midnight and the place had a constant flow of people, mostly our age.

When I pulled up to the table, Gretchen said, "Okay if I take notes? It helps me organize my thoughts and not forget things."

"Sure."

"Number one: Whoever cleaned up the murder scene doesn't know about the secret escape route from the Chesters' house."

"Agreed."

"Number Two: Those files in the secret room aren't fake. They are relevant."

"To what?"

"I don't know. But they aren't like the boxes in the garage. Those are definitely props."

"Agreed." I laid the key fob on the table. "Number three: There's another vehicle somewhere."

Gretchen nodded and typed. "Number Four: We have some label information about the garage boxes we can track down."

"Number Five: We have some pictures of sample documents in the secret room."

"This almost sounds silly, like that Clue game I played with my grandmother."

"Which one?"

She frowned at me. "The Chinese one. She was adamant I learn English as a toddler. We played lots of games where we had to speak English."

"How did you learn to pronounce the words—did she speak English?"

"We had a laptop program. She typed in the English word, and it spoke it correctly for us. She practiced, too." Gretchen laughed. "You should have heard us struggling with 'Candlestick.'"

Her smile faded. "She passed away when I was twelve. Can't believe it's been ten years."

"I'm sorry."

"No, Buck, it's okay. We all have to die. She did good while she was here and left me a ton of memories."

She looked at me for a moment. "You never talk about your family."

My stomach growled. We'd skipped dinner. Besides, I didn't want to get into my family. "Let's get our notes done and then get something to eat. I've got a quiz in Police Terminology at 9:00 am tomorrow."

She stared at me for a moment, then said, "Number Six: Why are we doing this?"

That was hard to answer. I didn't think I knew. Gut feel gets you killed in law enforcement. That was from a 101 introductory course.

I glanced at Gretchen. She was staring at me. Waiting for an answer, I presumed. "I'm not sure. It seemed like someone needed to. Otherwise, the Chesters just disappeared from the face of the Earth. Vanished. Surely someone cares."

"I bet the people who poisoned them care."

"That's a frightening thought."

"Yeah. Don't want to get opposite of them."

"It's not just the police or marshals. We don't want to get caught by them, either. But if we figure out who *they* are, then we might be able to figure out the why."

"So long as *they* don't figure out the *who*—who we are."

She was right. This was dangerous. It wasn't just the police who might get mad because we interfered with an investigation or even charge us with some minor crimes. Someone had murdered the Chesters. This wasn't a game or a lab class. This was real.

"Why'd you come along, Gretchen?"

"Maybe I was being polite, accepting your invitation. But a real investigation at a real crime scene seemed like good experience. Low risk late at night so not likely to get busted by other law enforcement." She leaned forward and propped her chin on her elbows. "But that creepy-ass house with that secret room and escape tunnel—there's some serious shit going on there. I don't wanna run afoul of the perps."

She'd summed it up well. We didn't really have a reason to pursue this. It was risky in several ways. There was probably a no-win in it for us. We should leave it alone, walk away.

"I can't dispute any of that. Except we left our coveralls on the floor of their foyer."

She closed her eyes and scrunched up her face.

"You want to call it a night?"

She sighed. "Think so. I'm done with classes after 1:00 tomorrow. You want to check in then? See how we're feeling?"

"Sure. I'm out at noon. Call me when you're done."

We both rose and started to gather our stuff.

A voice behind me said, "You kids should sit back down. We need to talk."

Gretchen's eyes nearly bugged out of her head. She froze and her face flushed.

I turned around.

"Tony?"

Uncle Tony pointed at the table. "Sit. I'm getting some coffee."

We sat down and waited for him to return. Gretchen said, "Why's he here? How'd he know where to find you?"

Gretchen knew I lived with my uncle, but I'd never shared any of my family information with her. Even tonight, I'd walked the block to Insomnia, and she picked me up here. Neither of us knew exactly where the other lived. We were classmates and lab partners, not really friends.

Tonight may have tipped over that line into the friendship zone a little. We were still partners, maybe in crime, but some of our chatter bordered on friendship. I suppose partners in law enforcement became friends, too, particularly when you depended on each other with your life. This investigation was really an extension of our lab, albeit a real-life one. At least that's what I told myself.

Tony returned to the table. He sipped his coffee and shifted his gaze back and forth between us. He settled on Gretchen. "Gretchen Kho, I presume?"

"Yes. And you're Uncle Tony."

He nodded and sipped more coffee, then looked at me. "Want to fill me in?"

"On what?"

"What you've been doing tonight?"

I wasn't sure how much Tony knew, but he was here. He knew where to find me. He knew Gretchen's name. It felt a lot like when I didn't get home by my curfew when I was in high school five or so years ago. I had learned that lame excuses didn't work with him. But I tried anyhow. "I guess studying won't fly?"

He pulled a small tablet out of his coat and tapped it a few times. He laid it on the table facing us. It was a map with twenty or so small red dots, each with a time timestamp next to it. The most recent timestamp was ten minutes ago, and the dot was over Insomnia. It was a trace of my location for the last several hours.

I felt like I was fifteen again. "You know where we were. Why'd you track me?"

"I'll get to that. But first, why were you at the Chesters' house?"

I glanced at Gretchen. "We wanted to see a real crime scene."

"You know the risks, right? You could get arrested for B and E."

"We do. We were just talking about the risks and how we should walk away from it."

"Buck, this is a homicide. A murder, actually. The perps are out there. They might, for whatever reason, decide to come after you. And you don't have a badge or backup."

"I know. We know." I glanced at Gretchen. "We're done."

Tony looked at Gretchen. She nodded. "Yep. We get it."

Tony shook his head. "It may be too late."

I felt my stomach roll. When I glanced at Gretchen this time, she was doing the bug-eye thing again. "What do you mean?"

"I looked more closely at that camera on our feline friend. It's WIFI enabled. Not something you can buy off the shelf. That little marble-sized camera is very sophisticated. I'm betting it's not the only one in the house. The Chesters were high tech. When you took those pictures through the kitchen window, I'd bet you were recorded. The feds, and maybe the murderers, likely have your face. Not to mention you traipsing through the house tonight."

I shrugged. "So what? It's after their death. I'm just a looky-loo at this point."

"They may not see it that way." Tony pulled his chair closer to the table and leaned in. "Look. Taking those pictures was a crazy decision. Spur-of-the-moment idea in a high stress situation. I get it, but dumb. We've already talked about it.

"Stealing the SD card from the cat camera—another level of dumb decision like misdemeanor versus felony decision. With potential jail consequences. A baffling decision, given your training and education.

"But going back to the house and breaking in—potentially being recorded doing that—you've announced yourselves as a party to the crime that warrants attention. From the feds or from the murderers, or both."

"We'll drop it, Tony. Okay? We're done with it. We realized we made some mistakes, but we'll walk away. I promise. I give you my word."

Tony smacked the table with his open hand. "No!"

The sleepy customers all turned to look at us. One of the barista's called out, "Everything okay over there?"

I waved. "Yep. Just making a point."

Tony said, "I *am* making a point. You two don't know what you're dealing with. Or how dangerous it is. And you're not trained to investigate, let alone defend yourself."

I'd never seen Tony so agitated, at least not since he told me my parents were dead. I felt awful for bringing this on us. But I didn't know how to fix it.

And then Tony dropped the bomb. "I got a call. On my private business line."

"From whom?"

"I'm not sure. Some three-letter agency guy. Had my boss on the line, too. But he knew me. And he knew what you'd been up to, Buck. Said you'd waded into troubled waters. And now you were going to have to swim." He downed the rest of his coffee.

"What does that mean?"

"You stirred the pot. Upset some hierarchy of feds associated with the Chesters. Put yourselves at risk with guys who took out the Chesters. Since you've done that already, they told me to make sure you didn't walk away. Keep stirring the pot."

"What? Why?"

"Don't know. But then my boss told me to assist in any way I could. My other tasks are side-tracked until this is over."

Gretchen said, "They want us to keep investigating and they want you to help us?"

Tony nodded.

I said, "This doesn't make sense. Meddling in an investigation at the federal level is a crime in and of itself. And they…" I stared at Tony for a moment. "They want us as bait to draw out the killers?"

Tony scrunched up his face and nodded. Gretchen shot a hand to her mouth to muffle something between a scream and an expletive.

We were in a world of shit much deeper than we'd anticipated.

* * *

We filled Tony in on our night and what we'd found. His face remained expressionless.

"We had just decided we should give this up when you walked in." I glanced at my phone. "I have a quiz tomorrow. Can we adjourn until tomorrow afternoon?"

Gretchen said, "Yeah, I need to get home. I'll call you tomorrow when I finish classes. Two-ish."

We gathered our stuff and headed towards the door. Tony and I watched while Gretchen got into her car and drove off.

Tony said, "You go on home. I'll be there in a minute."

"Where are you going?"

"Please. Just do it."

I walked home and went inside. My hunger was outweighed by my need for sleep, so I grabbed a banana. Chester came over and sat down, meowing at my feet. I opened another can of cat food and set it on the floor next to the water dish. A few minutes later, Tony came in and locked the door behind him.

"May I ask where you were now?"

"I wanted to make sure you didn't have someone tailing you."

"Tailing me? Why would anyone be tailing me?"

Tony shrugged. "Beats me. But there were two different cars that followed you home."

CHAPTER 6

Friday, April 28

When my alarm went off at 7:00 a.m., Chester was curled up next to me. I'd wrestled with sleep, worried about who would be following me. And why two cars? Could they be working together or were there actually two separate tails?

I dragged myself into the shower, dressed, and grabbed a bagel as I headed out the door. As I drove to school, I kept looking behind me to see if I could spot anyone following me. If they were, I wasn't good enough to identify them.

The quiz in Social Inequity was only ten short essay questions, but it covered a lot of material. We didn't have anything like a textbook. Instead, the professor, Dr. Shubra, provided a list of twenty sources of material we were to follow. During class, he picked a few topics, and we discussed the various views and opinions of the source authors.

One of the sources was a Substack newsletter by Kareem Abdul-Jabbar. Dr. Shubra cited it for one point of view about the ongoing Disney/DeSantis feud. It was balanced with Will Witt's *Florida Standard* online news outlet. When we discussed that topic, the passionate classroom discussion bordered on heated. Then Dr. Shubra redirected our focus to the socio-economic status of my classmates and how that affected their views on the subject. The next-to-last quiz question was: *How does socio-economic status affect attitudes towards law enforcement personnel?* He followed it with: *How does the law enforcement personnel's social-economic status affect their attitudes toward suspects?*

It was clear to me how socio-economic status affected attitudes toward police. But I had never given any thought to how that would affect the police themselves. Each officer had his or her own background, story, and views. I supposed that they wouldn't be in that job if they viewed police as untrustworthy, or even evil. But their attitude toward the population, citizens, and suspects could vary greatly. Given the danger and risks they sometime must take, I could see where those attitudes could result in questionable behavior, despite their training. Those examples were in the news frequently. They escalated the polarized attitudes across the board. It was a snowball of tension, and I wondered where it would end. In the Portland area, we already had major retail chains closing stores because they couldn't manage the theft and looting.

I was still thinking about this later as I pulled my backpack over my shoulder and walked out of my noon class in Media Law. As I filed down the stairwell with the masses, someone smacked my shoulder. I looked back to see Gretchen going up. She looked over her shoulder and waved. I lifted my hand and kept going so I wouldn't be trampled.

In the parking lot a black Suburban was parked next to my silver Honda Element. I could see vague shapes of two people in the Suburban, but the window tinting made it impossible to see if there was anyone in the back.

I waved to them and both doors opened. The two guys who got out were the same ones from yesterday at the Chesters'. The passenger side one was the genie, but today he wore a black turban. "Mr. Buchanan," he said, "may we have a word, please?"

I glanced at the driver and back to the guy who reminded me of the genie. "Sure." I walked around my car and the genie stuck out his hand.

"I'm Vikramjeet Singh. You can call me Vikram. This is Archie Koewler."

We shook hands. "I guess you know who I am."

Vikram smiled. He had perfect white teeth. "Yes, we do."

I said to them, "How should I address you both?"

"We're marshals, but you may use our first names, if you like."

"Okay."

"We'd like to ask you to give a recorded statement about how you found the Chesters yesterday," Vikram said. "Would you be able to do that today?"

"Here?"

"No. We would want to go somewhere private, please."

"Like where?"

"We have an office downtown, but that might be inconvenient for you. We can use any police or sheriff station."

As part of one of my classes last year, I'd toured a sheriff's station not too far away and it was on my route home. "There's a sheriff's station on Murray in Beaverton."

"Yes. Could we go there now?"

"How long will this take?"

"Probably less than an hour."

"Okay. I'll meet you there as soon as I grab some lunch."

"That's fine. Say, in an hour?"

"Okay."

They got into their Suburban, backed out, and drove off. I wondered if they'd be there for the interview or if Marshal Massey would be there to take the lead.

I texted Tony and Gretchen, telling them what was going on. As I drove out of the parking lot, I watched behind me to see if I had a tail. I couldn't be sure, but there was a white Chevy Silverado pickup truck way behind me. I thought there was one like that on my way to class this morning, too. But I wasn't sure.

I drove through a Jack in the Box and ate while I drove. When I got to the East Precinct Sheriff's office, Vikram was waiting. He handed me a visitor badge and walked me down the hall to a door on the left. The placard on the door read "Interrogation 5."

Marshal Massey rose from the table and extended her hand. "Mr. Buchanan. Please come in and have a seat."

I shook her hand and sat down. I expected a conference room, not an interrogation room. My hands started to sweat, and I felt hot.

Vikram sat in a side chair. Marshal Massey waved her hand around the room. "I suppose being in an interrogation room might make you a little nervous, but don't worry. It's just the easiest way to get a recorded statement."

There was a small three-button box bolted to the middle of the table. She tapped one of the buttons, then stated her name and identified Vikram and me, gave the date and time, and stated our location. Then she said, "This is the voluntary statement of Mr. Buchanan about what transpired yesterday at the home of Ray and Kay Chester." She nodded to me and sat back, arms crossed over her black blazer.

I walked through what I remembered while she took a few notes from time to time.

She said, "Thank you, Mr. Buchanan. I have a few clarifying questions if you don't mind."

"Sure."

"How long have you been delivering to the Chesters?"

"At least eight or nine months. The shop would have the records exactly."

"Weekly?"

"Yes. I might have missed one or two weeks. Holidays. Vacation. I'm not sure. The shop records would show that."

"Do you normally speak to either of the Chesters when you make your delivery?"

"Yes. Always. I have to see their ID before I can hand over the order. For my own coverage, I always take a picture of their ID with my phone. And of the order label."

"So, you have approximately 300 pictures of their ID and related delivery orders on your phone?"

"No. I purge them monthly. I average a dozen or so deliveries each day. You can do the math and see they'd add up."

"Then you have three or four pictures of their ID and order labels for this month."

"Yes. Do you want to see them?"

"Not right now, thank you. Do you always deliver from your scooter?"

"Only on days when it doesn't rain. Maybe half of the time unless it's pretty cold. I get some exercise that way. It's a pedal-type electric-assist scooter. I mostly pedal. It's a–"

"And this month, did you ride your scooter?"

"Umm. Last week and this week, yes. The week before last, no. I drove my car."

"When you make a delivery, is your scooter always in your sight?"

I knew what she was getting at. She wanted to know if someone could switch orders in my bin. "No. But the bin is a CannaBin latched to my scooter. And the bin is locked. There are several deliveries on my route where the scooter is out of my sight for a minute or two. Same when it's my car. But the bin has its own camera system, alarm, and battery. If it's tampered with, it makes a racket."

"It has an alarm?"

"Yes. And I can't detach it from the cradle in my car or on my scooter. Only the shop manager and security guard can do that. There are different keypads and codes for the bin lid and for the latch system. I can only open the lid for access to deliveries."

She frowned for a moment and tapped her pen against her lips. "I suppose you always lock your car?"

"Always."

"So you knocked, no one answered, you peeked in the side window and saw what you thought was a dead cat. What about that made you call 911?"

"The cat had been dead for a while. I saw a fly go in and out of its open mouth. The other cat at the window looked malnourished. I figured if the cats were like that, then something must have happened to the Chesters. They wouldn't let the cats get into that shape."

"What did you do while you waited for the police car to arrive?"

"I moved my scooter off the street, took a few pictures of it to record where it was, where I moved it. By then the cops had arrived."

"You were in front of the Chesters' house until they arrived?"

"Yes." I felt my face redden. "And I barfed into a bush by the steps."

Massey didn't react. "You didn't leave, hop the fence, take some pictures through the kitchen window?"

Shit. They've figured that out. I hadn't lied to them yet. My hands really started sweating now. But I didn't wipe them on my pants. That was a sure sign of lying. "Yes. You know I did that already."

"And those pictures?"

"They're on my phone."

"I presume you realized the Chesters were dead when you took the pictures?"

"Actually, no. I didn't look. You can see from the pictures that I didn't aim very well."

"Why did you take those pictures?"

"I'm not really sure. I guess I wanted to preserve whatever scene was in there before the police got there and started stirring it up."

"Why didn't you just look in the window yourself."

I looked at my hands folded on the table. "I didn't want to see dead bodies." I felt stupid. Juvenile. Why didn't I just look in the window? I knew the answer, though. "No. It wasn't quite that. I just didn't want to see the Chesters…you know…dead. Like that cat. With flies in their mouths." I took a breath and realized I had tears in my eyes. "Ray and Kay were nice to me. Gave me good tips. And stuff from their garden. Tomatoes. Peppers. They were sweet."

"They were a financial loss to you, as well."

"I don't pick my customers. Some tip, some don't. It's not like I get a choice. I try to treat them all well. Next week, the delivery list will change. It changes most weeks. A new customer, a regular who moved away. That's common."

"So why are you so concerned about the Chesters?"

"I liked them. I didn't want something bad to happen to them."

"Like your parents?"

I was stunned. "What do you mean, 'like my parents?'"

"They had a violent death. Were you afraid that Ray and Kay had met a similar death?"

I was momentarily furious, wanting to pummel this woman for her needless jab at my parents. But a resolute calmness washed over me. I stared at her for a moment, breathing evenly, then stood. "This interview is over. Please record the time."

I walked toward the door and waited. I knew it was locked from the outside. After a moment, it clicked, and I pulled it open.

"Mr. Buchanan, I'll need those pictures from your phone."

I turned back and smiled at her. "Get a warrant."

CHAPTER 7

"You said what?" Tony was pacing in our living room. I sat on the sofa sipping a bottle of iced tea. I'd just recounted the interview.

"It just came out. I was angry but really calm at the same time. But you know what? As I rerun that interview in my head, I think she was trying to provoke me."

"For what purpose?"

"I don't know. It was like everything was cool until, boom, she dropped that crack about Mom and Dad. She knew what she was doing. She knew how I'd react."

"Obviously she knew about your parents. She'd have to be stupid to not suspect they'd be a sensitive topic for you. But I'm not convinced it was on purpose."

"I am. She lost my cooperation and I'm not giving up on this investigation now. You think she'll still tail me?"

He sighed. "Since I don't know who was tailing you or why, I can't venture a guess."

"How do I lose them if they're still there?"

"Hard to do. They're professionals, trained to surveil. They know all the amateur tricks."

"Harder than in the movies, huh?"

"Much. And a lot more dangerous."

"You have the training, maybe you could drive me around?"

"Only in theory, Buck. I was never a field agent, though I attended the same training as everyone else."

"Was that in a horse and buggy, or a real car?"

"Funny, kid. Go to your room."

We both laughed. I think it was as much nervous laughter as it was the banter. Uncle Tony had always been cool. Sometimes he had to lay down the law when I was a teen, but even then, I knew he had my back and was truly looking out for me.

I also knew he was no field guy. At five-foot-six, he wasn't going to intimidate anyone with his physique. He was plenty strong, but he was a little guy. I was more like my dad, six-foot-three, 220 pounds. I didn't work out much, but I was big enough to keep the high school bullies at bay. And with all my biking, my legs were particularly strong.

My phone buzzed. Gretchen. "Hey," I said, "why don't you come over to my place? I'll update you and we'll figure out what to do next." I looked at Tony. "I think my uncle's on the team now, too."

"Sure you don't want to stay on neutral territory, like Insomnia?"

"No. Too much chance of being overheard. I think these guys are still following me. If you see a white Silverado pickup, I think that's one of them."

"Should I park around the block? Come in a back way?"

"Yes. Could you also dress like one of Tom Cruise's babes from those *Mission Impossible* movies?"

"Leaving my spandex at home."

I laughed. "There's no back way. Park in the visitor space." I gave her the address and hung up.

"She'll be here in twenty minutes."

Tony nodded and started up the stairs. "I'll see what I can find out about Massey."

"Can you find anything about the Chesters?"

"Already did. They don't exist."

* * *

When Gretchen arrived, we set up on the couch with laptops on the coffee table. Tony came down and joined us in his recliner as Chester the Cat strolled in.

I looked at Gretchen. "Do I need to lock him out?"

"No. I took an antihistamine on the way here. Should be good."

Chester sat in the doorway and began his self-grooming routine with his tongue.

I updated Gretchen on the interview with Marshal Massey.

"So, the U.S. Marshals are pissed at you and likely getting a warrant for your phone?"

Tony said, "Probably not. I found a record for a surveillance camera system bought by the Chesters. I expect they have that video, so they have all they need. They probably took the system, too. You guys didn't spot it?"

I looked at Gretchen. "We didn't see anything. I kind of hope it was gone so we aren't on it."

"It was dark." She glanced at me. "And we weren't looking for hidden cameras."

"No," said Tony. "The four cameras were regular wall mount types, about the size of your fist. You might look for screw holes if you go back."

"Go back?" we said in unison.

Tony shrugged. "We'll see what shakes out. You never know." He looked at some papers he had carried down. "Not much on Massey. She's been with them for fifteen years. Clean record. Lots of routine cases. Nothing stands out."

"How long has she been in Portland?"

"Whole career. She was a cop here for less than a year before she joined."

I thought about that for a moment. Massey was just an average person doing her job. There was nothing to make her seem unusual or that would suggest she might have other connections to the Chesters. "I don't know how this works, Tony, but let's say my 911 call at the Chesters' address triggers the U.S. Marshals because this is a WITSEC location. Any time that address comes up, WITSEC is immediately notified, and they go call off the local police so they don't blow the cover. Does that sound about right?"

Tony said, "Yes, very close to what I think happens."

Gretchen said, "So they don't even know the Chesters. Don't know the background, why they're in WITSEC, never met them."

Tony shook his head. "Probably not. Inside the US Marshal system, this probably triggered someone else who is the Chesters' handler."

"But Massey and Singh are the on-call guys who have to respond ASAP. That's why I had a second tail. The on-call guys are tailing me, and the handler guys are tailing both of us. But why wouldn't the handler guys just take over from Massey and Singh?"

"Excellent question," said Tony.

"Given what we saw at the house," said Gretchen, "the Chesters didn't expect to fool a serious search. If the routine guys, Massey and Singh, don't know anything about the Chesters or why they're in WITSEC they wouldn't bother to look beyond the obvious. They're focused on finding out who slipped them the toxin-laced weed that killed them."

She was likely right. "Only the handler guys know the background. When they go in, they're going to look a lot deeper."

"There's a couple of other options," said Tony. "First, some WITSEC people come from other agencies or even other countries. Their background may not be known even to WITSEC. They just hide them. Compromised CIA operatives, for example."

"Oh," said Gretchen. "The Chesters may be more than just someone who testified against a bad guy."

"Right. Second, and even more complicated, the Chesters may have still been involved in something that was outside WITSEC."

I said, "You mean they might still be operating as CIA operatives, even though they're living inside the WITSEC program."

"Yes, that's one possibility. They might also be running their own operation of some sort, one that is unknown to everyone who is supposed to be providing oversight and protection."

"Shit," said Gretchen. "This gets complicated. How do we sort this out?"

With each new possibility, there was a myriad of angles, and other groups of feds that might be involved. Or some other unknown group, good or bad. "We need to know who that second tail is," I said. "They'll have some of the answers. I bet they can tell us if the Chesters were on or off the books, so to speak."

Tony said, "But they've no reason to share with you, Buck. You're just a couple of rookie students who don't even have badges yet."

A knock on the door interrupted us. Given the situation, the hair on the back of my neck stood up. Chester the Cat stopped grooming and ran into the kitchen, away from the door.

Tony walked to the front door. He pulled his jacket aside exposing his shoulder holster. I hadn't noticed he was carrying his gun. He'd only armed up a few times in my entire life.

He looked through the peephole, turned to me, and said, "This looks like fun."

He opened the door. Two women in black suits stood there, each holding up a picture ID and gold badge. "Mr. Buchanan? I'm agent Diaz and this is agent Mendoza. May we have a word with you, please?"

*　*　*

Tony stepped aside and let the two women in. The presence of Gretchen apparently surprised them.

Diaz looked at me. "Good evening, Mr. Buchanan. May I call you Buck so there is less confusion with your uncle?"

Tony said, "Please call me Tony." He waved an arm towards the couch where wide-eyed Gretchen sat motionless. "This is Gretchen, Buck's friend. From school."

The agents nodded towards Gretchen. Diaz said, "Mr. Buchanan, Tony, we'd like to speak in private with you and Buck."

Gretchen stood. "I can leave."

Tony and I both laughed. She was more than anxious to be clear of any federal agent confrontation.

I said to the agents, "Ladies, give me a minute with Gretchen, please." I grabbed her hand and led her outside. A black Suburban was parked in the other visitor space next to Gretchen's MINI Cooper. "I don't know who these women are, but while they're here, let's see if we can find out if there are any more tails. You drive around the block to Insomnia and park near there if you can. Go in, get a coffee, then go into Mir Music. You know where that is?"

"Yeah, couple doors down from Insomnia."

"Right. It has some parking spaces behind it. Go out Mir Music's back door and just wait there. See if anyone comes out or drives around and looks for you in the alley."

"And if they do?"

"Try to get a picture. Then come back here. Even if they don't, wait fifteen or twenty minutes, then come back. But walk back, through the parking lot, not on the street. Don't go back to Insomnia or back to your car."

"Why not?"

"Just trust me, please. We need to sort out who's following whom. They don't know who you are or if you're involved. We want to keep it that way."

"I like the sound of that." The lights blinked on her car as she clicked her fob. I waited until she drove out of the parking lot before I went back inside.

The two agents were on the couch and Tony was in his recliner. I pulled a dining chair into the living room and sat.

"Thank you for allowing us to speak with you." Diaz looked at me. "I understand you had an official interview with Marshal Massey today. Everything go okay?"

"Yes." I couldn't tell if they knew I ended the interview and walked out. Diaz could be testing me or maybe she knew something didn't go well and she was fishing.

Tony interrupted. "Agent Diaz. Why are you here?"

"Tony, you've been with FinCEN a long time. Have you ever been a field agent?"

"I'm sure you know the answer to that question."

"Yes, well, have you ever worked with WITSEC?"

"Not in my FinCEN work. No."

"The U.S. Marshals do a very good job of keeping individuals safe. And hidden. Part of their success is because very few people know the real identity of those they hide. The information isn't stored in a data system, either. In your line of work, I'm sure you can understand that rationale."

Tony just stared at Diaz.

"When an individual comes from, say, another country, their original identity doesn't come with them. No one at the U.S. Marshals knows who they were or what they did that warranted WITSEC."

"A blind protect."

I got it. "If I understand you correctly, Massey doesn't know who the Chesters were before they entered WITSEC. All she is essentially concerned about is processing the crime scene and moving on. Someone killed them. Not her problem."

The two agents shifted on the couch. Apparently, what I'd said made them uncomfortable somehow.

I glanced at Tony. He was smiling. "My nephew cut to the chase. You're here because the Chesters were murdered. You're telling us the marshals don't know who they originally were. And, they probably don't care. Pursuit of the murderer isn't their jurisdiction. Do we have that right?"

Diaz said nothing.

"I presume it is your jurisdiction."

"Yes," Diaz said.

"Do you know who they were before WITSEC?"

"Even if I did, I couldn't answer that."

"Of course. Security. But they're dead. Who cares now?"

"I'm sorry. I can't answer questions about the Chesters."

"Interesting," said Tony. He glanced at me.

I said, "You came here to let us know there are two agencies, or two parts of one agency, involved in the Chesters' case. Is that it?"

"And to warn you. We don't know who killed the Chesters. We don't know what they know about the Chesters. But it seems you delivered the toxin that killed them. It makes you of interest to us in figuring out who and how this was orchestrated."

She said "toxin," not poison. That made me nervous. Could I have been exposed? It didn't hurt to ask. "Could I have been exposed to this toxin?" Out of the corner of my eye, I could see Tony nodding assent.

"No risk to you."

"Why not?"

Diaz looked at her folded hands. I hoped Tony knew more about detecting lies than I did. But when she didn't answer right away, I thought she might be concocting a lie as an answer. "The toxin had to be heated. Are you familiar with decarboxylation that converts inert THCA to psychoactive THC in cannabis?"

Gage had given me some training in the chemistry of cannabis. It was a mini version of the training for the budtenders who worked in the shop. I was just a delivery guy, so I didn't need to engage in the sales talk nor need to know all the background like they did. "Mostly," I said.

"The toxin was constructed similarly."

"It had to be smoked. No, heated to become active."

"Exactly."

Tony chimed in "How long is the toxin active?"

"Probably a few hours."

Chester the Cat must have been listening. He came to the door of the living room and began to meow. I pointed to him. "That's the cat from their house."

"The one with the camera on the collar?"

They'd done their homework. "Yes."

"Do you have the video from the camera?"

"Yes," Tony said.

I glared at him. We didn't want to share with these guys. We wanted to get information from them.

"We'll take that with us. Please."

"Sure." Tony got up and went upstairs. He returned quickly with the SD card which he handed to Diaz.

"Thank you. Do you have any other information or evidence that might be helpful to our investigation."

My phone vibrated.

Tony said, "That's the question you ask so you can come back and get us for obstruction of justice, right? But the answer is no. And the time is now four-twenty. Our discussion with agents Diaz and Mendoza is complete. I am Tony Buchanan, and my nephew Buck Buchanan, and I have freely and openly cooperated and answered all your questions. You may stop the recording now."

Diaz turned to look at Mendoza. Mendoza fiddled with her phone, apparently stopping the recording.

Diaz said, "We're on the same side here. I hope you'll continue to be of assistance." She stood and handed a business card to Tony. "Please contact me if you discover anything that might pertain to the Chesters' murder. Thank you for your time." They headed towards the door and Tony followed.

I looked at my phone. There was a picture from Gretchen—a white Silverado pickup truck.

* * *

The sprinkle had turned to a downpour by the time Gretchen got back to our house. She took off her windbreaker and shoes, then pulled off her beanie. She shook out her hair, droplets of water flying.

I smiled.

"Crazy hair, huh?" She tried to smooth it down, and finally pulled it back into a long ponytail. "If it was just straight, it would be okay, but it has kinks and waves that make it uncontrollable."

"You ever cut it off?"

She eyed me for a moment, then looked down. "Once. When I was twelve. I had braces. My dad said I looked like Jaws."

"I can see the resemblance to a shark, particularly when you're mad."

She stared at me for a moment, then made a face, baring her teeth.

We both laughed.

She said, "Not that one, moron."

"Oh. Jaws—the henchman in James Bond movies? The one who went around biting through cables and stuff."

"Yes."

"I can see why you keep it long. Was your dad a dick?"

"Sometimes." As she sat down, she motioned towards Tony who was sitting in his recliner. "How was your visit?"

I said, "Tell us your story first."

She curled her legs under her. "I did what you said. Got coffee at Insomnia, went through Mir Music and out the back. I stood there for maybe two minutes while it was sprinkling. Then a guy comes out the back door, glances at me, and keeps walking. I couldn't tell if I had startled him or what, but he had a split-second of stop motion when he saw me. He just kept walking, though. A white pickup rolled up. He got into the passenger side, and they drove off."

Tony and I said in unison, "What did he look like?"

"Definitely Latino. Shorter than me by a few inches. Lean. Muscular. Wore a black T-shirt and black pants. No facial hair."

"Would you recognize him?"

"Maybe. Nothing distinguishing."

Tony said, "Anything in his hands?"

She stared at the ceiling for a minute. "I don't think so."

"She got a picture of the truck," I said to Tony as I showed him my phone. "Think we can make out the license?"

"Maybe." He leaned forward. "Gretchen, you know you can bow out of this. Even though the feds have our back, there's still danger and risk."

I added, "I don't want you to get hurt, Gretchen. I want you to stay safe."

"I get it, but I'm not walking away now. We're a team, right?"

"At the risk of over-stepping my parental boundaries, don't do this because of your relationship with Buck."

Before I could object, she jerked a thumb in my direction. "He's just a lab partner. Nothing going on here."

I started to agree, but she put her palm up, like she was pushing me away. "Don't. Just don't, Buck. Anything you say is gonna be wrong."

Tony laughed. "She's probably right, Buck."

I felt reprimanded, like I was a little boy at a table with grownups who were patting me on the head. It made me angry, too. Gretchen and I were just friends, and not good friends. Just a step above lab partners, in my book. But I kept my mouth shut.

Tony said, "Gretchen, let's use the original picture of the truck on your phone. We'll go upstairs to my office and see if we can get the license plate number."

* * *

Upstairs, while Tony tapped away on his keyboard, I filled Gretchen in on our recent visitors.

She asked, "Did you take a pic of their business card?"

"No. What for?"

"Never know when you might want to call them."

Tony had laid it on the corner of his desk. I moved it to a worktable and took a picture of it. She leaned in and tapped her phone a couple of times.

"Did you take a picture?"

"No. I have a scanner app. It just added all the information to my contacts automatically."

Tony leaned back in his chair. "These guys are professional. The license is registered to a green Subaru wagon in Salem. They probably switched plates. Or just stole them."

I said, "Think the truck is stolen, too?"

"Not likely. Unless it's from another state. But with the way it's been around here lately, I'm not sure a street cop would pull over a suspected stolen vehicle. If the occupants weren't white, the cops might just look the other way these days."

"That's sad," said Gretchen. "But true."

We stood there silently for a moment, contemplating how downtown Portland had become the most dangerous downtown in America.

Tony said, "It's after five. Let's get some dinner."

I looked at Gretchen. "Amelia's?"

She waved her hand. "How about Thai House?"

Tony said, "Thai House it is. We'll walk. Make the tails suffer the traffic."

CHAPTER 8

Gretchen ordered Som Tum, a spicy green papaya salad. Tony and I both ordered Pad Thai, Thai-style fried noodles.

Tony said, "Gretchen, I don't know much about you. Would you mind filling me in—where you grew up, family—that kind of stuff."

She eyed Tony for a moment. "What do you want to know?"

"Well, you said the guy from the pickup was a couple of inches shorter than you. How tall are you?"

"Six feet even." She folded her napkin a couple of times. "My dad said we're distant relatives of Yao Ming, the basketball player."

"Your dad from Shanghai?"

"Yes. He's six-five, or was. Little shorter now that he's turned sixty."

"Your mom?"

"Filipino. She's five-nine."

"That's quite tall for a Filipino woman, too."

Gretchen nodded.

The server brought our dinner, and our conversation paused. I snagged a noodle with my chopsticks and slopped it into my mouth. The White guys at our table were chop-sticking it as best they could, and the Asian woman was using a fork. It was an odd picture.

As we dug in, Gretchen said, "You know, no one eats Thai food with chopsticks anymore—not even in Thailand."

I glanced around the restaurant. The only other chopsticks I saw was with a silver-haired elderly gentleman sitting in the corner.

"Thank you, Gretchen. But I prefer to be the poster boy for racial insensitivity."

She pointed her fork at me. "See, if you had just put your chopsticks down, it would have been fine. But your attempt at humor wasn't funny and screamed insensitive White boy."

As I laid my chopsticks down, I could feel my face turning red. I glanced at Tony as I started to reply. He shook his head subtly.

Gretchen said, "Listen to your uncle."

I picked up a fork and resumed eating my Pad Thai. I felt humiliated, but I also realized she was right.

Tony said to me, "I have some ideas, but I want to hear your thoughts first."

"About what?"

"The Chesters. Last night, you agreed that you were done with it. Still feel that way?"

I glanced at Gretchen. I guess she thought that was a signal for her to speak first.

She said, "I had a dream last night. You know when Mr. Chester is dying and tries to dial his phone. I dreamed he was calling me to ask me to figure out who killed him." She forked some Som Tum into her mouth, then pointed the empty fork at Tony. "This is how it is in law enforcement, right? Nothing's black and white, you don't always know who the good guys are. It has opened my eyes a lot. I can see why I might want to be a lab guy like you, Tony."

He laughed. "That's another side of the world, but it has its risks, too."

"I don't have any sentimental connection to the Chesters like Buck does, but I still think everyone deserves closure. Someone needs to bring their murderers to justice. And I don't think we've met anyone else who's likely to do that. But I don't like us being used as bait."

"Buck?"

"I still think about Kay Chester handing me a warm cookie on a cold afternoon last December. Maybe we'll find out they were bad people, but she went out of her way to be special to me. I feel like I owe her. Maybe despite the feds." I sat up straight. "You don't suppose some of these feds were in on their murder, do you?"

Tony's eyebrows shot up. "Plausible. And dangerous. We must work as a team. Keep each other informed. Share what we're thinking. No rogue stuff, okay?"

Gretchen and I both nodded.

"Guess I should keep carrying my gun?"

Gretchen's fork clattered to the floor. She did that bug-eye thing again, looking at me. She covered her hand with her mouth while she chewed and swallowed her salad.

A server showed up with a clean fork, handed it to Gretchen, and snagged the one from the floor.

Gretchen leaned towards me. "Why are you carrying a gun?"

"Protection."

"Why do you need protection?"

"Have you walked through downtown Portland by yourself at night lately?"

"No. And neither have you."

"Tony taught me how to handle a gun years ago."

He nodded agreement.

"I've carried it since I graduated high school. And the dispensary job has its risks, too."

"Yeah. I read where a sixteen-year-old with an airsoft gun held up a delivery guy."

"It happens. So, yeah."

She said, "I have a whole new level of disrespect for both of you."

I opened my mouth to protest, but Tony cut me off. "Thank you, Gretchen. He still needs some work in recognizing the cues of sarcasm, though."

I was confused. What was Tony talking about, sarcasm? When was she using sarcasm? Was that "disrespect" comment meant to be funny. Or complimentary. I didn't get it.

I turned to Gretchen. "Explain, or I'm going to shoot you in the foot."

She laughed, a mouthful of lettuce landing on her plate. Her face turned red, and she continued to laugh. Tony laughed, too.

I felt like the brunt of their private joke. They were laughing at me right in front of my face. It was an awkward moment, saved by the waiter bringing the check.

I handed him my credit card. When he brought the bill back, there was a business card-sized paper tucked on top of my credit card. It was blank except someone had written *Call Me* on it. When I turned the paper over, there was a hand-written phone number.

Tony took the paper. "Maybe our third-tier tail is having dinner here, too. Come on." He started for the door with Gretchen and me trailing.

Once on the street, Tony leaned in close to us. "Walk back to our place by separate routes. Tony, take Second Avenue. Gretchen, take Fourth Avenue and give me your keys. I'll meet you guys there."

It was a short walk, but going separate ways at least made our tails work to follow us.

Gretchen and I got to the driveway at the same time. We walked back to the house and went inside.

Gretchen said, "Do you suppose we're bugged now?"

"Doubt it. But Tony can scan for it when he gets here."

We sat down on the sofa and Chester the Cat came and sat on the coffee table in front of us. He looked around like he was waiting for something.

A moment later I heard the slider open in the kitchen. By the time I got up to see who it was, Tony walked in.

"How'd you get in that way?"

"The gate at the end of the wall."

"I thought that was locked."

He smiled. "Used to be. It takes you into the parking lot behind the next-door apartment building's dumpster."

It dawned on me that Tony had originally locked the gate to restrict my coming and going during my teen years, essentially eliminating any sneaking in or out. "When did you unlock it?"

"Couple years ago."

"You didn't tell me." I felt a little hurt and angry. If I was old enough and trustworthy enough, then he should have told me. It felt like he still didn't trust me. I looked at him. "Not cool."

"I get it. My mistake. I apologize."

I put it aside. We had other more pressing issues. "Are we bugged here?"

He went upstairs and returned with a wand-like device. He wandered around the house, waving it here and there. It beeped once every five seconds. After a few minutes, he came over to me. "Stand up."

I stood and he waved up and down in front and back. Nothing. He turned to Gretchen. She stood and he wanded her front. When she turned around and he wanded her back, the beeping became a solid tone near her butt.

"Check your pockets."

She slid her hands first into one back pocket and then the other. In the second pocket, she found a black credit card-sized piece of plastic. "I don't…"

Tony held up his hand, then made the shushing motion to his lips with his finger. He held out his hand and she gave the card to him. He took it to the refrigerator and tucked it inside the freezer.

"Will that kill it?"

"No. But it can't eavesdrop on us in there. Might need it later."

"I don't know where that came from."

"Don't worry about it. Pretty easy to do." He put the wand down on the countertop and pulled the slip of paper from the restaurant out of his pocket. He handed it to me.

"Her name's Cinna. Bar tender at Thai House, barista at Insomnia.

Gretchen started laughing, then threw a hand over her mouth and turned away.

I stared at the piece of paper.

"She wanted you to have her number, Buck," Tony said.

"Why?"

Gretchen howled with laughter and fell onto the couch, burying her face in a pillow.

"I guess she likes you, Buck. It's not related to the Chesters."

"Oh." I could feel my face turn red. When I glanced at Gretchen, she was sitting up but had tears running down her cheeks from laughing.

"What is so funny?"

She said, "I'm sorry. I didn't realize how innocent you are. Girls never give you their number?"

"No. Why would they?"

Gretchen nodded and held up both hands. "Okay. I apologize. I shouldn't have laughed. It was rude and uncalled for."

I looked at her for a moment. My humiliation wanted to morph into anger but that would get us nowhere.

I turned to Tony. "So, we're bugged?"

"Yes." He took his phone out of his pocket. "I guess we're involved whether we like it or not. I think we need samples of those documents at the Chesters' house. Before they disappear.

"Take this and go out the back way. Walk a couple of blocks, then use this to call an Uber. Or me, or the police, if needed. It can be tracked, but it's not connected to you. Try to keep it that way."

Gretchen said, "What about our phones?"

"Leave them here. If they are tracking them, we want them to think you are tucked in for the night, so they relax."

I said, "You want some pages or just pictures?"

"Either works. If we know what they are, maybe we can figure out who the Chesters were."

I looked at Gretchen. "We should change."

Tony tossed her car keys to her. She walked out and came back with a small gym bag. "No run today, I guess."

"You never know," I said. "The night is still young."

Tony pointed at the stairs. "First door on your right."

"My room."

"Your guest."

While Gretchen changed, I said to Tony, "I'm going to take that key fob we found and see if we can find the other vehicle they had."

"You know how to do a spiral search?"

"More or less. But it's a residential neighborhood. Walking alleys and streets is probably the best we can do."

Tony nodded. Gretchen came down in her black coveralls. I was glad we'd had to purchase two sets for that class. I went upstairs and changed into my mine. When I came back down, Gretchen had shed her coveralls. She wore red running shorts and a tank top.

I said, "New plan?"

Tony had his hands in his pockets. "She pointed out that the two of you in all black would make the Uber driver notice. Might even refuse to take you. Plus, dropping you at a gas station…" He shook his head. "Need to take the black stuff with you and change there."

She was right. "I'll be right back." I changed into some running shorts and a t-shirt, then pulled a small daypack from my closet. I rolled the coveralls and stuffed them into the day pack.

Back downstairs, Gretchen rolled her coveralls, and I shoved them into my bag. "Looks like we're going to get that run in after all."

"I'm good with that. If we aren't chased."

I liked her sense of humor. She used it when she was stressed. I was kind of surprised at how she'd stuck with this, too. She was a no-nonsense lab partner and kept her personal information to herself. I still didn't know where she lived. The information she shared with Tony about her parents was all new to me. And she only shared that because Tony asked. Maybe I should ask more personal questions. She probably felt the same about me because I never shared my personal information. If not for this crazy investigation, she would never have been to our house or known where I lived. Now she's been in my bedroom. I wondered how much she snooped around.

She tapped my arm. "Ready?"

"Need to get some flashlights." I opened the pantry and rummaged around in a bin for a couple of medium sized ones.

As I came out, Gretchen said, "Did you test them?"

I flicked each one on. They burned brightly. She didn't know how organized Tony was, nor how he had rubbed off on me. We changed our smoke detector batteries every six months, along with our flashlight batteries and emergency food and water. We even had a backpack under our beds with spare clothes and emergency gear in case we had to leave the house in a hurry during a disaster. Tony was prepared for contingencies. I guess he drummed that into my head because it was just part of his life. But the other guys in high school thought this was weird. None of them had spare water. Their flashlights rarely worked so we always had to spend time looking for new batteries.

Tony handed me a gizmo that looked something like a Swiss army knife, except it was black. "Might come in handy."

I tucked it and the flashlights into the bag.

We slipped out the slider and headed towards the back fence. I found the gate. It swung open noiselessly. We stayed in the shadows until we got to the corner of the parking lot. I scanned down the row of cars, looking for black Suburbans or a white Silverado. None. We walked out, turned right on Third Avenue, then left on Jackson. We walked a couple of blocks to the railroad tracks. I pulled out the phone and summoned an Uber. A Black guy in a silver Toyota Camry showed up two minutes later. We rode in silence for thirty minutes.

CHAPTER 9

The Farro trailhead on Denny was only a half-mile from the corner where the Chesters had lived. I pulled the backpack onto my shoulders. "I guess we could jog on the trail until it gets dark."

"How long will that be? I don't know what time it is."

"It's 7:22. I'm guessing sunset is another forty minutes. Time we have to kill."

"We could jog down by the Chesters, see if that key fob pings any cars."

"Sounds like a plan." I quickly learned "jog" had different definitions for the two of us. By the time we had "jogged" the half-mile to the Chesters' neighborhood, I was winded. "Do you know the difference between a jog and a sprint?"

"Yes. Doesn't look like you do, though."

"How much do you usually run?"

"Thirty miles a week. Four five-mile weekdays and a nine- or ten-mile weekend run."

"I sometimes run upstairs."

"But you bike a lot. Hills."

"Strength versus cardio. Think of me as a bodybuilder."

"Buck the Rock!" She laughed. "In your dreams."

I stopped and dug out the key fob. "Let's jog around, at a normal jog pace, and see what we find."

An hour later, we had no success, and my feet were getting sore. I had to embarrass myself further by asking to walk for a while.

We passed the Chesters' house again on Denney Road. Gretchen said, "What about the alley—where the manhole cover is?"

"I think it's a dead end. But let's see where it goes." We turned into the alley and started walking up the slope. "You know, this might be a driveway." Sure enough, at the end of the alley was a large one-story house. A transport van sat in the driveway. "Specialty Senior Care." I clicked the key fob. Nothing. I started to turn back.

Gretchen grabbed my arm. "Wait. That driveway goes on around the house."

As we passed the van, we could see another garage set back next to the house. We walked closer and clicked the key fob again. Nothing.

Gretchen pointed to the left of the garage. "There's a break in the fence there. Let's see where that goes."

"I think we're trespassing now. Second crime in two days."

"Shut up."

We squeezed through the opening onto another driveway/alley. It curved slightly to the left so we couldn't tell where it went.

Gretchen said, "I feel like some guard dogs are about to start barking."

It was dim under the trees, and shadows were getting long as dusk set in. "It is a little creepy here."

We broke into an open space. "This used to be connected to Anne Avenue. That's where those red and white barriers are, six or seven houses down from the Chesters."

On one side of the alley, eight or ten cars sat in a haphazard row. Across the alley was a small garage with no sign. It had two bays with windowed roll-up doors and a small office next to them. There was a car in each bay, but no lights and no sign of anyone.

I clicked the key fob. Again, nothing. Darkness was descending.

Gretchen said, "Where are we going to change clothes?"

"I don't want to walk back to the park."

"You mean *crawl?*"

"Funny. How about next to the senior care place's garage. Plenty dim there. No line of sight to any houses."

She pointed at a car across the alley. "Between those cars is fine. I don't like that creepy senior place."

The car she pointed to sat under a pop-up carport made of a metal roof and an aluminum frame. I'd seen them on sale recently at Costco. Unlike the mostly rusty old vehicles in the row, this one was a black late-model Jeep Grand Cherokee. I glanced at the logo on the rear gate. It was a Laredo 4x4 model. Not new, but maybe three or four years old.

We crossed the alley and stood between the cars. The one next to the Jeep was a Honda sedan. I set the backpack on the hood of the Honda and pulled out our coveralls. After we shrugged them on, Gretchen pulled on a beanie and handed one to me.

I got out the flashlights and gave her one. When I started to shoulder the backpack, she said, "Did you check these cars with the key fob?"

"Yeah. When we got here. No beeps. No lights."

"Looks like the perfect place to hide a spare car."

I looked around. "Yeah. Easy to get to. Some shady garage guy here to keep an eye on it. Probably gets some cash to ask no questions."

"Maybe it's inside the garage. Try again."

I pulled out the key fob. We both stared at the garage, and I pressed the button. No lights flashed. But we both heard a soft clunk behind us. I looked at the Jeep. No lights were on inside or outside. I tried the door. It was unlocked.

* * *

We pulled on gloves and climbed into the Jeep, me in the driver's seat, Gretchen in the passenger seat. No lights came on when we opened the door, even though dusk was rapidly giving way to a dark night.

I turned on my flashlight. "It's immaculate in here." I wiped my hand across the dash. No dust.

"Maybe the garage guy cleans it."

"Or Ray cleans it after every use. Can't have been long ago." I opened the console and shined the light inside. A Jeep key fob lay next to an iPhone. There was a charging cable from the phone to a jack inside the console.

"It's an iPhone. I thought there might be a burner."

"Why?"

"So he couldn't be tracked. But the Jeep can be tracked, too. I bet the iPhone isn't in his name. Or the Jeep."

Gretchen opened the glovebox. It was empty. She got out and looked at the license plate, then climbed back in. "Plate's current. Expires in November."

I opened the door and took a picture of the Jeep's VIN. "Tony can find out who owns this. Betting it won't be Ray Chester."

Gretchen picked up the console iPhone and pressed the power button. It a few moments, the phone came to life. "No password. You think that's odd?"

"Maybe. There's a lot odd about Ray's security."

"Let's check its GPS history." She tapped and scrolled for a few minutes, then turned the phone towards me.

"One place. Sand Island Marine Park. First day of the month for the last four months. Nothing else." She balanced the iPhone on her leg and took a picture of the GPS log with her phone.

"He drove to the marina in St. Helens, but he'd have to take a boat to Sand Island." We looked at each other for a moment. I finally said it. "He's got a boat at the marina."

She nodded.

I wondered what it was that Ray was up to. His half-assed security that even we were able to uncover made me nervous. Was there another more serious security layer we missed? This could be a wild goose chase just to throw us off. Still, it was all we had. I glanced at the phone again. "Any texts or emails?"

"None. No browser history, either."

"Calls?"

"One number. Outgoing. Twice last month. Within a few seconds of each other on the first of the month."

"Both short calls? A couple of seconds?"

"Yeah." She took a picture of the phone number and the call times.

"Just a signal. No talking. What time of day?"

"10:15 a.m."

"Broad daylight. While there are people in the garage, maybe even with the door open. As long as no one sees him come out of the manhole, there's nothing to tie him to Ray Chester. These guys at the garage probably know him—as someone else."

"Could have been Mrs. Chester?"

"I don't think so. This is the lowest model Jeep. No power seats. No memory. This seat is set manually with a lever under the front. It's a little close for me, but it would be way too far for Kay. She wasn't much over five feet tall. Definitely Ray.

"Can you figure out when he left here or when he arrived? That way we can guess whether he called from here, on the way, or when he arrived. Or something different."

Gretchen tapped and studied the phone. "Here. Definitely called from here."

"Try it."

"Call? At this time of day?"

If this was a signal to someone Ray met, calling at this time of day might tip them to something being off. "I guess not. Let's try tomorrow."

"Yeah. At 10:15. Just before we leave for Sand Island Marina."

"It's not the first day of the month, but I don't think we should wait until then."

"Agreed."

Gretchen powered down the phone and plugged it back in. I decided to take the Jeep's key fob with me, though. I didn't want the vehicle to disappear before we could make our trip tomorrow.

We climbed out of the Jeep, and I locked it with the fob we'd found at the Chesters' house. The Jeep made no noise, other than the clunk of the locks. Ray had disabled the lights and horn, either through the Jeep menu or by some other means.

We made our way back past the senior care center, down the driveway, and back to Denney Road.

Gretchen grabbed my arm, pulling me back into the shadows of some bushes. A white Silverado pickup cruised by slowly. We watched it turn right at the corner by the Chesters' house.

She said, "I think we need to get out of here. We'll have to get to those files another time when those guys aren't hovering around."

"Back to the park. Call an Uber?"

We stripped off the coveralls and beanies and I stuffed them into my backpack while Gretchen summoned a ride with Tony's phone. We took off down the street at a good clip.

As we got to the park a few minutes later, our Uber pulled up and we got in. While the driver was pulled over to the side to pick us up, a white Silverado pickup drove by.

* * *

It was 10:30 by the time we got back to my place. Before she left for home, Gretchen and I agreed to meet at the Denney trailhead at 9:30 a.m. the next morning.

When I walked into the house, Chester the Cat scampered over to me and began rubbing against my leg. I picked him up and scratched his head, wondering what we were going to do with him. Neither Tony nor I wanted the responsibility of a cat. I had felt sorry for him and wanted to get him healthy before trying to find a real home for him.

I fed him and refilled his water dish. Tony brought out a laptop, and we sat down at the dining table. I recounted our last couple of hours.

Tony opened his laptop. "What's the VIN of the vehicle?"

I pulled up the picture and read it off.

After a minute, Tony said, "Gabor Cupul, 11970 SW Denney Road, male, fifty-two years old."

I pulled up Google Maps and entered that address. "That's the garage next to the Jeep. You think that's the guy who owns the garage?"

"I don't know." Tony turned the laptop toward me. "Recognize him?"

It was a headshot from an Oregon driver's license. "Yeah. That's Ray Chester."

"I figured."

"Can you find out who owns that garage from the address?"

Tony typed for a couple of minutes. He leaned back and crossed his arms over his chest. "Gabor Cupul."

"I'm confused. Ray owns the garage under a different name?"

"Or Ray used the name of the guy who owns the garage to register the Jeep. I presume Ray had a driver's license to match."

"I wonder if the marshals found a driver's license with that name and Ray's picture."

Tony frowned. "I'd bet it's in that Jeep."

"Why?"

"Wouldn't want it to be found in his house. That could compromise one or both identities."

"Maybe this is Ray's name before he was in WITSEC."

"I doubt it."

"So you think he might have had a secret identity after WITSEC. What for?"

"There's this casually hidden cache of technical documents in a secret room at Ray's house. He wasn't trying too hard to hide them. He just wanted the nosy neighbor and casual visitor to slide by and not notice anything out of the ordinary."

"But why does he need another identity for that? Are those documents what got him into WITSEC? Maybe he stole them, and they're evidence against someone, someone who wants Ray silenced."

"Tomorrow is Saturday. Odds are they won't clear out the house on the weekend. But if they turn it over to a realty company to sell the house, they might."

I got his message. He wanted me to go back and get those secret documents tonight. He was afraid they might "disappear."

"I have work tomorrow at the sheriff's office," he said.

"You might be sick tomorrow."

Commitment was one of Tony's integrity pillars. He instilled that in me, early and often. If I signed up for baseball, I had to go to all practices and all games, no matter the weather or how much I hated the coach. I had to be in bed with a fever above 100 before he'd let me off. Missing work was another level. I smiled because I realized it was another level, not just for him, but for me, too.

I nodded. "You're right. I think an evening drive might make me feel better."

CHAPTER 10

There was no easy way to do this. I couldn't lug nine banker boxes through the tunnel and up through the manhole. I also couldn't hike them all over the fence. It was either the garage door or the front door. I suspected the garage door would make a lot of noise and it would be a big visual, should anyone glance my way. I opted for the front door.

I backed my Honda Element onto the Chesters' driveway next to Ray's old pickup. I killed the lights and sat there for a good five minutes, watching and listening to see if anyone noticed me. The house across the street was big and faced Denney. Their driveway, though, was entered from Anne Street. It led to a free-standing, double-car garage. There were only three small windows facing this way, and they were dark.

I looked at my watch: 11:15 p.m. I wanted to make this quick. The faster I went, the less chance of discovery.

I pulled on the beanie from Gretchen and popped the car door. I pushed the door shut quietly and walked across the lawn to the fence. I figured someone running would attract more attention than a normal walk, particularly at 11:15.

I scrabbled over the fence and made my way to the bedroom window. When we were here earlier, we'd left the deadbolt unlatched. I'd considered picking the door handle lock on the front door, but that would have left me exposed with my back to the street. Slithering through the window seemed to be a better option. And I was already familiar with the layout inside.

I went straight to the garage, moved the boxes aside, and crawled through the tunnel to the secret room. The nine boxes were still there. Pushing three at a time through the tunnel, I moved the first stack to the hallway. Three-high was too tall for the hatch in my car, so I stacked them two-high just inside the front door.

I got six of them in the hallway and started on the last threesome. I had two boxes in the tunnel and turned to pick up the last box. When I grabbed it, the box felt like it was stuck to the floor on one side. I swept over the box with the mini flashlight I was holding in my mouth. There was a piece of duct tape on the floor next to the box.

I got down on my hands and knees and looked closely. The tape seemed to go under the master bedroom wall. I popped the lid off the box and looked inside. More files. I pulled them out, one-by-one, laying them in a stack on the floor. The last one in the back seemed to be stuck, like the box. I pulled the papers out and looked inside the folder. There was something taped inside at the bottom of the folder.

At first, I was thinking about a booby-trap and considered running. But there wasn't room for an explosive. I thought it might be a flash drive, but the lump was too small. I peeled the tape back to reveal a cotter pin with a wire looped through the closed end.

I followed the wire. It went out the bottom of the folder, then out the bottom of the box. There was a small tube, like a drinking straw, under the duct tape. The wire ran through the straw and into the master bedroom wall.

I grabbed the stack of files on the floor, pushed the two other boxes though the tunnel, and carried everything towards the door into the hallway. As I stepped through, I could see a flashing red light coming from down the hallway. I'd set something off. It was a booby trap of some kind. I didn't know whether to check on the light and try to reset it or turn it off or move my files out to my car for a getaway. If I left the red light going, someone would eventually notice. Maybe I'd be far enough away that it wouldn't matter. Maybe not.

Cupping my hand over my flashlight to hide it from outside, I crept slowly down the hallway. At the open master bedroom door, the flashing light was much brighter. I pulled my gun and poked my head around the corner, ready to pull back. The light was coming from a small lamp on the dresser. Nothing else seemed amiss. Shielding my eyes from the flashing light, I stepped into the bedroom, and walked to the dresser. I felt along the lamp's base for wires. The only wire was attached to a lever on a shaft coming out of the lamp base. It went down behind the dresser and into the wall at the baseboard. There were no other wires so I decided it must be battery operated. I couldn't find any switches, so I tried depressing the lever again. The flashing light stopped. This simple warning system seemed to fit the whole approach of hiding these files. It would pass a casual look, but not a thorough search. Although I'd tripped the flashing light, even I could unravel what it was and how it worked. But somewhere in the back of my mind, this lamp bothered me. There had to be more to it than met the eye. It was constructed of six white spheres stacked on top of each other. The spheres were about three inches in diameter. The top one flashed brightly when you pressed the lever. There was no shade, so just sitting there, it looked a little odd. I decided to take it with me.

I dug out the multitool from my backpack, found the wire snips, and clipped the wire from the lever. I picked up the lamp and carried it out to the passenger seat of my car. After I loaded the boxes and our previously discarded coverall garb, I shut the front door and locked the deadbolt from the inside, then made my way back out the bedroom window and around to my car.

Driving down Denney Road, I kept looking in my mirror to see if anyone was following. I even took a few loops around a couple of residential blocks to see if I could spot anyone. No obvious tails appeared, so I headed home.

Tony was still up when I arrived. I carried the boxes to the kitchen and set them near the dining table. I brought the lamp in and set it on the kitchen counter.

Tony took the lid off the top box and started flipping through the files.

"Are you going through the papers now?"

"No better time." He looked at me for a minute. "You go on to bed. Get some sleep. You'll need it for tomorrow."

I agreed and headed upstairs. I was asleep in ten minutes.

CHAPTER 11

Saturday, April 29

Nine o'clock rolled around faster than I expected. By the time I showered and got downstairs, Tony was sitting at the dining table. He said good morning and handed me a yellow piece of paper on which he'd written a note. *We're bugged, but I don't want to remove it yet. Text me when you're done. We'll meet at Insomnia.*

I nodded and grabbed a bagel. "I'll see you after class."

When I pulled into the Denney trailhead parking lot, Gretchen's MINI Cooper was already there. I parked next to her car and got out. She wasn't in her car. I looked around the lot. There were a few other cars and a couple was taking gear out of their vehicle. But no Gretchen. I walked over to the trailhead and looked down the paved path. The folks who were getting their gear out walked by.

"Excuse me," I said. "Did you guys see where the lady in the MINI Cooper went?"

"No, sorry. It was here when we pulled in a few minutes ago."

"Thanks."

I went back and stood by my car for a minute, trying to decide what to do. My mind was racing and wondering if a white Silverado had been here. My phone dinged.

Had to use the bathroom. Be there in five.

In a few minutes I spotted her walking across Denney Road. She walked to her car and popped open the back. "Sorry I'm late. Thought there was a restroom here. What park doesn't have a restroom?" She pulled out a small backpack and swung it over her shoulders.

"No problem." I didn't know whether I should tell her how alarmed I was to find her car empty and her not around.

She turned towards me. "What's wrong? You look upset."

I grabbed my backpack and locked my car. "No, I'm fine." We started walking down Denney toward the Chesters' place.

She glanced at me again. "Come on, Buck, tell me what's wrong."

This wasn't going to go away until I gave her something to explain my near panic. I thought about making up a story just to placate her. But that was no way to treat a partner. Was that what she was now? Friend? Partner? I didn't really know.

"Okay, well, when I got to the parking lot your car was here and you were nowhere around. I was starting to worry, you know."

"Worry? About what?"

"About where you were?"

"What do you…oh. The white Silverado."

"That, and who knows who else is involved in this. Or even just a park perv who abducts women on the trail."

"You were worried about my safety."

"Of course!"

"Sorry. I keep forgetting about how dangerous this is. It seems more like one of our labs."

"These are real people and there's a murderer in the mix."

"Yeah." She was silent for a while as we walked. "You have your gun?"

"Yes."

"Is it loaded?"

"Of course."

"Aren't you afraid it might accidentally discharge?"

"I'd be more afraid I wouldn't have time to load it when I needed it."

"I guess."

"I don't think you can be afraid of guns and be in law enforcement."

"I'm not afraid. I'm unfamiliar."

"You've never fired a gun?"

"No. Never had a reason."

"What about self-defense?"

"I had a can of pepper spray once, but our dog got into it and chewed the cap off."

"I thought women were always worrying about self-defense. Didn't you take Karate or something?"

"We do worry. I guess there are lots of ways to deal with it."

"Head in the sand isn't dealing with it, if you ask me."

"Don't be rude. You don't know me and it's none of your business."

"I apologize. But it is kind of my business if we're going to be partners."

"Partners in what?"

"In this investigation. Where it's dangerous. Where someone's already been killed. Where multiple arms of law enforcement are crawling around. Where I have to rely on you."

She was quiet for a long moment, then she stopped walking and stared down the street. "Do you smell smoke?"

I sniffed at the air. Definitely smoke.

Before I could answer, Gretchen pointed down the street. There were several fire engines and police cars sitting in the street with their lights flashing. The right lane of Denney Road was blocked off. White smoke drifted into the air alongside the street.

Gretchen grabbed my arm. "Buck, that's the house."

"Keep walking." We walked up the street on the left side. As we got closer to the emergency vehicles, I could see she was right. The Chesters' house was gone, burned to the ground. The only thing left was a burned-out hulk of the old Toyota pickup sitting in the driveway. It was mostly black. Its tires were burned away, and the windows were gone.

We stepped around a knot of people on the sidewalk gawking at the scene. I paused to listen to a couple of middle-aged guys chattering.

A scruffy-bearded guy in a Trailblazer's robe said, "They coulda had a bunch of gas in their garage."

Another guy smoking a cigarette said, "No way. That sucker went up like fireworks. It was arson."

The scruffy guy said, "Ain't no reason to burn down a house out here."

The cigarette guy said, "I'm telling you, I woke up right at four. Explosion woke me. When I looked over there, the whole place was on fire, clear through the roof. It went up all at once."

Someone else said, "Maybe it was a meth lab. Some of those around."

Cigarette man said, "Nah, it was more of a whoosh when it went up. Meth lab would be more of a real bang. And localized, not the whole house at once.

I moved on down the street and caught up with Gretchen where she waited at the corner.

"Are we still going for the Jeep?"

"Yeah, but I don't think we walk down the alley. Too many eyes in the area." I pulled up my GPS. "We can walk on down to Queen and then come back through the residential section. Hit that blocked off alley at Butte."

As we walked, I repeated what I'd heard from the neighbors about the Chesters' house fire.

"You think it was arson? Somebody trying to cover up something?"

"Have no idea. I haven't had a chance to tell you yet—I was there last night."

"Last night? By yourself?"

"Yes. I got the files from the secret garage room."

"You didn't call me."

"Thought you needed your sleep. It was late."

"All that talk about partners—you don't get to make decisions for me. You have to ask."

There was an edge to her voice I hadn't heard before. It seemed to be anger. Her face was flushed, and her eyes were daggers. All because I tried to take care of her and let her get her sleep. Which she needed.

"Buck, switch positions. How would you feel?"

I opened my mouth to speak before really considering what she'd said. But I stopped. What if it was her who'd gone to the house by herself last night. I would be pissed. Angry with her for taking such a risk by herself with no partner, no backup, no help if something came up.

"I'm sorry. You're right. I should have asked. And I shouldn't have gone alone. I didn't consider the risk. And look what happened—the house burned down."

"You didn't do that, did you?"

"Me? No, I left by 12:30. Those guys said it started around 4:00 a.m."

"Maybe you triggered it?"

"I don't think so…" Could the flashing lamp have been a signal that self-destruct was imminent? People really didn't booby-trap their own house, did they? I'd probably been watching too many sci-fi movies.

"Why'd you go there last night?"

"I told you, to get the files in the secret room."

"You got them?"

"Yeah. Tony was up a lot of the night going through them, but we didn't get to talk this morning." Between Gretchen not being in the parking lot and the fire, I had forgotten about the note he handed me. If there was one bug, there might be more. In our cars, backpacks…anywhere. We'd have to have Tony sweep us thoroughly when we got home. I filled her in on our conversation via notes.

We rounded the corner and turned onto the other end of Anne Avenue. The smoke and equipment were still at the end of the street.

We crossed and came to the dead-end Butte. It had a red-and-white striped gate across it, like something the city would put up. It wasn't new, but it wasn't more than a few years old. We walked around it and came out right behind Ray's Jeep.

The garage doors were open and Latino music was blaring inside. I could hear an occasional air tool being used, like a drill or lug wrench.

I pulled Gretchen back to the red-and-white gate. "I think we should go into the garage and tell them we're taking Ray's Jeep. If we don't, they might call the police and report it stolen."

"Risky. But I agree. We ought to try to figure out if someone there is connected to the Chesters or if they just keep their car here."

"Do you think the garage guys know Ray as Ray or as Gabor Culpul?"

Gretchen stared at the garage for a moment. "Hard to know. Do they just a rent some random guy a parking space, or are they involved in this whole Chester thing in some way?"

"We could ask them how long they've been here. If they were here before the Chesters arrived, then they aren't part of this. They're just a garage located in an odd place off the streets, renting a parking space."

"So we don't really know what we're getting into if we talk to the guys in the garage."

"But we don't want them calling the police on us."

She nodded. "You have a story about why we're taking the Jeep?"

"Yeah, I'm Ray's nephew. Ray's in the hospital after the fire, but he'll be okay. He sent me to take care of some business for him."

"That's some major bullshit."

"Other ideas?"

She shrugged. "Who am I?"

"Sister. Ray's niece. Girlfriend. Whatever you want. But plausible."

"You think being your girlfriend is plausible?"

"How about hooker?"

She slugged me hard right in the solar plexus.

I gasped a couple of times, but still laughed, trying to ignore how hard she had hit me. "Partner doesn't work."

"Okay. Sister. No, that's stupid. Look at us. White boy and Asian girl. We can't be brother and sister. Same with niece. White people don't have Asian nieces."

"Actually, Ray and Kay were Chinese."

"You never told me that."

"Didn't seem relevant."

"So, I'm their niece and you're my…"

She paused too long. I felt my face flush from her stare. If you stare at a dog, making eye contact, it will eventually look away—that's how I felt. Like the dog. I glanced at the garage where an air wrench was making a racket.

She never finished the sentence. "Let's go." She started towards the garage.

While she was turned away, I rubbed the spot on my chest and wondered if I'd have a bruise.

I followed her through the office door. It was a mess in there. A beat-up Formica counter about six feet long divided the space. Stacks of paper—I guessed they were service manuals--lined one wall. The whole place smelled of oil and grease.

A slender Latino guy in what were once gray coveralls came through the door from the garage bays. He was wiping his nearly black hands with a red rag. He looked at Gretchen. "You a relative of Ray's?"

"Yeah. Why do you ask?"

"Saw you eyeing his Jeep."

"Right. Well, you know Uncle Ray's house burned down last night."

The guy's eyes flashed to me, then outside, then back to Gretchen. Wheels were turning in his head.

"Yeah," he said. "We saw it when we came in this morning."

"He's in the hospital, but he wanted us to take care of some business for him. I'm his niece, Wei." She tipped her head towards me. "This is my sometimes boyfriend, sparring partner, and handyman."

What the hell was she talking about? She was using a fake name with this guy. Why? Or maybe Wei was her Chinese name and Gretchen was just an American name. It wasn't good to not understand what your partner was saying. I'd have felt less demeaned if she'd just said I was her friend. But she put me in roles, all of which were expressed as subservient, like I was along for the ride to do her bidding.

He extended a greasy hand towards me. "I'm Brian."

I said the first name that came to mind. "Toby." I shook his hand and could feel the grime gift he'd given me on my hand. I wiped my hand on my pants.

"Sorry to hear about Ray. Nice guy. Don't see him much. Once a month when he goes for his drive."

Gretchen said, "I don't know how he pays for the parking space. If he pays you monthly, I'll make the payment for him."

"No, we're good. He paid for a year. Until June"

"Okay, well we won't bother you more. Nice meeting you." Gretchen turned towards the door and brushed by me.

"Brian, what kind of repair work do you do here?" I asked. "I have an old Chevy that seems to be broken more than it's running."

He looked at me and glanced outside, I presumed he was watching Gretchen. "Transmissions and differentials. All the heavy gear stuff. Mostly for other garages, but if you got a problem, bring it in. I'll look at it."

"Thanks. Have you been doing this long?"

He didn't answer immediately. He just looked at me with a cold stare. "Long enough."

I took the hint and left. Gretchen was already climbing into the driver's seat in the Jeep. I had planned to drive, but it made sense, given what she'd said to Brian. I wiped my hand on my pants again. It left a black streak.

I climbed into the passenger seat. "What time is it?"

"10:07."

"I was asking if it was boyfriend, sparring partner, or handyman time."

She looked at me for a moment. "Male egos are such a delicate thing."

"Who's to navigate and who's to steer?"

"Sounds like a sappy song from the sixties."

"Eighties. Dan Fogelberg."

"Can we move on?" she asked.

"Sure."

"I called the number twice and hung up each time after one ring. Plugged the location into my phone's GPS." She backed out and headed down the alley.

I wasn't sure she realized I was joking about what time it was. She seemed to think I was whining. What she had said was clever and rolled off her tongue like it was true. Plausible. It surprised me, though, putting me into an unexpected role in front of Brian. But I had to admit it did make me feel a little subservient. I hoped Gretchen didn't mistake my cooperative partner approach to mean I was submissive. She'd led plenty of times in our lab work. That didn't bother me. We switched back and forth easily. Maybe it was her use of "boyfriend" that set me off. I'd never once hit on Gretchen. She'd made the boundaries clear from the start. We were barely friends. That was fine. I just wanted a competent lab partner so I'd get good grades.

We rolled along in silence for twenty minutes. Karen, as I thought of the GPS voice, occasionally gave instructions.

Gretchen let out a loud sigh. "Are you going to sulk all day?"

"What? I'm not sulking. Just thinking." I stared out the window at the occasional house as we climbed through the pass on Route 127.

"About what?"

I wasn't sure. "Nothing."

She laughed. "Compartmentalized emotions. Is that your nothing box or your sulking box?"

"I don't know what you're talking about."

"Men. They compartmentalize their emotions. They don't integrate their feelings and thoughts. And they have an empty compartment where their brain is essentially in neutral thinking about 'nothing.'"

"I still have no idea what you're talking about."

"Didn't you take any psychology classes?"

"Of course. But I never heard of your 'compartmentalization.'"

"We must have taken different courses." She turned her head and looked at me for a moment as she braked at the light.

"Watch the road," I said.

"Are you upset?"

"No."

"Yes, you are."

"Why are you trying to tell me what's in my head, what I'm thinking?"

"Because you're in a mood. Sulking. I need your head back on what we're doing."

"It is. I'm fine."

The light turned green, and we turned left on Route 30.

She sighed again. I glanced at her face. She had a furrowed brow. Angry face. Her right hand fiddled with some kind of bracelet on her left wrist while she drove with her left hand.

I closed my eyes for a second. We had to focus on this case. It was dangerous. Being distracted could get us in trouble. Hurt. Even killed.

"When we get back, I'll ask Tony to find out who Brian is. See if there's a connection to Ray."

"Can't you just text him?"

"Too easy to intercept."

"Ha! Your house is bugged and you're worrying about them intercepting your text."

"That's exactly why I'm worried. If they went to the trouble to bug us, they could just as well tap all our phones."

She glanced at me. "We should have ditched our phones."

I groaned. "Yeah, you're right. They could be tracking us right now. This just got riskier."

Karen interrupted to tell us we had arrived. Gretchen slowed as we rolled by the marina parking lot on the right. I didn't see a white pickup or a black Suburban. Ahead, on both sides of the street, were some camper trailers that looked semi-permanent.

"Let's drive on past, see if we can park out of sight."

River Street ended in a kind of turnaround that looked over the Columbia River. Next to that were a dozen parking spaces along the riverbank. Gretchen drove to the far end and parked.

I said, "Let's sit here for a minute and see if any of our known tails show up."

She turned off the ignition and picked up the key fob from the console. "What do you think these other keys go to?"

I watched for cars in the mirror while we talked. "Given we're at a marina, the big one might go to a boat."

"Or a locker."

"The little one looks more like it goes to a cheap locker or box. Can't be much of a lock. But the middle two look more like deadbolt keys."

"You think Ray has a boat here?"

No cars had appeared behind us. "Let's see if anyone knows."

We climbed out and locked the Jeep. The three cars in the lot were empty. We walked by them down River Street, past the boat ramp, and through the marina parking lot. There were two side-by-side brownish buildings at the end of the marina walkway. One looked like a storage barn with a roll-up door. The other was a small office with a sign overhead that read "Dockmaster." A bell above the door rang as we walked in.

A brownish Formica counter ran across the front. The back half of the office was partitioned with an open door in the middle of the wall. A woman rolled into view on a desk chair. She had a near-buzz haircut and a red-and-black checkered shirt. "Can I help you?" she said, as she got up and walked towards the counter.

"I'm Toby and this is my friend, Wei."

"Liv Hendrickson. I'd shake, but we got out of that habit with Covid."

"Understand."

"How can I help you?"

Gretchen said, "My uncle's house burned down and he's in the hospital. I'm trying to take care of his business while he's laid up. We came down because I think he has a boat here. Just wanted to make sure it's okay."

"Sorry to hear about your uncle. What's his name? I can look him up and see if he rents a space."

"Ray Chester."

She smiled. "I know Ray. Is he gonna be okay?"

"Yeah, just got some burns and bruises. He'll be out in a few days."

"He comes by once a month, always on the first. Pays his slip bill, buys a six-pack, and goes for a ride in his boat."

"Oh, yeah, Uncle Ray liked his beer. He had a favorite, too. Can't remember it, though."

"Juice Box IPA. He always asks for that but we don't always have it."

"That's it. Bugs me about bringing some when I visit. You have any today?"

She pointed at a cooler. "You'll have to check."

Gretchen said, "Toby, can you take care of his slip fee, please?" as she moved towards the cooler.

I wondered if that was a calculated move by Gretchen to get me to pony up the money. I said, "Do we need to pay his slip fee? You said he pays each month."

"Yeah. $136. Not due until the fifth if you want to wait."

That was more than the eighty dollars I had. "Wei, do you have some cash I can borrow to pay Ray's slip fee?"

She had the cooler door open and was looking at the beer inside. I was hoping she just didn't hear me rather than not recognizing her 'Wei' name.

Liv said, "There's an ATM on the outside of the shop if you need it."

I walked over to Gretchen and said, "Find it?" She jumped. With the door open the cooler was noisy.

"No. I don't think they have any."

I pointed. "It's the one with the little man in the top hat."

"Oh. Sorry. I missed it." She grabbed the six-pack.

"Do you have any cash? Need to pay the slip fee."

"How much?"

"$136. I have about eighty."

A little smile slid across her face. "I can cover it. You get the beer." She handed it to me and walked to the counter. "$136?" She pulled out a wallet and handed Liv two one-hundred-dollar bills.

Liv said, "Be right back. I'll get your change and receipt."

I set the beer on the counter. When she came back with the change, I paid for the beer.

Gretchen said, "I guess we'll take the boat out for a little spin. Keep it seaworthy."

Liv laughed. "Enjoy. Sorry to hear about Ray. Tell him we'll take care of his boat for him."

I said, "One thing, Liv—where is Ray's boat?"

"It's just inside the gate on the left. C-2. You have his keys?"

I held up the ring.

"Gate's locked. Make sure it closes behind you, please."

"Got it. Thanks for your help." I held the door for Gretchen. Before we walked down the path toward the gate, I scanned the parking lot, but didn't recognize any vehicles that could have been our tails.

* * *

The large key fit the marina gate. Inside to the left was Dock C. Ray's boat was the first one. It was a twelve-foot aluminum jon boat with a 3.6 HP outboard motor.

Gretchen pulled the gate shut and stood staring at the boat. "You know how to run this?"

I stepped into the boat, then held her hand as she stepped in. "Yeah. Tony and I used to fish in a similar one. You sit in the front. When I get it running, just lean forward on your knees and untie us."

I picked up the gas can that was sitting against the transom. It was empty. Another smaller can poked out from under the seat. It had a hose to the engine and when I pulled it out, it was about half-full. I lowered the propeller into the water, turned on the choke, and pumped the gas line bulb a few times to prime it. The smaller key fit the ignition and I switched it on. The engine started on the second pull. "Okay. Untie us."

I backed out of the slip, then headed along C dock, past the small boats tied up there. We cleared the dock, and I headed across the channel. In less than two minutes we were sliding alongside the Sand Island dock. I held onto the dock while Gretchen climbed out and tied us off.

She pulled up Sand Island on her phone GPS. There was a picnic shelter to our left.

I held up the key ring. "Two more unknown keys. One for a real lock, like a deadbolt. The other for more of a locker or a boat storage chest." I looked around the boat. "Nothing here."

She eyed the keys. "Let's try the restrooms. I bet they're locked in the off-season." She pointed towards the picnic shelter.

"That way. There's three of them, one on each end, one in the middle of the island."

We trudged along the trail for a few minutes. Campsites were scattered among the trees. I wouldn't have wanted to carry my camping gear all this way from the dock. It was still off season—the campgrounds wouldn't open until Memorial Day weekend—so there was no one else on the island. I wondered who camped here. And why.

The first restroom was a cinder-block building with an asphalt shingle roof. There was a brass deadbolt just above the handle on each restroom door. The key easily slid into men's restroom lock, but it didn't turn.

Gretchen said, "Try the women's."

"I'm sure Ray came here. Not Kay."

She rolled her eyes. "Just try it."

It wouldn't turn either.

She led the way to the mid-island restroom. It was identical to the other one. I tried the men's door, but it wouldn't work. I started to turn away, but then decided to try the women's door. It didn't work either.

We headed down-island to the last restroom. I slipped the key into the men's door, fully expecting it to turn. But it didn't. I wiggled it. Slid it in and out a couple of times. Nothing. I had thought we were onto something and would find a clue to the real Ray or Gabor. Or whoever he really was. But nothing. Dead end.

Gretchen held out her hand.

"What?"

"Keys."

I handed them to her.

She stepped over to the women's door and inserted the key. It turned. She pushed open the door. "Misogynist."

"Maybe they both came. Ray definitely drove."

"Or whatever he came here for is in this restroom. You coming?" She walked inside and the door swung closed.

I pushed open the door and stood there looking inside. There were four stalls and two sinks. Gretchen pushed open each stall door and glanced inside. At the fourth stall, she said. "Come here, Buck."

I felt like I was violating some gender code of ethics by being in a women's restroom. I was pretty sure I was committing some crime by being here. But I walked over to her and looked to where she pointed. Just beyond the fourth stall were two white boxes attached to the wall. Each had a picture on it and a sign that read "50 cents." They were mini vending machines.

"In case your male brain can't recognize feminine hygiene products, the one on the left is a tampon. The other one is a pad."

"I'm not twelve. I know what they are."

"I bet they have condom vending boxes in the men's restroom."

She inserted the key into the tampon box. Even though she wiggled it back and forth a few times, it didn't open. She tried the pad box. It opened on first try.

There was a stack of maybe thirty pads, each in a small, flat box. Gretchen picked up the top one and examined it. "It's been opened." She flipped open the end flap and pulled out the pad, turning it back and forth in her hand. She handed it to me.

I didn't really want to take it, but I was cornered. I had no sisters. There were no women in my house as I grew up. I understood menstruation, at least intellectually and from a biological point of view. But I had no real experience, other than high school girls who sometimes made jokes about "being on their period." I was even uncomfortable walking down the drugstore aisle where they had feminine hygiene products. To be honest, I was even embarrassed about buying condoms in the drugstore. The one time I'd needed to buy them, I'd driven out to the truck stop on the Interstate where they had a vending machine in the restroom.

Gretchen shined her iPhone light into the box. "Empty. There has to be something here."

"Are they all open?"

She handed me the empty box, then picked up the next box on the top. When she turned it over, I felt cold chills. There was a number written on the bottom in black Sharpie. It was a phone number.

* * *

Gretchen took a picture of the number and put the box back.

We stood there for a moment, trying to decide what to do now. Outside, the buzz of a small motorboat grew louder.

Gretchen snatched the pad and empty box from my hand and stuffed it back together. She laid it on top of the stack, closed the vending box door, and locked it.

I was already at the restroom door, holding it for her. The boat noise had grown increasingly louder. We ran for the trees away from the noise. The noise suddenly stopped. The trees were relatively small and far apart. Most of the underbrush had been cleared, I guessed to make room for more campsites. But near the edge of the trees, there were two bushes. We dove behind them and peeked back towards the restroom.

Nothing happened for a couple of minutes. Then a woman came into view between the trees on the far side of the island. She'd apparently come upstream and beached her boat on the other side of the island.

She threw something like a large stick, and a big black dog burst out of the weeds. It gave chase to the stick and returned it to the woman. I checked the wind. It was blowing right at us. The dog shouldn't be able to smell us unless he followed our trail as we ran here.

I looked behind us for an escape route. The only place was down the short beach to the water. We'd have to jump in if the dog came at us.

The woman was sauntering slowly our way, throwing the stick, and letting the dog retrieve it. It was a large Rottweiler.

I zoomed the camera on my phone and snapped a picture of the woman and dog. Nudging Gretchen, I whispered, "Jump in the water behind us if the dog comes after us."

She looked up into the tree trunk near us. I shook my head. "Woman might be armed."

Gretchen slid off her backpack and slipped her phone into an outside pocket. Then she shoved the backpack into the weeds around the bushes.

We watched while the Rottweiler and woman played fetch. She drew closer and closer to the restroom until she said something to the dog. He immediately went to her side and sat down, looking up at her. She walked to the restroom door with the Rottweiler at her side. She said something else to the dog. He turned, faced away from the door, and sat, looking around and sniffing. The woman unlocked the door and went inside. She was only there a couple of minutes. When she came out, she pulled off some gloves and said something to the dog. They both ran back in the direction they had come. Shortly, the boat motor noise resumed. We listened as it receded downstream.

Gretchen retrieved her backpack.

"Why'd you hide that?"

"It has my phone and Ray's phone. If we had to jump in the water, I didn't want to get them wet."

I was starting to think she was smarter than me. She thought ahead. Had a plan. It was good to have a partner like that.

"Let's go back inside the restroom. See if she did anything."

"Can't hurt. We're here anyhow."

She handed me the keys and slung her backpack over her shoulder.

Inside, the pad with the number and the opened one were both gone. Gretchen checked the others—twenty-six of them. They were all sealed and had nothing written on them.

We looked around the restroom. It was empty. There was nothing else the woman could have done.

Gretchen said, "I gotta pee. May as well do it here."

"I'll wait outside."

"No. Wait right there." She walked into the end stall and closed the door.

"I don't want to hear you pee. I'll be outside."

"Don't make me come out there with my pants around my ankles."

I laughed. "That's a funny visual. Think you could beat me to the boat that way?"

She didn't answer. I could hear her pee hitting the water in the toilet. "Does this bond us in some new way?" I asked.

When she walked out, she said, "You always crack jokes when you're nervous?"

"I never noticed. Maybe."

"They're lame. Just zip your lip and let the moment pass quietly." She washed her hands, then pulled out a couple of paper towels and dried them. She dropped the towels into the trash can.

We hadn't looked in the trash can before. It was the kind that had a door you pushed in to open it. I grabbed the top and pulled it off. Inside was Gretchen's wet towels. Under that was a maxi pad box and an unfolded pad. I pulled out the whole plastic bag from the trash can and dumped everything on the ground. Nothing new appeared.

Gretchen picked up the box and the pad. "I think it's the one that was open. Why'd she unfold the pad?"

"She was looking for something inside."

"What? Did she find it? I didn't feel anything inside the pad when I handed it to you. Did you?"

"How would I know what a pad is supposed to feel like?"

She stared at me for a minute, then waved her hand in the air. "Some other time. Let's go."

"Some other time, what?"

"Drop it. Let's get out of here before that dog comes back."

"They aren't coming back."

"Maybe. We need to call that phone number, though. And I don't want to do it from here."

"Should we take the box? Maybe we can get her fingerprints and find out who she is?"

"Tony has a fingerprint lab upstairs?"

"No."

"I don't have any forensics connections. Do you?"

I didn't, but maybe Tony did. Or his fed connections who dangled us as bait would assist.

Gretchen interrupted my thoughts. "She wore gloves. But we know how to reach her, anyhow. Just dial that number on Ray's Jeep phone."

"Yeah. And bring a big box of dog treats."

We heard a buzzing in Gretchen's backpack. She pulled it off and fished out her phone. The noise continued from her pack. She fished out Ray's phone. It was ringing. Caller ID said it was a blocked number calling. While we looked at the phone, it stopped ringing.

We continued to watch the phone, expecting it to ring again and signal…something. We didn't know what. But it had rung several times. Not just a short one or two rings.

"I think we should call them back."

Gretchen handed me the phone. "I don't think you're wrong, but I'm not doing the calling."

"Why?"

"I don't know what to say."

"But you knew just what to say, *Wei*, when you walked into that garage."

She shook her head. "That was different."

I considered she might be bipolar. One moment, she was way ahead of me with contingency plans and insight I might never reach. The next moment she was afraid to dial a phone. I looked at her face. She seemed frightened. Maybe we were in over our heads and needed each other to keep us afloat.

I punched redial. The phone rang once. A woman answered. "Get out of there now. Keep that phone. I'll contact you." She hung up.

I handed the phone to Gretchen. "I think we better go."

* * *

Half-way back to the pier, I said, "Do you think we should go back to the marina?"

Gretchen stopped. "We have to. The Jeep is there."

"Yeah. And maybe one or more of our tails. That woman's voice on the phone—she sounded scared."

"Thank you for that. You have a such a calming way in stressful times."

"And you resort to humor, too. I like that."

"No, I don't. You're the one who makes lame jokes when you're stressed."

She stared at me for a moment. The look on her face told me she might cry. I couldn't blame her. We were in over our heads. Although Tony and his feds were backing us up, we were out here flailing around in dangerous territory. There weren't any feds lurking behind bushes who could jump out and save us if that Rottweiler had attacked us. Ray's house had burned down. Someone had probably set it ablaze. Or Ray could have booby-trapped it. Either way, this wasn't a Portland State training lab. This was real. And that white Silverado wasn't with the feds.

An explosion slammed our ears. We both automatically ducked and dropped to the ground. But it wasn't close. Gretchen pointed through the trees. "Big plume of smoke coming from the marina. Looks like the office."

"Guess we can't go back there."

"But we have to get the Jeep. The police will run the plates of all the vehicles in the lot."

"I don't think that would be a problem, but we'd be stranded. We couldn't explain being here or prove that it was our truck. We need to get out of here fast."

Gretchen jumped up and started jogging towards the pier.

We hopped into the boat and slid downriver along Sand Island, eyeing the fire on the pier. I spotted a private dock not far from the marina and pointed it out to Gretchen. "We'll pull in there. If they ask, we'll tell them the police won't let us into the marina. We'll be back to move the boat tomorrow. Use the Wei and Toby names."

Gretchen perched on her knees as we crossed the channel towards the private dock. There was a thirty-foot Bayliner tied up on the inside of the dock. We landed on the outside, and Gretchen tied off the bow line. I tossed her our packs and jumped out.

We ran down the street, cut through an unfenced backyard, and pawed our way through some bushes.

Five minutes later, we stopped at the entrance to the park. Down the street, fire trucks and police cars blocked our way. Just past the trailer park, I spotted a white pickup. "Are those the guys who were following us?"

"Hard to tell from here."

"Let's not find out." We dashed across the parking lot to the Jeep and jumped in. I put it in four-wheel drive and turned right, crossing into the rear parking lot of the trailer park. At the back edge, a slope led up to Wyeth Street. I gunned the Jeep, and we climbed right up, then turned down Wyeth Street.

A little higher now, we looked over the trailers and spotted the white pickup sitting between the trailers. It was still too far away to confirm as our tail, but I knew it was them.

The office was in full burn-down. Several firetruck streams of water rained on the rubble where we had stood an hour ago.

Gretchen said, "I wonder if that lady got out."

"Liv. Liv Hendrickson. We'll ask about her tomorrow when we move the boat."

"You think that's them in the white pickup?"

"Yes. I can sort of feel it. I just know in my gut that it's them."

"Yeah. Me, too."

CHAPTER 12

The ride back to the Jeep's garage parking spot was quiet for a while. Gretchen finally said, "What are we going to do with the number from the maxi pad?"

"Have Tony check it first. See if he knows to who or where the number goes."

"Any ideas about how this works? Was Ray getting the number from the woman, or was he delivering the number to the woman? Was there something in the pad we missed?"

"I've been thinking about it, too. Let's say Ray gets the number from the restroom. He calls it to get something else or report something."

"How's he call? Not on his Jeep phone."

"Burner. He gets a new one every month, too."

"That's kind of clever. You figure that out or read it somewhere?"

"I don't really know. I might have read something like that some years back. But it makes sense, right?"

"Yeah. That's good." After a long moment, she said, "Where does he buy his burners? Same place every time? And where does he dump them?"

"Maybe he buys a new one on his monthly run to the marina."

"If he stopped somewhere else, it would show on his GPS history. But he didn't."

"Right," I said. "And what about gas for the Jeep? He'd have to stop at a station sometime. Let's say it's forty miles each way, eighty miles roundtrip."

I did the math in my head as we passed a gas station. "Has to fill up twice a year, at least. And he needs to buy gas for the boat. That tank was about half full."

I glanced at the gauges. "Jeep's nearly full. Above three-quarters."

"It was filled on his last trip. But no GPS stop in his history."

I slowed and turned onto Route 127.

Gretchen said, "Wouldn't he get boat gas at the marina?"

"Yeah. There was an empty can on the boat. A four-gallon one. That's it! He buys his gas at the marina and fills the Jeep and the boat from that can. Eliminates another stop."

"Okay. Burner phone."

"He could get it on Amazon."

"No," she said. "That would leave a credit card trail. He'd pay cash. Has to buy it over the counter somewhere."

"Where?"

"I don't know."

My head hurt. This was an endless puzzle. Each time we pulled one thread, others showed up. Clarifying, connecting, and sorting the information was daunting. I could see why some used wall boards where they posted evidence on notecards and connected them with string and push pins. It was too much information to track for my brain alone. If this was really what chasing crooks was about, I didn't know if I had the stamina. "Does this wear you out?"

"What?"

"Trying to figure out how these puzzle pieces fit? It seems endless. We get one piece and then we have to figure out a dozen more."

"Not as much fun as I thought."

We passed a sign for Portland Community College. I said, "Why'd you choose criminology?"

"Pre-law. I don't want to be a cop. You?"

"I'm not sure. Tony worked for the Treasury Department as an investigator. He never talked about the details as I was growing up, but he did share one story. His financial tracing work was the key in catching that guy who blew up the federal building in Oklahoma City back in 1995. It always seemed interesting, chasing bad guys. But being in the field is different. Dangerous. But I guess I prefer a little excitement, not just sitting behind a computer."

"You want to be a cop?"

I had never really thought about that. As a senior, I knew I would need to find a job, but going to a police academy wasn't on my radar. "I don't think so."

"About time you decided. Don't you graduate in two weeks?"

"Yeah. Have you applied to any law schools?"

"I started a year ago."

"And?"

"Got a lot of rejections. Accepted at a few lower tier schools." She looked out the window and quit talking.

"So, what's your plan?"

"Guess I'll have to find a job. I don't have the money for law school. And I can't see going into that much debt at my age, even if Biden ends up forgiving part of it."

"What kind of job?"

"Probably serving at a restaurant. Quick cash and evening hours. That way I can take part-time classes when I have the money."

I felt bad for Gretchen. She was a smart woman in a situation where she couldn't pursue her dream because of money. I knew lots of people like that. Dreams got squashed by the weight of making a living. Is that how life really works?

As I slowed to exit on Sunset Highway, I glanced in my mirror. A white pickup was closing in on us fast. By the time we completed the cloverleaf loop to merge onto the highway, he was right on my tail. He cut into the lanes behind me and sped off ahead of us. It was a Silverado with two guys in it. I was glad Ray's Jeep had tinted windows.

* * *

We parked Ray's Jeep in his spot in the garage and walked back to Denney Park. Thirty minutes later we parked our cars at my house. Before we got to the front door, Tony came out, holding a finger to his lips to shush us. He motioned us to walk with him.

When we got to the street, he said, "I don't want to disturb the bugs in the house right now. I think it's to our advantage to feed them misinformation as needed."

Gretchen said, "Do you know who's listening?"

"Not yet."

I said, "I'm starving. We didn't get lunch. Let's go to Wilson's and have a burger."

At the restaurant, we ordered, and Gretchen gave Tony the phone number from the maxi pad box. "Maybe you can figure out who owns this number. Where they're located?"

"Probably. I'll look it up when we get back."

By the time we'd updated Tony on our trip, our burgers had arrived. While we ate, Tony sipped a beer and filled us in on what he found in the file boxes.

"Most of the material is related to a device that's hooked to a submerged communications cable. The device is supposed to detect any big metal object, like a submarine, that gets close to the cable. They put one of these devices on each end of the cable and they can tell where along the cable the submarine has been detected."

Gretchen said, "Are they trying to track submarines?"

"No. They're trying to detect the approach of a submarine that might be planning to cut the cable, I think."

I said, "Why would anyone cut the cable?"

"Sabotage. Disrupt communications. Terrorists. There are more than 500 submerged cables worldwide. And they carry more than ninety percent of the international Internet traffic and phone calls."

What did Ray have to do with this? I presumed he was holding this information as proof for whatever got him into WITSEC. But I couldn't see an angle where this information gave him leverage over anyone. It was probably classified information, but he couldn't use it against our government or its agencies. They already knew about it. They built it. Or someone built it for them.

CHAPTER 13

Sunday, April 30

Tony was sitting at the dining table when I came down. Chester the Cat was lying on his lap, asleep. Tony tipped his coffee cup towards me. "Good morning."

I did some hand motions toward my ears and my mouth, trying to ask if the bugs were still listening.

"No, I took care of them."

"Should I ask how?"

"There were two. Just audio, no video. I fried one in the microwave. The other's in a box in my office. There's a 24-hour false track playing through a small speaker in the box with it."

"What's a false track?"

"Someone took the time to record a full week of nominal home noises. You play it back next to a bug and the listener thinks things are normal."

"Doesn't it need our voices?"

"It has them."

I just looked at him. He knew the question. Chester awoke and slid to the floor. He came over to me and started rubbing against my leg.

"It's something I created years ago. I update it from time to time with new voice snippets from us."

"Why?"

He shrugged. "My work deals with a lot of criminal and underworld types. You know I sweep for bugs here all the time. We never know when someone might infiltrate us. It's pretty common for everyone in my department."

"So, are these bugs related to your work or to Ray Chester?"

"I'm not certain, but probably Ray Chester."

"Who planted them?"

"We had a visitor. A break-in when we were at Insomnia. Came in through the slider."

"You caught him on camera?"

"Not exactly. They did something to the cameras that blanked visible light. All I got was an infrared signature moving in the house."

"Maybe the guys in the white pickup."

"Not them, but maybe related."

"How do you know not them?"

"It was a woman."

My first thought was whether it could be Gretchen. Obviously not, because she was with us at Insomnia. I also thought it was weird that she'd be my first suspect. Maybe my subconscious didn't completely trust her. Even after all the stuff we'd been doing together in this investigation, I still didn't know much about who she really was.

It might have been the woman we'd seen on Sand Island. But I couldn't imagine how she'd connect us. Unless she was part of the law enforcement groups who'd visited.

Tony interrupted my contemplation. "Something's been bothering me about the documents you brought from the Chester house. These documents are all U.S. Some even have the Naval Research Lab's information in the cover, so I'm sure the device is or was being built there."

"I've never heard of them. I thought CIA and NSA did all the secret government programs."

"NRL has a long history of satellite space programs. They also developed the SOSUS underwater surveillance technology and GPS. But they're good at staying out of the news. Anyhow, that's not my point.

"Some foreign countries might be interested in the technology. They might want to protect their own cables, or they might want to learn how to thwart our protection. But it's not the kind of technology that warrants WITSEC. Besides, what are these documents doing in a random house? They aren't even classified."

I saw where he was going. "It's like the boxes in the garage. They'll pass a casual look, but not a real investigation. Those documents aren't really what they were protecting."

"Exactly! But one of the boxes didn't have documents. It had what looked like some camping supplies. Tent stakes and stuff. And a plastic bag of burner phones."

"Burner phones? How many?"

"Eleven. Good idea to have one or two if you're camping, right? No place to charge your phone, so you can use a burner if your phone goes dead. But…"

"That's not why they were there."

He looked at me with a big grin. "Nope. But I didn't sort out their purpose at first. And I wouldn't have looked closer if I hadn't found a thermal igniter under the cap of one of the butane cans. If it gets above 100 degrees, the can opens, and the ignitor starts it burning. There were two of them like that. They cause the others to explode, and suddenly, the whole box is burning at butane temperature. 3500 degrees. Seconds later, all the boxes are engulfed."

"Whatever they were really hiding was in that box."

"It was the burners. All but one turned on. They keep their charge. They all had made one call. All different numbers. All on the first of the month over the last year. But not normal numbers. They were all twenty-one digits. Only the last seven digits changed each month."

"How do you dial a twenty-one-digit telephone number?"

"It's old school. The numbers select AT&T as the carrier to call a number in Diego Garcia, a British island in the Indian Ocean where the US has a base."

"Why go to all that trouble?"

"Probably security. Maybe it guarantees the call goes via a particular satellite or secure route. Or maybe the receiving end makes sure you're calling via the prescribed route. Something like that."

"Who's on the other end?"

"A computer. All the old numbers are dead—number not in service. The number you got from the bathroom today has an automated voice that recites thirty-two numbers once and hangs up."

"What are the numbers for?"

"My guess—it's a public encryption key. Ray used it to encrypt data he uploaded somewhere."

"Why not just leave the key in the box on Sand Island?"

"Extra level of security, I guess. You have to know the long dialing prefix for the number to work. I wouldn't have known or guessed it if I hadn't seen the burner numbers he called."

They were the burners Ray used to make his monthly call to the number he got from the maxi pad. I'd been right about that. But I didn't understand why he was saving them. He could have dumped them anywhere and no one would have ever known. Why did he keep them? And why were they valuable?

"I went through the rest of the stuff in the box," Tony said. "Took the lanterns apart. Flashlights. Even sawed the batteries in half. Had me stumped. Made me think of Sherlock's maxim about after excluding the impossible, whatever remains must be the truth."

"The dead burner phone."

Tony pointed at me. "Elementary, my dear Watson." He sipped his coffee. "It had a tiny nub flash drive hidden inside."

"Have you looked at it? What's on it?"

"No idea. It's encrypted."

"Can you break it, Tony?"

"Not in my lifetime. I'm pretty sure it's using symmetric encryption, and we'd need a 128-bit key."

"128 bits. That's sixteen characters. I don't suppose there was a slip of paper in the box with the key written on it?"

Tony laughed.

Someone knocked at the door. When I opened the door, agents Diaz and Mendoza smiled back at me.

* * *

Chester the Cat watched the two agents as they walked towards the table. When Diaz sat down with her back to Chester, the cat hissed, and ran behind the couch.

We took our places like we were getting ready to play cards. I chuckled a little because, like our typical Hearts game, this had the feel of a game, too. Bluffing and deception plays were frequent in both. But I had never imagined law enforcement to work this way. Apparently, territories or missions or something dictated an odd kind of caste system where one agency could trump another agency, depending on the case. Who wanted us to continue as bait, and where did they fit in this three-letter sea of feds? I felt certain that this pair saw us, not as bait, but as troublesome meddlers.

Diaz was eyeing me. She was dressed in a black suit with a white shirt, reminding me of the Queen of Spades.

"Something amusing, Mr. Buchanan?"

"Call me Buck, please. And yes, there is. We usually play cards here. I was just thinking about who would win."

"Interesting. We have a few cards to play today, so why don't we get right to it. We need your cooperation. But we can't tell you why or any more about the Chesters."

Tony said, "Okay. Lay your IDs on the table and let me take a picture of them. Then I'll run upstairs and verify your credentials. If everything turns up good, we'll be more than glad to assist."

Diaz frowned, but she pulled out her ID and laid it on the table. "I'm doing this to demonstrate we are who we say we are as a good faith gesture." She looked at Mendoza. Mendoza produced her ID and laid it on the table.

Tony used his phone to take a picture of each. He went upstairs, leaving me with the two agents.

"Would you like coffee?" I asked.

Both women nodded.

While I fixed coffee, I searched for something to talk about. Chester the Cat meowed and scampered over to the slider, giving Diaz a wide berth.

"Why do you think the cat doesn't like you?" I asked.

"I have a Schnauzer. It smells him on me."

I looked at Mendoza. "How about you? You have any pets?"

She glanced at Diaz. "This is stupid."

Diaz stared back. "It's harmless. He's in FinCEN so he can access the datacenter. Seems to be a fair way to ensure them of our authenticity."

"Interrogation room would work just as well."

I sat cups of coffee in front of each of them.

Diaz took a sip. "Coffee's better here." She nodded her head toward me. "Tell him about your pets."

Mendoza glared at Diaz for a moment, then looked at me. "I have four Pit Bulls that would each tear off a limb from your body if I let them."

"I'd love to visit your place. Sounds like loads of fun."

Diaz said, "They're retired police dogs. Old and fat. Give 'em a treat and they'll lick your face off."

"Think I'll skip that test."

"You should," said Mendoza. "They don't like men."

I was about to ask if that was a learned thing from Mendoza, but Tony came back down the stairs and said, "Okay. Let's continue."

Diaz looked at me and said, "The Chesters' house burned down yesterday."

"Really?" I just wasn't up to feigning surprise. It was too much work, and I didn't need to impress these agents. At least, I hoped I didn't. Unless they thought I was involved in that. I had an alibi—I was here, asleep. Tony could vouch for me.

"Yes. Odd. Just two days after their murder. Do you suppose it was burned on purpose?"

"I wouldn't know. Aren't you the investigators? What do you think?"

"We tend to avoid conjecture and instead rely on facts. In this case, we know it was arson because there were numerous spots where accelerants were used. Someone wanted to torch it and ensure everything was destroyed."

Tony chimed in. "Sounds like the murderer is covering his tracks."

Diaz nodded. "It does look that way. But there are other scenarios. For example, maybe there's someone else—not the murderer—who wants to cover their tracks."

"Plausible. But wouldn't you need suspects and motives for that to be a real alternative?"

"We have those. Don't you agree?"

It was my turn to step in. "Is there a point to this or are you just fishing for information you think we have?"

Diaz frowned. "Is there information you want to share with us?"

Tony said, "I think we shared our information already."

"Yes. Your video confirmed our theory. The cannabis was laced with a toxin. It killed the cat, too. And it was fast acting."

Diaz glanced at Mendoza.

"You get that from the video, or did you test everything?" I asked.

Diaz said, "I guess you earned that A in Criminal Investigation."

"I earned all my grades."

"I'm sure," said Diaz. She leaned back from the table and glanced at the cat peeking out from behind the arm of the couch. "Look, the Chesters were in WITSEC. Pretty obvious when U.S. Marshals show up and relieve the police. There are some who would harm them for what they did. Nothing unusual about that for WITSEC.

"As you have surmised, the Chesters weren't routine WITSEC, though. They were involved in some very complicated and delicate situations. As a result, their deaths have alerted several organizations who don't like to be alerted. These organizations work very hard to make sure nothing unplanned or unanticipated occurs."

Tony laid a small Ziploc bag on the table. Inside were broken parts that looked like a smashed hearing aid. "Maybe we can help each other. Who bugged our house?"

Mendoza examined the bag, then handed it to Diaz. Diaz looked at it casually, then slid it back to Tony.

"Why would anyone bug your house?"

"I was hoping you'd know. We don't. Presumably, it's connected to the Chesters."

Diaz looked at Mendoza. "Recognize it?"

"Chinese. You can buy it online."

"You see, Tony, I don't really know what we're dealing with here. I can't imagine why anyone would bug your house as it relates to the Chesters. On the other hand, I don't know if maybe you bought this yourself and are just screwing with us. That's why we seem to keep dancing around."

"I could show you the other one. It's still active."

The agents exchanged glances.

"It's upstairs in a decoy box. Same model as this one. $2.29 plus shipping from China. Not what I expect from our agencies. So, who bugged us?"

Diaz said, "Why have you left it active?"

"Might want to feed some misinformation."

"Well, the device is readily available. Could be a jilted lover or something similar."

Tony smiled. "Nope."

"I don't think it's related to the Chesters."

"They were planted while we were at a coffee shop just down the street yesterday. Coincidence?"

I was getting impatient. We were all dancing around because we weren't sure who could trust whom. "Look, you don't trust us, and we don't trust you."

"Why don't you trust verified agents of the U.S Marshal's office?" said Mendoza.

I started to answer, but Tony cut me off.

"Because you've been on special assignment for the last nine months and spend most of your time at Joint Base Bolling next door to the Naval Research Labs in D.C. Not a typical post for U.S. Marshals. No reason for that to relate to the Chesters. But you are suddenly in Oregon investigating their deaths. That makes it probably related to the Chesters. Something sensitive. Secret. But you can't tell us about it. So we look at this from the information we have. Everyone is a suspect until ruled out. And in our eyes, your badges don't rule you out."

Both agents' mouths fell open. After a few moments, Mendoza said, "We aren't at liberty to share information with you—even if you are clever and have access to information you shouldn't have."

Tony said, "There's more. You want to hear it?"

"No. Particularly not if you've been bugged."

"We're clean now. Unless you two are wired."

"Us? Why would we be wired? We can remember whatever you tell us. Or write it down."

"How about if I scan you both for bugs?"

"That's ridiculous," spat Mendoza.

Diaz said, "Sure. Go ahead." She stood up. "Scan me."

Tony went upstairs and returned with a silver wand about two inches in diameter and a foot long. He scanned the front of Diaz. She turned around, and he scanned her back. The wand made a low rumble sound and never changed while he scanned.

Tony looked at Mendoza. Mendoza said, "No way. We're agents for the United States government. Some tech nerd is not going to scan me."

Diaz said, "Yes, he is, Mendoza. Step over here."

"Not happening. What are you thinking? This is absurd." Mendoza stood and started for the door.

"Mendoza," said Diaz, "please don't make this a problem." She emphasized the word "problem."

Mendoza wheeled around. "This is personal and uncalled for. You know that."

Diaz stared at her for a moment. "Wait for me in the vehicle."

Mendoza stormed out, slamming the door.

Diaz sighed. "I apologize for her outburst and lack of cooperation. There are some personal issues with Mendoza that have no bearing on this case. Or on you. Just let it go. She is not bugged. I can guarantee that."

I said, "Agent Diaz, we don't know what's going on. I don't think you do either. You know about Marshal Massey and her group. You know about the first responder police officers. Do you know about the other two in a stolen white pickup who have been following us? Or the others in the shadows who remain unidentified? With so many players, you see why we don't know who to trust. Who are the good guys?"

She pursed her lips, glancing from me to Tony and back. Then she walked to the door as Chester the Cat rubbed against my leg. She turned as she opened it. "Maybe it's you." She shook her head. "Maybe you're the only good guys."

CHAPTER 14

Monday, May 1

The next morning, I scrambled some eggs while Tony showered. Chester jumped up to the counter next to the stove and I set him back on the floor. "No cats on the counter, Chester. You stay on the floor. This is not like it was at the Chesters'."

I wondered how long they had had Chester the Cat. He looked young, maybe a year old. Probably got him when they moved to Portland. Did they want a cat or was it to support their cover? Maybe they had to leave a cat behind.

He rubbed against my leg and meowed. I filled his water dish, and he drank a little. Then he sat down next to the slider and looked back at me.

"Okay. I get the message." I opened the door, and he scampered outside.

The microwave dinged. Tony would complain about me microwaving bacon instead of frying it. I didn't think it tasted much different. But the cleanup of the grease was a no-decision for me. He'd eat it microwaved.

As I served up two plates, he came downstairs. His hair was wet. I knew he worried about it getting thinner, but it was getting grayer, too. He looked tired today.

"You get any sleep?" I asked.

"Some." He sat down and picked up a piece of bacon. He just looked at it for a moment, then took a bite. Inside, I smiled but said nothing.

A thumping at the slider reminded me of Chester and I let him back in. He came over to the table and began licking his paws.

Tony looked down at him. "How's the cat doing?"

When he asks a question while we are eating, something was up. It was a sure sign of an approaching topic he wanted to discuss. "Good, I guess. I don't know much about cats."

"Allergies bothering you?"

"No. Maybe him staying downstairs helps."

"He's short-haired, too. You planning to keep him?"

"No plans at all. This situation seems to have disrupted everything." I was sure Tony didn't want to talk about the cat. He was leading up to something.

"That's true. You keeping up with schoolwork?"

"Yeah. I met with my presentation team last night. Just have to do the in-class presentation on Wednesday. I have to write a couple of papers and then finals next week. Maybe a little studying in between."

"How's the personal life?"

I laughed. There it was. Asking about my personal life was his way of seeing if I had any dates or social life. At least that's where I thought he was headed. "Nonexistent right now. Too much on my plate."

"And Gretchen…how is she?"

He caught me by surprise. Gretchen. He thought she was part of my "personal" life. "Good, I guess. We don't hang out, Tony. It's all professional. Lab partners investigating this Chester thing together. Nothing else going on."

"You sure?"

I set my fork down. "What are you saying?"

He pointed his fork my way. "You sure that's how she feels? Women are funny. You can't always read them. Sometimes they give off the opposite signal, expecting you to step up and take the initiative."

"I don't think so. She introduced me as her part-time boyfriend to that guy in the garage. When I teased her about it later, she punched me in the chest. She obviously works out. I have a bruise."

Tony smiled. "See, she likes you. She'd have punched you in the face if she was offended."

"No, it's not like that."

He shrugged.

"Tony, it's not. And she's made it clear she wants it that way. I do, too. It's more comfortable to work together this way. I don't have to deal with that whole emotional thing and try to guess what she's thinking. We keep everything out there so there's no misunderstanding."

"I'm just asking." He stood and carried his plate to the sink. "I'm always on your side, Buck. You know, you've become more like a little brother than a son to me. Seeing you work this case makes me realize how grown up you are. Reminds me of…well, reminds me of younger days."

He was going to say, "your father." I reminded him of my father. Even though I still missed my parents, Tony had stepped into my life and filled most of that void. Deep down, I wasn't sure how much I missed them anymore. It was just something I was supposed to feel. Really, Tony was my parent—father and mother. And we had grown a new dimension to our relationship. It was more brotherly. "I barely remember them anymore."

Tony leaned on the sink, his back to me. "I know. Maybe I failed to hold them in our lives as much as I should have." He stood there quietly for a moment.

"We make the best decisions we can with the information we have at the time."

Tony turned and smiled. "Where have I heard that before?"

That's what it said on a framed sign on the wall by the stairs. It had been with us since I moved in twelve years ago. It came up often when he was trying to teach me to make good decisions as a teenager. He let me make plenty of mistakes and suffer the consequences. I had often wondered if this was how a real father worked, or if it was different with him and me. Given what I'd heard from my friends about their fathers, Tony was tops. He was at every game, every school performance, every back-to-school night. Unlike a lot of fathers, Tony was there—always there.

My phone vibrated. It was an email from an unknown sender. I was about to delete it when I noticed the subject: *Meet at Insomnia.* I studied the sender email address, but it was just random numbers and letters with a domain of the same random characters. The message read, "11:00 a.m. today."

I showed it to Tony. "Forward it to me. I'll see if I can find out who it is."

While I was washing and drying the dishes, I texted Gretchen and asked her to meet at Insomnia at 11:00. She agreed.

Tony came down the stairs. "Dead end. Untraceable. Be careful. I'm going to try to trace our bugs."

"I'm meeting Gretchen there. Safety in numbers."

* * *

I called Gretchen and told her about the email. I asked her to go on into Insomnia and find a seat where she could see the whole place. Unless something went wrong, we wouldn't acknowledge each other so as not to tip off whoever set up the meeting if they didn't already know we were connected. Plus, a backup was always a good option.

When I arrived at Insomnia, Gretchen's car was parked a few spaces down the street, right behind a brown UPS truck. The hair on the back of my neck stood up. Visions of being thrown into that brown truck played through my head. I imagined the Chesters still in there.

A guy in a brown uniform came out of Heritage Bank across the street. He crossed and climbed into the truck and pulled out into the light Main Street traffic. I was relieved, but still spooked. I didn't want to have a UPS phobia forever.

Gretchen sat at a side table facing the front window. She had her back to the rest of the room with her laptop open. No one would notice her staring at us, whoever 'us' was, via her laptop camera.

I ordered a coffee, giving the name Toby. The barista, a slim young woman with long, brownish-blond hair, looked at me for a moment. I glanced at her nametag. Shylah. Not Cinna who slipped me her number at Thai House.

Still, Shylah knew my name because I was here so often. But I didn't want to have that discussion right now. So, I spelled it. "T-O-B-Y." She frowned and wrote it on the cup.

While I waited, I looked around. There were no familiar faces. When they called Toby, I picked up my coffee and headed towards the back table. At first, I didn't notice the guy coming out of the restroom. As he walked closer, I glanced at his face and nearly dropped my coffee in surprise. It sloshed on my hand, and he said, "Sorry. My fault." He handed me a couple of napkins.

I started to wipe the coffee off my hand but saw there was writing on the top napkin. I walked on to the table and set the cup down. Folding the napkin with the writing and setting it aside, I used the other one to wipe off my hand and the cup. By the time I sat down, the guy was gone.

I sat there for five minutes, just sipping, and looking around. People came and went. Some sat at tables chatting. A couple of others had their laptops open. Nearly everyone was looking at their phone or a screen of some kind.

No one approached me. I didn't want to look at the napkin in case someone was watching. I figured I'd just pocket it when I left. But I glanced anyhow. It was an address and a time. 8:00 p.m. My phone dinged with a text from Gretchen. *What's on the napkin?* If she knew I looked, then anyone else would know, too.

I texted back. *Meet at my house.* I got up, dumped my coffee in the trash, and headed out the door.

I started around the corner and realized the spot where the UPS truck had been was now occupied by a white Silverado pickup. As I walked by, I looked inside. The driver, a Latino man wearing a black cap, was just getting out. The passenger side towards me opened and I jumped, half expecting someone to leap out and grab me. But a ten-year-old boy in a soccer uniform stepped out. He glanced at me, then slammed the door. He and the man walked on down the street chattering in Spanish.

When I got home, Gretchen was already there, standing outside the front door.

"Did you knock?" I asked.

"No. Just waiting for you."

"Did you see the white pickup in front of your car?"

"Yeah. Scared the shit out of me at first."

"Me, too Not the same one."

"It had Washington plates."

She was more observant than I was. We walked inside. Tony was back at the table with a laptop. I pulled out the napkin and showed it to Gretchen.

She asked, "Where is that address?"

"Don't know." I handed the napkin to Tony. "Can you look this up, please."

He typed for a moment. "Sikh Center of Oregon. South Beaverton." He typed and clicked some more. "Twenty-minute drive."

Gretchen said, "The guy who handed it to you wore a turban."

"Yeah. His name is Vikramjeet Singh. He's one of the marshals from the Chesters' on Thursday and at my taped interview with Massey. He's the one who fed Chester milk at the scene. I thought he was a good guy."

"Maybe he is. But why does he want to meet?"

"We seem to be swimming in feds who have different agendas they won't share. I guess Vikram has another one. And I bet he won't share either.

* * *

Gretchen came by and rode with me to the Sikh Center. We chatted about our classes and the remaining work before graduating.

I said, "I wrote drafts of two papers this afternoon. It felt like I got a lot done. They're not due until Friday."

"You usually wait until the last minute?"

"No. I try to stay ahead of it so if something comes up, I have some flexibility."

"You're a planner," she said.

I didn't know what to say to that. I didn't even know if it was a compliment or a criticism, so I let it hang there for a moment. She was right, though. My calendar App on my phone was how I organized and ran my days. It was the most used App on my phone. "What about you?"

"Not a planner. Obviously."

"Why obviously?"

"You called me on this Chesters thing, and I jumped right in."

"I thought you just wanted to hang out with a charming guy." Before she could slug me, I raised a defensive arm. "Don't hit the driver."

She glared at me for a moment, then started laughing. "You deserve it, though. It's just because I value my life."

"What about mine?"

"Not so much."

There was something in her tone that hurt a little, like there was some truth in what she said. I hadn't thought of her as narcissistic, but that crack stung, and I had to consider it. I'd dated a girl once—just once—who was very narcissistic. When I was a freshman, she was in my Business Law intro class. Dark hair, lots of makeup, very good looking. I ran into her, literally, one day at the bookstore. More accurately, she ran into me because she was rushing and not watching where she was going. We chatted, I asked her out, and we had dinner. The conversation was all about her. At the end of the meal, I walked her to her door and said goodnight. When she went inside, she slammed her door. The class ended a few weeks later and I never saw her again.

Gretchen didn't seem to be that type. I glanced over at her. She was looking ahead of us and had a little smile on her face. I noticed she wasn't wearing earrings.

I said, "Personal question?"

"Forget it."

"Are your ears pierced?"

Her hand shot to her ear, and she pulled her hair over it. She was silent for a while. "Why would you ask that?"

"Just curious. Almost all women have pierced ears. You don't?"

"I don't wear any jewelry."

"Why not?"

She started playing with that bracelet on her left wrist. Guess she didn't consider that "jewelry."

The GPS interrupted to tell us to turn right on River Road. We were in farm country now. Uniform trees in rows filled the field on the left side of the road. A sign for Hoffman Farms Store passed on the right.

"Females in law enforcement still take a lot of shit," Gretchen said. "Being less feminine reduces the comments and stares. If I dressed like that golfer Paige Spiranac, I could still do the same job, but the men would harass me to death. I couldn't work like that."

"I can't disagree with you. On the ride-alongs with the sheriff's office, there are some Neanderthal guys there who even make me uncomfortable. I'm surprised they still work there."

"They work at the jail?"

"I don't know."

"That's where they often put most of the assholes. I guess the prisoners can't complain as much as regular citizens whom they might offend."

We went through a roundabout and transitioned to Scholls Ferry Road.

She said, "Why don't you have a girlfriend?"

"Unlike you, I don't hit people who ask me personal questions." I'd never hit a woman. I'd thought about that a lot a year or two back. In the line of duty, I wouldn't have any problem hitting a woman if the situation warranted. These days, though, any use of force could get a cop into trouble or even in jail. It had become nearly impossible to navigate those waters and stay afloat long-term. Most of my classmates were heading towards jobs that avoided any kind of policing in the streets.

"Hey! You still with me?"

"Yeah. I was just thinking about something."

"Obviously. Get back in your driving box. Focus on that for now."

The GPS said to take the next right turn. I slowed. It was a gravel road through an open field that led back to some buildings shielded by trees. A wall along the left side seemed to be like a dam, holding back the crawling condo construction from spilling onto this empty brown field.

Gretchen said, "This doesn't look creepy."

It was 8:05 p.m. Shadows were getting long. The gravel crunched under the tires as we drove along. The closest building looked like a regular ranch house. A few lights shined in the windows.

The road led between the trees and ended at the back of the house. No black Suburbans were parked there, but a white Chevy panel van and an older gray Honda seemed to hunker together. I stopped a distance behind them.

To our left were two garage-type buildings. One looked to be a detached two-car garage that matched the off-white of the house. Behind it was a much bigger gray building, more like a farm equipment storage building with a ten-foot-tall roll-up door.

Vikram walked out the back door of the house and waved.

Gretchen whispered, "Do you know anything about Sikhs or their religion?"

"No. You?"

"Nothing."

We got out of the car. Vikram showed no surprise that Gretchen was with me. He wore a white shirt rolled up a little at the sleeves.

He extended his hand towards Gretchen. "Miss Kho. Welcome. Thank you for coming."

Gretchen glanced at me. Vikram grabbed my hand. "Thank you, Buck. I appreciate your cooperation and taking the time to make this journey. Please come in." He held the door, and we walked inside.

Vikram said, "If you would, please follow me." He led to a conference-like room. There was an oval center table with ten chairs surrounding it. White marker boards filled two walls. A projector hung from the ceiling over the table. A laptop was open at the head of the table.

Vikram waved an arm towards the chairs. "Please. Have a seat. Would you like some water?"

We both declined. Vikram shut the door and my ears popped. I recognized the sensation. We were in a soundproof room, also likely shielded electronically so no signals got out or in. It was like Tony's office. Vikram sat down in front of the laptop and closed the lid.

"Thank you for coming. I appreciate your trust and you driving all this way."

I said, "No problem."

Vikram seemed nervous, but that would be natural for this circumstance. I wondered if this was his house and the whole Sikh Center thing was a ruse to avoid taxes or something else. This was clearly not a worship center. Yet we were in a conference room. I hoped Vikram had some explanation.

"How is the cat you rescued from the Chesters' house?"

"He's fine. Doing well, eating, running around."

"What are your plans for him? Will you take him to a shelter?"

"I'm not sure yet. We'll see how it works out. So far, my allergies haven't been too bad, but we keep him on the first floor."

"Yes, I see. You sleep upstairs. That is good."

There was an awkward pause in the conversation. Finally, Gretchen said, "Vikram, why did you invite us here?"

He frowned and opened the laptop. "Would you please turn off your phones and put them on the table?"

I glanced at Gretchen. I could tell she was nervous, but we both complied.

"Thank you, "said Vikram. "Buck, as part of my full disclosure, I acknowledge your revolver on your ankle, which is legally licensed."

"I don't really like people nosing into my personal business, Vikram."

"Of course. I would feel the same way. But we need to have full disclosure. Honesty. Straightforward conversations. It is necessary to share what the agency has gathered about you and Miss Kho."

Gretchen seemed to squirm in her seat. "You may skip me. I'm good. Let's get on to the purpose of this meeting."

Vikram smiled. "Of course."

He seemed to be moving his laptop on the table. Just a tiny bit, here and there. And he moved the lid several times, just a hair more open or closed. I looked at the lid closely. There was a small black dot about the size of a pencil eraser on the back of the lid. It was a camera lens.

I said, "Vikram, who else is joining us?"

"I'm sorry?"

"Who is watching and listening through your laptop?"

He glanced at the laptop display, then back at me. "You and Miss Kho seem to be far more perceptive than is expected from a couple of college kids. My employer has spent a good deal of time thoroughly investigating both of you because we suspected you might somehow be agents of a foreign interest."

"What?" I smiled and looked at Gretchen. She wasn't smiling.

Vikram held up a hand. "But that is not why I asked you here. We are trying to find out who murdered the Chesters. I think you can help us. Could you walk us through Thursday up to the time you called 911?"

Gretchen said, "You're not going to tell us who else is watching?"

He looked at his hands, glanced at the laptop, and said, "No. That is not going to happen."

"Why?"

"You have no need to know."

"We have no need to be here."

He said, "You've been thrown into a situation with considerable personal risks, and you have limited, if unexpected, skills. I'm the only one who has your back, the only one you can turn to if you need help."

I said, "Vikram, I think you are an honest and a good man. That's why we are here. We trust you. But having someone else secretly watch this discussion undermines that trust."

He shrugged. "As I said, there is no alternative. And you could greatly assist us in finding the murderer."

I looked at Gretchen. I could see she was fuming and ready to walk out, but Vikram was right. We were just ordinary college kids who'd stumbled into this whole thing. But now more than ever I wanted to know where this went. Who killed the Chesters. And why. And who was in the white pickup tailing us. Vikram might not have all the answers, but he knew things we didn't.

I put my hand on Gretchen's arm and said, "It's okay, Wei."

Her head snapped around and she glared at me. After a moment, she looked at my hand on her arm. I pulled it back. She snapped that bracelet on her left arm and smiled at me. Shit. She was telling me she was going to pummel me later. I could feel the sweat breaking out under my arms.

I turned to Vikram. "Proceed."

An hour later, Vikram had exhausted his questions about how and what I did on Thursday. He closed the laptop. "Could you please show me the pictures you took on that day? If you'll be so kind, I think you can use Smart View on your phone to project them onto the screen next to us."

On the TV, a popup appeared, and Vikram clicked on "Allow." The screen flickered, and my phone screen showed on the TV.

I navigated to my gallery and opened the first picture in the series of pictures for Thursday. I captured the whole bag label that had the customer's name and address, the product information, and the price.

He said, "Isn't some of this information about tracking the product from the seed to the customer delivery?"

"Yes, the UID or Unique Identifier. It's the number issued by the government for tracking and monitoring. Almost everyone uses a software product named 'Metrc' to track product and confirm regulatory compliance."

He nodded and I scrolled through the remainder. When we got to the Chesters', he said, "Could you go back to the first one, please? Let's walk through each one so we understand the process better."

I started at the beginning and moved to the driver's license for Maureen Malone. "She was my first delivery, on Whitford Lane. My first six stops were on the east side of the freeway. The Chesters were my seventh stop, the first on the west side of the freeway."

We walked through the deliveries with a few questions and answers along the way.

When I got to the Chesters' order, I noticed the UID ended in 907. I was certain the Malone order UID was different, even though they were both eighth-ounce weed.

After a few more questions, Vikram said, "Thank you for sharing your information."

I stopped Smart View and closed my phone. I couldn't wait to look into why the UID was different on the Chesters' order, but not knowing the answer and not knowing who else was watching meant I wasn't going to share my discovery with them right now.

I said, "Why do you have a SCIF in this house?"

Gretchen looked at me. "A what?"

"SCIF. Sensitive Compartmented Information Facility. Didn't you notice the door on the room? It's like the door to Tony's office."

She still looked confused.

"It prevents electronic signals from escaping so you can't be monitored from outside. It's like a big Faraday cage."

Vikram stood and looked at the floor, shifting from foot to foot. "I am truly sorry that I cannot share more information with you. It is as it must be." He withdrew a business card from his pocket and slid it across the table. "Should you need to contact me, you may use this number."

I picked up the card. It was plain white. In the middle was his name. *Vikramjeet Singh.* Below was a phone number. Nothing else. I turned it over. Blank. "This doesn't look like what I expected from the U.S. Marshals. Not quite the same as Marshal Massey's card, either."

"Yes. Not quite the same."

I looked at Vikram for a moment. He didn't meet my eyes, but glanced at Gretchen, the floor, his laptop, then settled on the door. I took that as an invitation to leave.

We filed out and retraced our steps to the back door and outside.

"Thank you for coming and for sharing your information." He shook hands with each of us, then turned and went back inside the house.

We climbed into my car before we spoke. As I buckled my seatbelt, Gretchen was furiously snapping the bracelet on her left wrist.

"What are you doing?" I asked. She seemed to be gritting her teeth.

"Trying not to hit you."

"Hit me? What for?"

"Wei?" She rolled her eyes. "Trying to placate me. It felt like you were telling the dog to sit."

"Is hitting routine with you?"

"I try to communicate in a language that my partner will understand."

"It makes me want to not speak at all."

"That would be a good start."

It was dark so I couldn't see her face.

"Are you really riled up right now, or is this just retaliation, punishment for a perceived offense that couldn't be administered at the time of the crime."

"It depends."

"On?"

"How you apologize."

"For what? I wanted to stop you from objecting to the people on the laptop. It wasn't going anywhere useful. And if I had said that, we would have had a long discussion. What I did worked."

She slammed her fist into the dash.

"Stop it!" I said. "Don't hit stuff."

"Or what? You gonna hit me back? Try again."

I looked out the window at the smaller building. My temper was starting to boil, but that was stupid. She was angry with me, but that shouldn't make me angry, too. I blew out my breath. "You're being unreasonable. You have no reason to be angry with me. If you think I said something demeaning, I can't argue with your feelings. But there was no such intention. I was trying to manage the situation as best I could. I'm sorry if—"

I saw movement on the top of the garage. A dark shadow slid along the roof and disappeared behind what looked like a four-foot golf ball. I recognized it as the cover of a small satellite antenna. I pulled out Vikram's card, held it next to the dash so I could read it, and dialed the number.

"Vikram, there's someone on your garage roof by the satellite antenna."

I could hear him breathing, but he didn't say anything for a moment. "Buck, you should drive away. I appreciate the call." He hung up.

I put the phone back in my pocket. I was sure he was protecting us. Someone who shouldn't be there was on top of Vikram's garage roof.

I backed out and turned around, heading out the driveway. I said to Gretchen, "When I get to the end of the driveway, I'm gonna turn right and drive along the road to the first entrance to the condos. I'll pull over and then you drive."

"Why?"

"Because I'm getting out. I'm going to go help Vikram."

"With what?"

"The guy on his garage roof."

I texted Vikram to let him know I was coming back up the condo side of the wall on foot. I figured I could get beyond the garage and climb over. Whoever was up there was going to be watching the house, not watching behind him.

I got out of the car. The street ran right along the wall all the way to the back of the property. The lights from the condos gave enough light that I could see a tree hanging over the fence near the back. It looked like a good place to cross over.

Just before I got to the tree, a dark figure leaped from the wall onto the street in front of me. As he landed, he immediately started running away, towards the back.

I knelt on one knee, grabbed my weapon, and pointed it towards him as I yelled, "Stop!" He kept running, getting farther away. I thought about firing a warning shot until a pocket of blacktop exploded into my right calf.

Things slowed. The small flash of orange light from the top of the wall by the tree, the blacktop exploding, and a muffled thump sound came together as I realized someone was shooting at me. With a silenced weapon.

I rolled to my left, and another pocket of blacktop exploded near me. I fired three rounds where I'd seen the flash of light. The sound of my weapon was deafening in the quiet of the early night.

I jumped up and ran behind the nearest car for cover. The guy who was running down the street was long gone by now. A moment later, there was a loud whoosh before flames shot into the air from the other side of the wall. The blast and heat nearly knocked me over. My phone vibrated. No caller ID popped up, but the number looked familiar.

"Hello."

"Buck. Are you okay? Where are you?"

"Vikram?"

"Yes, yes."

"I'm fine. What's on fire?"

"The garage. Was that your weapon firing?"

"Yes."

"They are gone now. The police will be here shortly. Slip away and go home. I'll be in touch."

He hung up. I holstered my weapon and realized my leg was bleeding. Running or even walking wasn't a good idea.

I looked up at the street sign, then down the street into the condos. There was a swimming pool and park just beyond the condo where I was hiding. I limped down the street and dialed Gretchen. She answered on the first ring. "What happened?"

"GPS to 17400 Sabrina. Come through the condo complex, not down the side street. Cops and firetrucks are going to be swarming soon."

Sirens wailed in the distance. In a moment, flashing blue and red lights lit the sky.

Headlights flashed from my left. I limped over to the car and climbed into the passenger side.

Gretchen looked at me and tapped on her phone a few times.

"Not the hospital," I said. "Back home first."

It took a while to get out of the condo complex because the only entrance to the street was the one I had run down. A cop finally moved his car and waved us through.

I guess I crashed because later Gretchen said I started snoring almost immediately.

When we got to my house, she helped me out of the car. I put my arm around her shoulder and limped to the door, keeping the weight off my leg. She parked me in a dining chair.

I called out for Tony but got no answer. "Door at the end of the upstairs hall," I said to Gretchen. "There's a doorbell button on the wall to the right of the door."

A moment later, Tony came flying down the stairs. He took one look at my bloody pants and went to work.

He pulled off my shoe and sock. The sock was squishy with blood. He dropped both into a trash bag.

"Give me the other shoe and sock." He dropped those into the bag. "Pants, too. We don't want any evidence lying around.

I emptied my pockets on the table, then dropped my pants to the floor. Tony worked my left leg free, and I hobbled my right leg out.

"Shrapnel wound?" He unstrapped my ankle holster and laid it on the table.

"Yeah. Round hit the blacktop and blew it into me."

"Looks like someone took a bite out of your calf. Not too deep, but a lot of blood."

Chester jumped onto the dining table and stood looking down at my leg. I didn't have the energy to make him get off of the table. I looked around.

"What happened to Gretchen?" I asked Tony.

"Bathroom."

"Do I need to go to the hospital?"

"Not unless you object to a calf scar."

"I think my leg scars have scars from my soccer years. Another one won't matter."

He nodded and went about dressing the wound while I told him the story.

When he was done, I stood up and tested my weight on the leg. I'd had worse pain.

I stood there in my boxers as Gretchen came down the stairs and started giggling.

"What are you laughing about?"

She pointed. "Your legs. They're so white they're blinding."

I started to make a sarcastic retort, but I noticed her red eyes. She'd been upstairs a long time. I hobbled over to the foot of the steps where she stood. She had her hand over her mouth like she was trying not to laugh.

"How about helping me upstairs so I can cover the objects of your mirth?"

"The what?"

"My blinding white legs."

She took my hand and slung it over her shoulder. I could have walked up the stairs, but I figured having her help me was a good thing. I couldn't explain. It was a feeling without logic. At my bedroom doorway, I hobbled to my dresser. I found a pair of pajama pants and pulled them on.

Gretchen remained at the doorway, arms folded across her chest. "You played soccer."

"Yeah, in high school."

"You any good?"

"We got third in the state my senior year."

"Not bad."

"You ever play sports?"

"Not the kind you're thinking."

"What about the other kind?"

"A little."

"Could you be more elusive?"

"Probably." She walked over to my shelves and started reading through the book titles lined up there. "*EMI Control Methods and Techniques.* Bathroom reading, I guess. Didn't know you were such a nerd."

"You were telling me about your sports."

"No, I wasn't."

"You know about my sports."

"Are we keeping score?"

"Not yet. Maybe later."

"You're annoying."

"Touché."

"Some other time."

"Why not now?"

She looked at me, crossing her arms again.

"Where the fuck did you go and what did you do? I heard gunshots. You got hit in the leg. And I'm stuck in the car with my thumb up my ass." She glared at me.

I held up my hands. "Pity the weak and infirm."

She grabbed my hand in a control grip. "You going to tell me, or do I have to beat it out of you?"

Tony stuck his head in the door. Gretchen released her grip. He held up my phone. "This is dinging." He tossed the phone to me and walked on down the hallway.

I looked at my phone. "It's a text from Vikram. He wants to meet. Oregon Buddhist Vihara. On Walnut."

"When?"

"Tomorrow. 9:00 a.m."

"Good. Let's go to Elmer's for breakfast. We can walk from there to meet him." She glanced at my leg. "At least, I can."

"My leg hurts. I'm exhausted." I pulled back the covers on my bed and crawled in. "Good night."

She stood there, hands on her hips, glaring at me.

I closed my eyes. I was nearly asleep when I heard the bedroom door close.

CHAPTER 15

Tuesday, May 2

My bedroom door flew open. "Get your shoes on." Gretchen turned and called, "You, too, Tony. You're driving."

Twenty minutes later, after we ordered at Elmer's, Gretchen propped her elbows on the table and her chin on her hands. She stared at me.

Tony laughed. "That's your cue," he said to me.

I told the story as best as I could remember. It seemed like there were some gaps, particularly about the whole ride back. But I started in. "After I got out of the car, I ran down that street using the wall to shield me. But before I got to a tree where I could cross over the wall, a guy in black jumped down in front of me and started running away. I yelled at him to stop, and then another guy in the tree started shooting at me. I returned fire. And then the garage went up in flames."

Tony started quizzing me. "Did Vikram know you were coming down the street?"

"Yes. I texted him."

"Where was your backup?"

"I didn't have one."

"Sure, you did. What was Gretchen doing?"

"She was in the car where it was safe."

"Why?"

"Because I didn't want to risk her getting hurt."

My words just hung there. Tony and Gretchen exchanged glances, then looked back at me. The silence felt endless. I realized what I'd just said and what was going on. I might as well get it out on the table and deal with it. It was my problem. "Okay, so that was a bad decision. I can see where my…feelings about Gretchen got in the way of safe procedures. We should have gone together." But in my head, I was thinking about how I would have felt if she'd been hurt, or shot, or even killed. I wasn't sure I'd made such a bad decision.

Gretchen said, "Do you need a new partner?"

Our food came and we started eating. My leg throbbed and I had lost my appetite. She was right. She always was. If I couldn't keep her in my partner role, both intellectually and emotionally, then I needed to find a new partner.

Tony said, "I think you can both see how field work can really mess with emotional attachments. It's why law enforcement has such crappy marriage statistics."

"I don't have an emotional attachment." I pushed some Canadian bacon around on my plate.

Tony said, "Buck, you'd have the same issue if I was your partner. You'd have tried to leave me in the car, too."

He was right. I didn't have many people in my inner circle. I closed my eyes. Was I including Gretchen in my inner circle? I guess so. And for some reason, I sort of had the Chesters in that group, too.

Maybe I was emotionally deficient or broken. My only parent figure was my uncle. It was certainly unusual to grow up like that. But just because I didn't have bonds with a lot of people didn't mean I couldn't form them. Or that I was somehow broken. I was as normal as the next guy with both parents, a gang of brothers and sisters, and a busload of relatives. I did wonder what that felt like. But it had always seemed so stifling. Trying to juggle so many personal connections seemed like chaos to me.

I looked at Gretchen. She was forking her veggie bowl into her mouth like a fireman shoveling coal into a boiler. She was frowning but I didn't know why. It felt like it was my fault for not understanding. There was a vague sense of *déjà vu* when I thought about the girls I had dated. Briefly. Maybe I needed therapy to figure this out.

I stuffed a chunk of tasteless Eggs Benedict into my mouth and swallowed it. Gretchen finished her bowl and shoved her plate aside. She rummaged in her purse, then held out two Tylenol. I didn't argue. I sat back in my chair and crossed my arms over my chest. My thoughts flew around, hopping from point to point about the Chesters' case. It let me ignore the elephant in the room that was dripping with emotion.

"Hey, I forgot to mention something." I pulled out my phone.

Gretchen said, "That's a surprise."

I ignored her and scrolled through my pictures. I laid the phone on the table. "Look at the UID for the Chester delivery the previous week. It ends in 907." I scrolled back to the Malone delivery. "This is the same product delivered on the same day to Malone. Ends in 572." I picked up the phone and scrolled back to the pictures from the week before. I laid it on the table. "So three weeks ago, a week before the Chesters' laced product arrived, the Malone UID ended in 907" I scrolled again. "And the Chester UID also ended in 907."

Tony said, "What was it this past Thursday?"

I scrolled through the pictures. "492."

"Does the UID change each week?"

"For this product, yes. Sometimes twice a week. Whenever we sell out of a batch. Each batch has a different UID."

Gretchen said, "If I follow, you're saying the product UID that killed the Chesters was originally delivered to someone else. They laced the product and then slipped it into your deliveries a week later."

"Yes. Everyone's been thinking that the Chester order got switched in my locked delivery bin somehow when I had my back turned or was making a delivery. But that's not the case. See, I also take pictures in the shop of each order. It's my receipt for pickup proof." I scrolled to another picture. "What I picked up from the shop was what I delivered. There was no switch along the way."

Tony said, "Obviously, someone in the shop must be involved. Whether they're involved in lacing is a different question. Someone could have paid them to make the switch without their knowledge of what was going on."

"And they probably took the other one home, if I was betting," said Gretchen.

"Why do you say that?"

"They wouldn't want it discovered at the shop. Might screw up inventory or someone's audit."

Tony said, "Wouldn't they just toss it into a dumpster? Why take it home? Or does it make a difference?"

"Maybe not, "she said, "but later it might become relevant. So, it's a note for now."

Tony looked at his watch. "Ten minutes. You better get going with the gimp. I'll get the check."

"Thanks," we said in unison.

It was a little over two blocks to the Oregon Buddhist Vihara. I was walking slowly, my calf still throbbed but the pain was somewhat muted by the Tylenol.

As we crossed Oak Street, and headed down First Street, Gretchen said, "I'd hit you again, maybe several times, but you're injured."

"Why?"

She said quietly, "I do keep score."

"That's frightening."

"Let's keep our focus here and work as a team, okay? Equal partners. None of this emotional bullshit. Just think of me as Tony number two."

I laughed. "Bad choice. I realized I'd have done the same with him. He's a combo package of father, mother, and all my family rolled into one. I'd never put him in jeopardy."

"You don't have any other family?"

"Nope. Just Tony. And Chester the Cat."

"Now the cat is family?"

"Chester is a good cat. Stays downstairs. Completely housebroken. He's grateful."

We turned up Walnut Street. She grabbed my arm. "Wait a minute. Do you think I should be grateful because you didn't take me with you down that street last night?"

Interesting question. I didn't know the answer right off. Maybe? I realized she didn't see it that way. That was like the complete opposite of what she thought. At least I thought it was. I was confused. I finally found a neutral answer I thought would be acceptable. "I wouldn't presume to think you should or should not feel any particular way."

She slugged me in the chest, but not as hard as usual. She stomped forward, furiously snapping the bracelet on her wrist.

Vikram opened the door before we rang the bell. "Come in."

He escorted us into a vestibule area where a golden buddha statue sat atop a light brown stand. A spotlight shone down on him, making him the focal point of the dim room.

He pointed down a hallway. "This way." He led us into a small conference room. A round Sam's Club table and four folding chairs filled the room. He produced three bottles of water and set them on the table.

I took one. It was cold and I held it to the spot on my chest where she had just hit me.

She looked at me and realized what I was doing. She shook her head and said, "Such a baby."

Vikram said, "Buck, are you injured?" His eyes went wide as he glanced at the bottle held to my chest.

"This? No. I just have a sore spot on my chest. I did get a small gash on my calf from a bullet ricochet last night, but it will be fine."

Vikram said, "I am so sorry you became engaged in that situation last evening. I had hoped you had cleared away before those men arrived."

"Who were they? What did they want?"

"Another time, perhaps. Right now I must focus on ensuring your safety. Those men may discover who you are and come after you. I cannot be sure, but I believe you returned fire and may have struck one of them."

"How do you know he was hit?"

"If he wasn't injured, he would have returned your fire. Instead, he hastened away. By the time I circled behind the garage, he had cleared out. Then the police and firefighters arrived. But it was too late. The building was doused in accelerant, probably gasoline."

"Vikran, you know the Chesters' house burned down, right?"

"Yes. I suspect it was the same men. But I cannot figure out how they identified my location. And I am concerned that they may have tapped our meeting transmission, which would implicate you even more. So, I am going to engage Marshal Massey and ask her to place you in WITSEC temporarily. We need to hide you so no harm comes to you."

Both Gretchen and I started to protest, but Vikram held up his hand. "Let me finish. If we do that, then the events of last night must not be revealed to Marshal Massey. Can you do that?"

I looked at Gretchen. She must have gotten it sooner than I did. She said, "You weren't wearing your U.S. Marshal hat last night?"

Vikram looked confused. "I always wear a turban as part of my Sikh religion."

Gretchen smiled. "I'm sorry. That was a euphemism. I should have said, you were not working as a U.S. Marshal last night?"

Vikram looked at his hands. His eyes darted from me to Gretchen. "That is correct."

"And you won't tell us why or in what capacity you orchestrated our meeting last night."

He smiled. "Thank you for understanding."

I said, "Vikram, it would make us feel much more at ease if you could confirm that your other work is not linked to a foreign interest."

He studied the table. "Will it make a difference about whether or not you will accept WITSEC?"

Gretchen said, "No. We aren't doing that in either case."

"Then my answer is of no consequence."

"Yes, it is. Whether we trust you or not depends on your response."

"How would you know if I simply lied and gave you the answer I think you want to hear?"

"You're a professional. You could be trained to lie effectively. Even overcome a polygraph. But I think your faith comes first. Besides, you saved a cat's life."

Vikram pursed his lips for a moment. "Your reasoning is true."

I said, "We're just a couple of college kids who fell into a mess of feds swirling around the murder of an old, sweet couple." I glanced at Gretchen. "And one of the feds asked us to not step aside while the others tell us to quit getting involved."

He nodded.

"Vikram, we don't know who to trust."

"The men who burned down my garage destroyed my secure communications capability. I had a secure satellite link that is gone, as well as the building contents."

Gretchen said, "We're both sorry for your loss, but won't the government pay for it?"

"No. None of it existed, as far as the government is concerned."

"Who were the men who burned it down?"

"Probably the same ones who burned the Chesters' house. I am concerned that they might do the same to your house, Buck. So far as I know, they have not identified Ms. Kho, or she might be in danger, too. Hence, the WITSEC offer. It is still open."

"Why are they burning places?"

"To destroy evidence. They don't know where it is located, but they hope to destroy it by destroying the likely locations."

"What is the evidence and why do they want to destroy it?"

A pained look washed across Vikram's face. "I cannot tell you that information."

Gretchen said, "Do you know where this evidence is?"

He shook his head. "They may well have destroyed it in one of the fires. But I have no idea where it is or if it still exists."

"I'm confused," said Gretchen. "If they thought it was in the Chesters' house and they burned it down, wouldn't they think they had destroyed it? Burning down your garage or our houses could be for a different reason."

"Reasonable logic. These people tend to go to extremes and make sure they cover every alternative. They are dangerous people. You should not be involved with them. Please consider WITSEC to protect yourselves. And your families."

* * *

When we got back to my place, Gretchen headed home while Tony and I tried to trace the dispensary order that got the Chesters killed.

Tony said, "Walk me through these labels."

"A label on a cannabis delivery order has a lot of numbers and letters that seem like gibberish to most people. But each cannabis plant has a tracking number issued by the government. It's called a UID—unique identifier. With that number, the product can be traced all the way back to the individual plant or seed.

"In the dispensary, we sell products by UID. Once we sell all that UID—all products made from that plant—we switch to another plant with a new UID. The product itself might be a tincture, gummy, or, like in this case, regular flower—what most people think of as weed or grass. For flower, we typically sell all the product for one UID every three or four days."

"Okay. Got it. What do you need from me?"

With Tony's help, we hacked into the shop's inventory computer system. We confirmed that the flower UID I delivered on April 13 ended in 907. The flower UID I delivered to everyone on April 20 ended in 542. Except the Chesters'-- it ended in 907. Someone had pulled aside a 907 order from April 13, laced the content, and altered the original label with Ray Chester's name and delivery date to April 20. An additional someone, or maybe the same person, must have swapped the real April 20 Chester order with the laced one. The question was, where did they get the 907 order they laced? It had to be in the April 13 deliveries to get the label they altered.

Most of my deliveries were regular customers. They typically came in and set up a schedule in person. Sometimes someone else set it for them if they were disabled.

I had proof that I had made all my deliveries on April 13. None of the regulars complained about not getting their product or receiving the wrong product. It had to be one of the new name orders that requested delivery, probably under a false name. On April 13, there was only one. A woman named Natalie Durbin at the OliveTree Inn.

The OliveTree isn't the Ritz. Cars in the parking lot frequently look like someone is living in them. I often wondered if the homeless shelter gave out vouchers for the OliveTree when the shelter was full. Every time I've delivered there—and that's the only reason I would go near the place—the pool has been out of order and covered with green slime.

I couldn't remember Natalie Durbin. But when I scrolled through my pictures for that week, I found an ID with the name Wayne Durbin. Then I remembered. He'd said Natalie was in the shower and he'd take the delivery. He handed me $80 in cash and told me to keep the rest. The bill was $78.93. But I smiled and told him to have a good day.

Tony searched for Wayne and Natalie Durbin. They didn't exist. The addresses on their DL didn't exist either. Were they the ones in the white Silverado burning places down?

CHAPTER 16

Wednesday, May 3

At 10:30 a.m. I headed over to the OliveTree. Although I had a box of latex gloves in my car, I snagged the heavy-duty yellow ones from under the kitchen sink and stuffed them into my pocket. I didn't want to pick up any diseases or bugs at the OliveTree.

This was a "recon" mission, as Tony called it. In and out quickly with enough information so Tony could get to the hotel's computer and video systems. I had no plans to search for Natalie Durbin or go to room 130 where I had made my delivery. Tony was parked down the street and I had him on my phone's FaceTime in case I needed backup.

I circled the Olive Tree to see if a white Silverado pickup was parked there. Tony and I had agreed that if it was there, I'd abort the recon. But there was no Silverado, so I parked in the front by the office and walked in, a bell ringing above the door. A middle-aged Indian man greeted me with a toothy smile.

"Good afternoon. I am Sanjeet. How may I help you?"

I showed him my dispensary ID. "I made a delivery here on April thirteenth. A little over two weeks ago. I wonder if you have any information on the Durbins who were in room 130 that day?"

Before he could answer, an elderly woman burst into the office. Her hair was wet, and she had chunks of white stuff splattered in her hair and over the shoulders of her floral top. She was shouting before she even got in the door. "Those assholes above us flooded their bathroom and the ceiling just caved in on me. Look at me! The whole ceiling just fell down. There's water running everywhere. And the damn cockroaches are running for their lives."

Sanjeet glanced at me before darting around the counter. He grabbed the lady by the arm and pulled her out the door as he began to jabber at her. All the while, she kept ranting at him. He led her along the pool in the center of the courtyard and in the door of an open room.

I went around the counter where I could see a computer display. Tapping the space bar brought up a splash screen. *Hotel Management by DuckHost* splayed across the screen. There was a button for login. When I clicked, a password prompt appeared.

I opened my phone and searched for WIFI networks. OliveTree came up on the list first. It was unsecured so I connected. After opening a browser, I typed *What is my IP address.* I took a screenshot of the result and headed for the door.

With this information, I was pretty sure Tony could hack into the hotel's system and find the data we needed.

* * *

We gathered at 5:00 p.m. Gretchen's hair was still a little wet and hung limply down her back. It was weird to see her without a beanie, and she had on a different shirt and sweatpants. Her jaw dropped when she walked into Tony's office. "It looks like a control center or a spaceship. Who do you work for again?"

"U.S. Treasury. Financial Crimes Enforcement Network (FinCEN). It's a link between law enforcement, financial, and regulatory communities. In short, I look for money laundering and other financial crimes."

"I guess you're a super hacker?"

"I have access to many systems regular people don't. Some are law enforcement. Others are banking or payment processing systems."

I joined in. "Sometimes he does a little gray work, too." I showed him the screenshot I'd captured at the hotel. It took about three minutes before he was inside the system at the OliveTree Inn. He found the guest registration database and searched for April 13.

There she was. Room 130. Just like the dispensary label said. Natalie Durbin. She'd checked in the day before and checked out the following day, the fourteenth. Two nights. Time enough to set up the delivery by me and get out of town.

"Presuming she laced the product, how does she get it back into the dispensary and into my deliveries the next week?"

Tony said, "Let's see if we can find her on video." He poked around for a while and eventually found the video system hosted on another computer at the hotel, but the video history was uploaded to a cloud.

"I can't go hacking into a cloud. First, I'd be detected, and second, it's illegal, even for me. So we have to see if we can get the video through the hotel's server."

It took twenty minutes, but he finally got the hotel computer to retrieve April 13 from the cloud. From there, he transferred it to his system. After a lot of back and forth, we figured out that Natalie left her room at 7:30 a.m. and was back at 7:42. She was carrying something, which we guessed was the take-away breakfast provided by the hotel.

At 11:30, she left again. Her room, 130, was in the middle of the building next to the cross-hallway. The cameras were at either end of the building, so she was as far from them as possible. And the video quality was crappy.

When she came and went, we didn't get much more than a fuzzy image and only a few frames of video because she ducked into the cross-hallway immediately.

The inner courtyard cameras were apparently inoperative because the history had empty files for both of them on that day. We did, however, catch her on the lobby camera. It was decent resolution, but we only got the back of her head. When she went out the front door, we lost her, but a moment later a reddish sedan drove by and left the hotel.

Nothing else happened until I arrived on my scooter at 12:48 p.m. You could see me knock on the door and go through the process of getting the necessary pictures. The guy had said he was Natalie's husband, and she was in the shower. I had no reason to doubt him. On the video, I handed him the order, although you never saw him on the camera. He stayed inside the room out of the frame. I left on my scooter at 12:54 p.m.

I pulled up my pictures of the delivery. We looked at his ID. Wayne Durbin from Florence, Oregon. While Tony looked him up, Gretchen pulled up her GPS and searched for Florence. It was a coastal town at the mouth of the Siuslaw River east of Eugene. Population 10,000. Tony's search was less successful. None of the Wayne Durbins looked like the guy from the ID. And the address in Florence didn't exist.

We resumed our video search. Natalie came back to her room at 4:22, went inside for an hour, and then an Uber Eats driver showed up. He handed her a package and that was the last we saw of her that day.

I said, "That gives me an idea of how to get the order into the dispensary. Fake a food delivery. But you'd need someone on the inside to receive it and make the switch."

Gretchen said, "Do they often order food there?"

"Yeah. Probably once or twice a day."

Tony said, "Let me pull down the previous day's video and see if we can get a look at Natalie checking in."

It took another twenty minutes, but he finally brought up the front desk cameras. There were two of them, both higher resolution than the outside cameras. One was focused closely on the cash drawer, apparently to ensure no one dipped their hand into the till. The other was a wider shot of the lobby, but the area in front of the desk was centered and had decent resolution. I hoped we'd see her face.

Tony played the video at high speed, scanning for our target. There were only seven check-ins that day, so it was fairly easy to find her. But she knew what she was doing. The camera was high on the wall, next to the ceiling behind the front desk. Natalie wore a white ball cap, pulled low over her face. The most we ever got of her was a tiny part of her chin as she walked away.

Gretchen said, "She looks a lot heavier here than she does on the other video."

"Yeah," said Tony. "I thought so too. She might be wearing a body suit to throw off her appearance. She's a pro."

"What about breakfast? Can we catch her there?" I asked.

Tony went back to April 13. We knew the time she left her room, so it was easy to find her. She had the cap on again, pulled low. She came in, looked around a bit, poured herself a cup of coffee and grabbed a pre-packaged muffin. Then she walked back out.

Gretchen said, "Go back." She pointed at the screen. "There's a mirror behind the breakfast counter. Can you zoom in enough to pick up her face in the mirror?"

Tony tinkered for a couple of minutes and pulled up a clipped part of the video focused on the mirror, but with Natalie's face and shoulders filling most of it. The resolution was poor, but Natalie looked familiar.

Gretchen opened her phone and scrolled through her pictures. She opened one and zoomed in on the woman with the Rottweiler on Sand Island.

We couldn't be sure, but it definitely looked like Natalie.

"What about Wayne?" I asked. "When does he arrive or leave?"

Tony said, "Has to be after Natalie checks in, right?" He pulled up the camera outside room 130 from April 12 and moved to the time when Natalie checked in. We saw the heavy version of her pause at the teal-colored hotel room door, unlock it, and go inside. An Uber Eats guy showed up at 7:21 p.m. He scanned through the remainder of the day, through the night, into the next morning until Natalie left to grab her free breakfast. No Wayne.

Tony pulled up some of his tools and ran one on the April 13 video. A box popped up with two numbers: 12:05-300 and 12:57-300.

"What are those numbers?" I asked.

"Times when the video sync timer is interrupted. That means clips of 300 seconds, or five minutes, were deleted at each of those times."

"When Wayne entered and departed. Someone erased him coming and going."

"Correct."

"So someone at the hotel is in on this—they erased Wayne."

"Maybe. Could be anyone with access to the video system at the hotel. Or any decent hacker. Consider all options, remember?"

"Or the feds."

Tony frowned. "Let's see if we can find him somewhere else."

He pulled several other camera feeds to see where the camera was pointed. He found one that covered the parking lot next to room 130. At the side of the frame, there was a picnic table adjacent to the OliveTree freeway sign. It had a sun cover, and an obvious cigarette disposal-type trash can.

At 10:32 a white SUV parked near the smoking area. A man got out and sat down at the picnic table. He was too far away to make out any features other than he wore a tan cap. At 12:07 p.m. he got up and appeared to walk across the parking lot, out of the frame. Fifty minutes later, he came back into the frame and got into his car. He was carrying something in his hand that could have been my delivery order. He sat in the car for a couple of minutes, then started up and drove off. Tony tinkered with the video resolution, but it was too low to make out the model of the SUV, let alone a license plate.

We played the videos back and forth. Tony did his best to enhance the resolution, but we couldn't get a better look at Natalie Durbin. The same was true of the guy who came and went while she was out, the guy I'd delivered to and whose ID picture I had on my phone. At least I'd recognize him if I saw him again.

Tony backed out of the hotel system and shut down. After two hours, we were tired of staring at the screens and hungry. I made ham and cheese sandwiches on wheat bread. Gretchen ate without comment, although I saw her sniff the sandwich before she put it in her mouth.

I set a jar of dill pickles and a bag of potato chips on the table. We'd made no progress on identifying the woman at the hotel. But we had raised doubts about whether she had placed the cannabis order or laced it with toxin. It looked more like Wayne Durbin, or whoever he was, was the culprit.

Tony pulled the potato chip bag towards him and dumped a handful of chips on a napkin. "That hotel is really isolated for being in the city."

"Yeah, there's an open field on one side and the freeway on the other."

"Kinda like Vikram's house in Mountainside," said Gretchen. She pulled the bag to her and studied the ingredients label.

"No traffic cameras or store cameras anywhere in the area. Not a coincidence," said Tony.

I fed Chester and filled his water bowl.

Tony said, "Maybe change the litter box, too? It's starting to smell."

Gretchen slid the chip bag away and looked at me. "Payback for saving his life."

I changed the litter box and came back to the table. Chester was sitting at the door watching me.

"He sat there smirking at you the whole time," said Gretchen.

She was right. He did have a kind of smirk on his face like he was amused. But I said, "That's his thank you face, Gretchen. Right, Chester?"

He meowed in return.

"You're welcome, boy," I said.

He walked over and rubbed against my leg. You could hear his purring all the way across the room.

Tony said, "Buck doesn't have the same effect on women."

"I noticed," said Gretchen. She glanced at me and finished her sandwich. Wadding her napkin, she cleared the table and put the plates in the dishwasher. She walked over to the trashcan and opened the lid, peering inside.

"Full of paper plates. You guys live like bachelors." She walked to the refrigerator and opened it, looking inside for a moment. "You ever cook?"

"I made eggs yesterday. And toast."

"He did," said Tony. "Waffles the day before. Eggos. In the toaster. But in all fairness, he learned it from me. Bachelor all my life."

Gretchen leaned against the counter, smiling. "What do you do on holidays?"

Tony waved toward the pantry. "We have holiday paper plates—Fourth of July, Thanksgiving, Christmas, New Years. Birthdays, too."

CHAPTER 17

Gretchen and I both had classes on Wednesday. I got home a little after 5:00 p.m.

Tony had one of his mystery meat casseroles coming out of the oven. He bought a dozen at a time and kept them in the freezer in the garage. A guy named Tootles he knew up in St. Helens sold them from his meat processing store. He used the scraps from the various deer, elk, antelope, bear, and cougar people brought in. That's why it truly was mystery meat.

Chester watched as Tony set the casserole on the table. His whiskers were twitching, and he looked at the chair like he wanted to jump up there.

"Chester." He looked at me. "You stay on the floor. I'll get your dinner so you don't bug us while we eat." I got a can of tuna cat food and dumped it into his dish. When I placed it next to his water dish, he came over, sniffed it, and walked back over to the table. He sat there with his tail swishing while we ate.

Tony served the casserole on our plates. "Obedience isn't a cat's forte."

"Yeah. Kinda reminds me of Gretchen." I sniffed my plate and poked at a chunk of meat with my fork. "What do you think this one is?"

Tony shrugged. "No way of telling. Tootles keeps all the scraps in the same bag."

I forked some into my mouth. It was hot, but it was also tasty. Chester meowed. I pointed towards his dish. "Yours is over there." He didn't move but his tail kept swishing. "I was thinking about the female brain. If you could visualize it, I think it would look like a witch's brew, all swirling and steaming with dozens of thought threads tangled together. Impossible to unravel or understand."

Tony said, "On the other hand, they say that the male brain is single-minded. Only focuses on one thing at a time."

"Yeah, Gretchen said something about that the other day. Asked if I was in my nothing box or my sulking box. I looked it up. Seems it's mostly comedians who use that for their routines."

"It's made the rounds in pop psychology. I don't know if it's a real thing or not."

My phone dinged. It was a reminder for my team meeting tonight for my Crime Analysis lab. "I have a meeting for a class in fifteen minutes." I started shoveling in the casserole.

"At Insomnia?"

"No. They wanted something closer to Portland. At least a little bit. A Mexican place called Juan Colorado on TV Highway."

"Not that far."

"Yeah, but I need to run. Gotta get my bookbag and stuff."

* * *

Ethan, Ayana, and Ben were waiting when I got to Juan Colorado. They sat around a four-top in the back, coffees and laptops at the ready, surrounding the usual chips and salsa. I got a coffee and joined them.

Two hours later, we had our joint presentation worked out. Ben had control, and after he did the final formatting, he planned to upload our presentation tonight.

We walked out together and headed to our cars. I noticed a MINI Cooper backed in next to my driver's side. Like Gretchen's, it looked black with a white top. As I approached, I could see the outline of someone sitting in the driver's seat.

I clicked my fob to unlock my car. As I walked between the two, the window of the MINI glided down. I looked inside.

Gretchen said, "Work all done?"

"Yeah. What are you doing here?"

She was glancing around and fidgeting. "Nothing. Well, waiting. I guess, waiting for you."

Ben drove by and tooted his horn.

Gretchen jumped. She was drumming her fingers on the steering wheel now.

"Okay. Well. I'm gonna go home now. You need anything?" This was creepy, like she was stalking me. She was clearly upset but I didn't know what to do.

She didn't look at me. "Get in the car, Buck."

"Right. See you later." I turned to open my door."

"In *my* car, Buck. Please. Just get in. Now."

I turned back. "In your car—why? What is going on with you?"

"I know, I know." She motioned to me. "Just get in. Please."

I clicked my fob to lock my car and got into her car. "Where are we going?"

She pulled out, then gunned it, as much as a MINI can be gunned.

"You're not going to tell me where we're going?"

There was a light at TV Highway. When it turned green, she went straight across the intersection into the Arbor Roses apartments. She took the first right, followed by another immediate right on Elina Ave. That dead-ended at a left turn at Albertine Street. She slowed a little. When we reached the end of the street, she went directly into the driveway ahead, angled right, and punched a garage door opener on her visor. The door opened and we rolled inside. There was an older red Taurus in the other space of the double garage.

She killed the engine and got out. "Come on." She pushed the button on the wall, shutting the garage door.

I climbed out and realized I was still holding my bookbag. I walked around the car to where she held the door to the inside of the house.

"Living room. Go sit down. I'll make some coffee."

I watched her pull three cups out of a cabinet.

I dropped my bookbag on the floor. When I bent over to pick it up, I also snagged my revolver from my ankle holster.

Gretchen had her back to me, busy with the coffee. Keeping the gun hidden from view with my bookbag, I walked casually into the living room.

A large black Rottweiler sat next to a chair. He stared at me, glanced at my bookbag, and growled. A woman sitting in a chair raised her index finger in front of him. The Rottweiler went silent. She said, "Please join us, Mr. Buchanan. Bien won't bother you if you'll holster your weapon."

* * *

It was Natalie Durbin. She was small, maybe five-three, 110 pounds. She wore a white T-shirt and jeans. Her brown shoes looked like low-cut hiking shoes from REI.

The room was a typical townhome living room with space for one chair, a couch, two end tables, and a fireplace over which a flat screen TV hung. It looked like rent-a-room furniture, bland, beige, not too sturdy. No pictures.

Gretchen came in and handed each of us a cup of coffee. She sat on the couch nearer to the woman.

The woman said, "Miss Kho has been kind enough to host me while we awaited the completion of your classwork, Mr. Buchanan."

"Buck, please. And you are?"

She smiled. "Not Natalie Durbin. Miss Kho has filled me in on some of your adventures." She took a sip of her coffee. "Quite good, dear."

She set her cup down on the table. "My name is De'Aijree Keeva. But most people just call me DJ. I'm keen to learn the why behind your investigation into the deaths of Ray and Kay Chester. Would you be so kind?"

"They were my customers. And I found them..."

"I supposed they tipped well, too. It was a financial loss, personal to you."

"Yes, they tipped well. But it wasn't that."

"Curious." She looked at Gretchen. "Is he always this magnanimous?"

"Like I said, I haven't known him long. We were lab partners in a couple of courses, but that was it until he invited me into this investigation."

"And what would you say now? Is he one of the good guys?"

The hair on my neck stood up and I got goose bumps. Agent Diaz had used those words.

Gretchen said, "He seems to be. Most of the time."

I rubbed my chest where she'd been hitting me.

"But he's getting better."

The woman clasped her hands together around her crossed knee. "Do you know who killed them?"

I said, "No. From the agents' point of view, I think you're the leading suspect."

"Which ones, specifically? Massey or Diaz?"

Did that mean she was law enforcement, too? Maybe undercover? How else would she know the names of the agents? Was she another player in the fed mix to unravel. How did anyone ever solve a crime in this kind of chaos?

"Diaz. I haven't seen Massey lately, and I don't think she cares much."

"And Vikram? What does he think?"

"I don't know. He thinks we're in danger from the people who burned down the Chesters' house and his garage. Probably the same ones who burned down the marina office, too."

Her face sobered. "He's right about that—who burned it down and that they are dangerous. I suspect they're very curious about you two. Why are you involved and what do you know—that sort of thing."

"We don't know much." I looked at Gretchen and she looked at her feet. I wondered how much she told this woman, DJ.

When I leaned forward, the Rottweiler, Bien, turned his head to look at me. "DJ, who are you? How are you involved?"

"I'm a friend of the Chesters. And, like you, I'd like to know who killed them."

"All the evidence points to you."

DJ's eyes grew wide for a moment. "Me? How do you figure that?"

"You were at the OliveTree Inn. I delivered an order to you on April thirteenth. You laced the cannabis with toxin, and then switched it with the Chesters' order on April twentieth."

She smiled. "For amateurs, you do ferret out a lot of information. But I didn't kill the Chesters. And you didn't deliver any order to me."

"No. But I did deliver it to a man in room 130 who posed as your husband, Wayne Durbin."

She frowned. It seemed I'd delivered news she hadn't known. She was quiet for a moment, trying to process what I'd just told her, I suspected.

The doorbell rang. Bien leaped to his feet and looked at DJ. She held her index finger in the air again.

Gretchen got up to answer the door as we watched. When she opened the door, special agent Massey held up a piece of paper and said, "Miss Kho. I have an arrest warrant for DJ Keeva. And a search warrant to look for her in your home. Please stand aside."

Massey marched inside followed by three other agents. She glanced at Bien, then walked directly to DJ and said, "DJ Keeva, you're under arrest. Please stand up."

DJ stood. "Before you touch me, Massey, I suggest you allow me to instruct the Rottweiler. Otherwise, you'll probably lose at least a hand."

Massey hesitated and looked at the dog. Bien stared back at her, his hackles bristling. "I could just shoot him."

"It's too late to draw your weapon."

Massey was silent for a moment, glancing from dog to DJ and back. "Fine. Secure the dog."

DJ said, "Miss Kho, would you please come over here and stand next to me?"

Gretchen walked over to stand next to DJ. She took Gretchen's arm and turned so she and Gretchen faced Bien. DJ opened her right hand and put it flat on Gretchen's chest. She looked at Bien and said, *"Führer Hauptling. Führer Hauptling. Anerkennen."*

Bien walked to Gretchen and licked her hand. He glanced at DJ, then sat down and stared at Gretchen.

"Now just tell him to stay. *Bleib.*"

Gretchen looked at Bien. *"Bleib."*

He licked his lips and looked around.

DJ turned to me and said, "Stay in touch. We have more to talk about." She turned her back to Massey and held her hands behind her.

Bien watched as DJ was cuffed and the agents walked her out. At the door, Massey turned for a moment. "You kids should stay out of these things. Wait until you carry a badge."

Bien growled. She shut the door.

* * *

Gretchen stood with her hands in her pockets, leaning against the doorway between her kitchen and living room. "This investigation keeps giving us pets."

I walked over in front of her. She had tears in her eyes. "You need a hug?"

She glared at me. "Want to lose a limb? I have backup now." She glanced at Bien.

I raised both hands in defense. "Just trying to be nice. You must be scared. I am."

"I'm mostly angry."

"At?"

"Myself. DJ. Massey. You."

"What did I do?"

"You got me into this?"

"Your choice."

"Just shut up, Buck. Let me talk."

I smashed my lips together and leaned back against the opposite door frame.

"DJ practically forced her way in here. I recognized her from the island and the video. I knew who she was, and I was afraid of her or what she might do, particularly with him." She pointed at the dog. "She asked where you were, and I told her. She told me to go get you when you were done. She wasn't nice. She didn't ask. She just told me. With this dog, Bien, I decided that's what I had to do."

"Why didn't–"

She held up her hand. "She told me not to tell you she was here. She said it was safer that way. For both of us. I didn't know what that meant, but she frightened me. I decided to go along." She paused and looked around the room. "Having you here made me feel safer."

Bien seemed to sigh, like he was bored with this conversation. He laid down with his head on his paws, looking at us.

I thought about giving Gretchen a hug anyway, but I wasn't sure where Bien stood on that subject.

She snapped her bracelet. Bien raised his head at the sound.

"What is that thing?"

"It's called a SnappBandZ. Alternative to me kicking your ass." A smile crept across her face. "But not as much fun."

We stood there for a moment in awkward silence. Bien cocked his head as he looked at us. I knew exactly how he felt.

Gretchen said, "Massey must have followed the same investigation we did and tracked down DJ at the hotel. But DJ was framed, wasn't she?"

"Looks that way. I doubt Massey knows about the guy posing as DJ's husband. Eventually, they'll ask me if I delivered the order to her. That'll undermine their case completely. We can show them the video of the guy if we need to."

She looked at Bien. "What am I going to do with him?"

"You'll need some food. A big, big bag. A bowl for that and for water. Maybe a bucket. He's a small pony." I looked around the room. Apparently, I was allowed to talk now. "Is this your place?"

"Why?"

"You said you were here when DJ knocked on the door. Just trying to understand what's going on."

"Yes. I live here."

"Been here long?"

"Four years. Since I started at PU."

"Roommate?"

"No. Why?"

"Taurus in the garage."

She bit her lip and looked away.

"Not DJ's car?"

"No."

I walked to the living room doorway and leaned against the frame. It was so frustrating when I ask a simple question and she plays this game and won't answer. Or gives something evasive. I took a few deep breaths.

"Is this you being angry or what?" she asked.

"I can't get a straight answer from you. No, that's not it. I don't get answers about simple, routine stuff. It's not like I asked for a DNA sample."

"The Taurus is my car."

"Was it that hard to tell me?"

"Please stop."

She turned her back and snapped that bracelet several times.

My phone dinged. I read a message from Tony. "Checking in." I texted him back and told him I was with Gretchen and would call soon. "I guess I need to get going."

She stood there with her arms crossed over her chest, looking at the floor. It was another awkward silence for a moment, then she said, "If DJ knows where I live, then other people can find out, too. I'm not sure it's safe to stay here."

I flicked a thumb toward Bien. "There's a kennel down the street."

Bien raised his head and looked at me, like he knew what I was saying.

"I can't do that."

"Sure, you can. Not your dog. You didn't ask for him. He was dumped on you."

"DJ had no choice."

"Well, not many. Could have been me."

"No. She told me he won't take commands from men."

"Is he female?"

Gretchen said, "Wait here. I'll be right back." She stomped up the stairs. Bien and I watched her go. She banged around upstairs for a few minutes, then bounced back down the stairs, two at a time. She tossed a small backpack at my feet and said, "Take that."

I looked at the backpack, then back at her.

"Please," she said.

"Where are we going?"

"Your place."

"And Bien?"

"Him, too." She looked at Bien. *"Hier."*

Bien sprang to his feet and trotted over to her. She rubbed his head for a moment, then looked at me. "Let's go."

"Do you speak German?"

"Nein, du idiot."

* * *

Gretchen walked in behind me with Bien trailing her. I spotted Chester sitting by the slider. His head popped up and he looked our way. When he saw Bien, he trotted over and started rubbing against Bien's leg. Bien looked at Chester for a moment, then at Gretchen. I think he was asking if he could eat Chester, but Gretchen just patted him on the head.

Tony said, "Did you guys buy stock in Petco?"

I gave Tony a big hug. "Thanks for taking care of me. And my craziness."

"I draw a line at snakes."

We took both animals out the slider and let them do their business. After that, Chester followed Bien everywhere he went. Bien didn't seem to mind that much.

We updated Tony on the evening, then Gretchen said, "I don't feel safe at my place, so Buck offered to let me stay here."

I opened my mouth to object; I had done no such thing. But then I realized that Gretchen was probably scared. DJ knew where she lived. The marshals knew where she lived. The guys in the white pickup could know, too. Practically, she was safer with us. I really should have offered.

Tony's eyebrows went up. He glanced at me. "Chivalry runs deep in the Buchanan family."

She didn't smile. She picked up her bag and marched up the steps.

"Where is she sleeping?" asked Tony.

"I thought the couch."

"Maybe she's just using your bathroom."

We headed up the steps. Gretchen was just coming out of my bathroom. She'd changed into a Duck's t-shirt and gray sweats. She walked over to my bed, pulled back the covers, and crawled in, her back to me. I wasn't sure what to do, so I went into the bath and brushed my teeth.

When I came back out, the lights were off, and the bedroom door was closed.

"Get into bed," she called from the bedroom. "Do you need more instruction?"

"Nope." That could mean lots of things to any red-blooded twenty-two-year-old college guy. But we had history and boundaries. I was certain I understood what she meant. Still, there was a little voice in the back of my head that kept asking me over and over what she meant. My sane, rational, adult voice wished there was a brick wall down the middle of my bed because I didn't want to accidentally cross that line and get pummeled in my sleep. I stripped to my boxers and slid into the other side of the bed.

For a while, I lay there hyper-aware of Gretchen lying next to me. I could feel her body heat and hear her light breathing. I couldn't remember ever sharing my bed with anyone, even as a child. I think the newness kept me awake while I reviewed the events of the day. At some point, though, I dozed off.

CHAPTER 18

Thursday, May 4

When the alarm sounded at 6:30 am, it took a moment to recall last night and why the shower was running in my bathroom.

I got up and turned on the bedroom light. A moment later, Gretchen came out of the bathroom wrapped in a towel. She had another one wrapped around her head. "Good morning. Sleep well?"

"Yeah. How about you?"

"You snore."

I didn't know that. "Sorry."

"Didn't bother me. Hope my laughing didn't wake you."

"Laughing at what?"

"Your snoring. It's almost like a song. I found it funny."

My face felt hot, so I knew it had turned red. There was nothing to say, though.

She pulled the towel off her hair and started toweling it dry as best she could.

"I have a hair dryer."

"I know. Go ahead and shower if you want. I can wait."

I'd never really noticed her arms and shoulders before. Her shoulders were broad and muscular, like her arms. She must work out a lot to have that kind of physique. When she turned her back to me, I noticed a scar between her shoulder blades poking above her towel line. It was along her spine and looked serious.

My solar plexus knew not to ask.

When I came out of the bathroom, Gretchen was sitting on my bed dressed in another t-shirt and jeans. The bedroom door was open. "I let the critters out while you were in there. After I dry my hair, I'll go get some food for Bien."

"Where did you learn German?"

"High school. And a two-week trip to Berlin."

"Know any other languages?"

"Some Spanish. Mandarin. Tagalog enough to chat with my relatives. You?"

She spoke five languages. I felt a little stupid in her presence. "Just English."

She went into the bathroom and fired up the hair dryer.

I got dressed and went downstairs. Tony was sitting at the dining table with coffee. "I made coffee—enough for three."

"Thanks. Gretchen will be down in a minute. She's drying her hair." I glanced at Tony. He was staring at me. I knew what he was thinking, but he was too much of my parent to ask. "Completely platonic, Tony. Totally. And if I even joke about anything else, she hits me to remind me it's going to stay that way." I rubbed my chest where she'd hit me. It was still sore this morning.

"She likes you. Maybe not in that way, but she likes you, nonetheless."

I shrugged. "What's not to like?"

"Don't be cocky, Buck."

"It was a joke." I poured a cup of coffee. It was uncomfortable to talk about. It wasn't the teen thing where I was sort of afraid to talk with girls. Now it was more about how to move from casual conversation to exploring whether the girl had any interest in dating. In Gretchen's case, she had made that quite clear.

"He's even funny when he sleeps," said Gretchen as she reached the bottom of the steps.

"What do you mean?" said Tony as he gestured with his coffee cup. "I made coffee."

"His snoring is more like a song. Sort of a lullaby. Sweet."

My face flushed again. I looked at her. "Is this where I punch you?"

"See. He's funny now, too." She poured her coffee and sat down at the table. "I need to get some dog food for Bien."

At the sound of his name, he stood up from his spot next to the slider. Chester, who was curled up asleep next to him, stood and stretched that carefree cat stretch that makes you think they are oblivious to the world around them, or they just don't care.

I sat down at the table. "I was wondering if we should go visit DJ? Or even bail her out? We know she's innocent."

Tony said, "I could look and see if they've set bail, but I doubt we could raise the money, even on a bond."

"Not our problem, anyhow," said Gretchen. "If the real murderer thinks he got away with it, now that DJ is arrested, he might be easier to track down."

"How so?" asked Tony.

"I don't know. Just in theory. Maybe too many movie plots."

"No, it makes sense. But I would think the murderer disappears now. Monitor things from afar. No need for any more risk."

I said, "Are you thinking the guys in the white pickup? They seem more like muscle or monitors. I don't think the guy at the hotel is one of them, but they might be working together."

"The guys I saw in the pickup were definitely Latino."

"Not the guy at the hotel. Maybe European. More than six feet tall. A little brutish. And scary. Like a Russian hit man."

Gretchen laughed. "You have some imagination."

"Why?"

"You go from tall to hit man. What happened to 'just the facts?'"

"I'm trying to paint a picture."

The doorbell rang. We looked at each other for a moment, then I rose and walked to the door. Looking through the peephole, I could see a young guy about my age. He wore a gray, short-sleeved shirt with a name embroidered above the pocket. I opened the door.

"I have a delivery for someone name Kho." The name on his shirt was Greg.

"I'll take it."

"It's in the car. I'll get it."

I watched as he carried two bags of dog food towards me. I stood back and let him carry them inside.

"Just put them on the floor. I'll move them later."

He handed me a piece of paper and walked out. I glanced at the paper. It was a receipt from Western Pet Supply in Beaverton. He'd had a long drive.

"Hey," I called. "Here." I pulled a twenty out of my wallet and handed it to him.

As I shut the door, I looked at the receipt more closely. Each thirty-pound bag cost just over $100. Bien ate the good stuff. And DJ had some connections. "Tony," I said, "can you check and see if DJ is out. I don't know how she could have arranged this if she wasn't."

Tony went upstairs. Gretchen fished a salad bowl out of the kitchen. She grabbed one of the bags in one hand and carried it to the table. She studied the back of the bag, then poured some of the food into the bowl. When she set it on the floor near the slider, Bien walked over and looked at it. Chester drifted by and sniffed, then walked away. Bien stared at Gretchen.

"Guess he has to be commanded to eat." She stood there for a moment. *"Nimm Futter."*

Bien dove in and finished the bowl in short order. Then he drank his water bowl dry. He walked to the slider and, looking over his shoulder, gave a quiet bark.

Gretchen opened the door and walked outside with him. In a few minutes she came back carrying a grocery bag of poop. As she walked towards the front door she said, "I wish guys could be trained this well."

There was a lot I wanted to say. Questions to ask. While she was dropping the bag in the dumpster outside, I ran through several ways to start the conversation. When she came back in, she stopped and looked at me. "What?"

"I, uh, have some questions."

She stood there with her hands on her hips, almost glaring at me. "About?"

"Well, about you. That car in your garage. Why you're here. Maybe we need to clear the air, so to speak."

She turned and marched up the stairs. "I don't have time for this. And you need to go to work."

I looked at my watch. It was already 8:30. The dispensary opened at 9:00. I needed to get going.

* * *

Overnight, the temperature had dropped into the forties. The predicted high for today was in the sixties, so it felt like a good day for scooter deliveries. I put the scooter rack on my car and loaded my scooter before driving to the shop.

It had been a week since I'd discovered the Chesters. This was my first time back in the dispensary. We were sure someone here had swapped packages a couple weeks ago, but the video for the camera in the staging area had a two-hour gap. We decided I'd raise too much suspicion if I started asking questions. Besides, everyone who worked here had access to the staging area where my deliveries were kept. Everyone was a suspect.

Going through today's deliveries at the dispensary, I ran across one for the OliveTree hotel. The product was the same one the Chesters bought. Nadya Soon. Room 130. The hair on the back of my neck stood up. There was something creepy about another delivery there. And the same room. The delivery to DJ's room was my first there in several months, even though the clientele were probably active in the drug market. Cannabis, though, was not the kind of drug they sought. It was mostly meth and heroin, I suspected.

In the back office, I scanned each delivery and took a picture of each order's label. Then I loaded them into the CannaBin sitting on its charging pedestal. I cleared the bin lock and set my own code, then locked the door. The battery indicator said one hundred percent. I was good to go.

I pushed a button on the wall. In a couple of minutes, Gino, the security guard, walked in.

"Hey, Gino. Ready to go."

"Hey, Buck. Scooter today?"

"Yeah. Gonna be in the sixties and no rain. May as well get in the exercise while I can."

He punched in his code on the CannaBin latch, then lifted it off the pedestal. It began to beep.

We went out the back door and he slid it into the latch on my scooter. After he punched in his code, the bin stopped beeping.

"Thanks, Gino. See you later."

Before I got started, I called Tony.

"I think I need backup on one of my deliveries today."

"Which one?"

"Room 130 at the OliveTree Inn."

He was silent for a moment. "Hold on."

I could hear his keyboard clacking in the background. When he came back on the line, he said, "Their whole vid system is out right now. Convenient. I'll be by that smoking table in twenty minutes. What time will you be there?"

"I'm not sure. I'm going to do the route backwards so OliveTree will be an afternoon drop. I'll text you when I get a good idea. Maybe 2:00."

"Okay. I'll be there by 12:30."

"You think I should call Vikram? Or Massey?"

"Not Massey."

"Why not?"

Tony sighed. "I don't trust Massey. Something is off there."

"What about Diaz?"

"Neither of them seems to be in the loop. I guess I'd pick Vikram. Call him while I get moving. I want to see who shows up in that hotel room."

"Delivery says Nadya Soon."

"If I find anything, I'll let you know."

We hung up and I called Vikram. There was no answer, so I left him a message to contact me as soon as possible. I also texted him.

The shop's App had arranged the delivery order for me. But it didn't take elevation into account. And it had me use major highways, which I avoided when on my scooter. So, it took me fifteen minutes to rearrange the drop schedule to accommodate my scooter.

By the time I kicked off, it was 10:15 am. I crossed the freeway and rode to the end of Denney. My first delivery was to Sussex Village Apartments. By the time I'd finished the west side deliveries, it was 1:48 pm.

I texted Tony and let him know I'd be at the OliveTree in fifteen minutes.

Vikram still hadn't answered my messages to him.

I left Creekside apartments and pedaled to Taco Time on Allen Boulevard. I grabbed a couple of chicken tacos and wolfed them down before I went to OliveTree. I wanted to come in from west Allen Boulevard because I usually arrived from the east.

I wheeled into the driveway of the OliveTree and spotted Tony's black Tundra sitting up front in the left parking lot. He'd parked out of sight of the lower right lot and smoking table. I went around to the right side towards room 130 on the lower level. There was a guy in a hoodie sitting at the smoking table. He was looking at his phone and didn't look up when I pulled in. I figured it was Tony, but I couldn't be sure.

I pulled to the curb and popped my kickstand. That's when I noticed the white Silverado pickup sitting two spaces over. Maybe I should have called the police, but I wasn't sure what I'd tell them. Me seeing this pickup frequently wasn't something they'd care about. I couldn't even prove it had been following me.

I glanced at Tony at the table. He had his back to me, but his phone was up. I was guessing he had the camera on and was watching via that.

I took out the order for the OliveTree and took another picture of it. As I walked towards the door, I wandered by the white pickup and took a picture of the inside from the driver's window. There was nothing on the seats. It looked completely clean inside.

My hands were sweating. I walked up to the door of room 130 and considered pulling my weapon from my ankle holster, but if this wasn't some kind of setup, I could get in a lot of trouble with the shop. Customers didn't like to be greeted with a gun.

As a precaution, I stood to the side of the door and knocked. I didn't want to get shot through the door, either. I waited. There was no noise coming from the room. I knocked again and called out,

"Delivery." Nothing. No noise. Maybe "Nadya" was in the bathroom. Or at the front desk.

I knocked again, harder. The door moved a little. It wasn't locked or latched. I stood even farther to the side and, using one finger, pushed the door open. An odd rusty smell drifted out of the dark room. I didn't need to look. I knew the smell. Somewhere inside, there was blood. Probably a lot of it. There was no need for me to enter. I shivered. This was where the police needed to take over.

Looking over my shoulder, I checked for Tony. The hooded guy at the smoking area picnic table was gone. I looked up and down the parking lot for him. He'd disappeared.

If it wasn't Tony, who was it? In any case, I didn't think he could have gotten around me on either side without me noticing. The only direction he could have gone was away from me, through the weeds to the freeway.

I ran across the lot, jumped over some weeds, and landed at the concrete wall that bounded the freeway ramp. A gray Volvo wagon was just pulling into traffic from the wedge between the offramp and freeway. It was too far away to read the license plate.

Where was Tony? My stomach churned as panic tried to overtake me. I ran back up the slope, across the parking lot, and around the front of the hotel. When I got to Tony's truck, I yanked open the passenger door. On the floor of the truck, Tony was lying sideways, bound and gagged. Blood was dribbling down the side of his head. I wiped my nose and fought back tears. He was alive.

I ripped the duct tape off his mouth. "I'm here, Tony. You're gonna be okay. Where are you hurt?"

"I have a lump on my head where he hit me, but otherwise I'm okay."

I pulled out my knife and sliced the duct tape binding his hands and feet. Then I helped him crawl out of the truck. He touched his head and grimaced. He grabbed me into a bear hug. "I thought he might kill you, Buck. But he didn't kill me even though I saw his face. So I had hope."

I hugged back. Tony was my world. Had been since I was eleven. In evaluating the risks, I hadn't considered the risks to him. I wouldn't make that mistake again. I owed him everything. My eyes watered.

Then panic slammed me again. I pulled back from Tony. "Where's Gretchen?"

"She went back to her place with the dog before you called."

I looked him in the eyes. He must have known what I was thinking.

"I don't see any reason to think she's at risk. This was a setup to get you here. But I still don't know why."

* * *

We walked to the back of his truck and opened the tailgate. It made a fine resting place. I told him about room 130, and he agreed that we needed to call 911. Ten minutes later, a patrol car pulled in and we flagged it down.

Gonzalez and Copeland, the cops who showed up at the Chesters last week, must catch all the murder calls in the area. When Gonzalez got out, he said, "Ain't you the kid called us last week?"

"Yes, sir. Buck Buchanan."

"You got some kind of nose for murder."

"I hope not."

I explained what had happened and the smell in room 130.

Gonzalez looked at Tony's head. "You got a nice laceration there, too. Think you're gonna need some stitches." He called in and requested a 10-40 ambulance. I knew that meant no siren, no lights.

At their request, Tony and I got into his truck and I followed the patrol car to the other side of the hotel. They parked behind the white pickup, blocking it in place. I backed into a parking space next to the smoker picnic table, across the lot from the hotel.

We watched them draw their weapons and go into the room, their free hands going to cover their nose and mouth as soon as they opened the door. They were back out in thirty seconds. Gonzalez was on his radio standing by the door. Copeland made a beeline to us. "You called it, kid. Two male Latino subjects."

Tony said, "Homicide?"

"Throats cut. Side-by-side on the bed." He pointed towards the door. "That your scooter?"

"Yes," I said. "You guys going to process this one, or will the U.S. Marshals take over?"

"Can't tell. They just show up when they want to. We do our job until someone tells us otherwise."

"Okay. I'll call my boss to come get the deliveries. I guess we'll be here a while."

He nodded. "Soon as the wagon gets here, I'll have them take care of his head. Meanwhile, please stay put."

"Right."

I texted Gage and asked him to have someone come to get the rest of the deliveries. There were only two remaining plus this one for room 130. I'd set it on the seat beside me after carrying it with me on the run to the freeway and then to Tony. Gage said he'd be here in ten minutes.

The ambulance rolled in, and three guys got out. Officer Copeland chatted with them, pointed our way, and the trio walked over to our truck.

"Who has the head injury?"

Tony climbed out. "I do. But I can walk over to your truck."

They walked to the ambulance and opened the back doors. Tony sat in the opening and two guys began looking at his head and taking his vitals.

A drizzle of rain crawled over us. They moved Tony inside the ambulance. My scooter and the deliveries inside its container wouldn't mind the water. Even though I checked the weather daily, getting caught in the rain was common in Portland.

Another patrol car and a black Chevy blazer pulled in. The new uniformed officers strung yellow crime scene tape across the parking lot, blocking it off from public access. They strung another tape across the lot on the other side of the white pickup.

Sanjeet, the toothy Indian hotel manager, was in animated conversation with Officer Gonzalez and the new guy from the Chevy Blazer. I wasn't sure a double murder would do much to hurt the business at the OliveTree, although I thought that was what Sanjeet was talking about. He didn't want this on the news. But he was too late. A KATU news truck pulled up next to the yellow tape and their satellite antenna mast began inching skyward. I expected Sanjeet would be on the news by 4:00 p.m. this afternoon.

In a few minutes, they had Tony patched up. As he walked towards me, a lady hopped out of the news van with a microphone in her hand, followed by a woman with a camera pointed at Tony. The one with the microphone called out. "Sir, excuse me, could you please tell me who you are and how you were injured?"

Tony didn't even turn his head. He kept walking and never looked their way. When he climbed in on the passenger side, he said, "I hope those news people don't identify us. We don't want to be connected to this."

"Probably too late." I jerked a thumb over my shoulder. "The lady with the mic is taking our license plate number." I'd watched her in the mirror. She pulled out a pad and pen, then moved along the tape to the rear of our truck and wrote down something.

"How's your head?"

"Hurts. Big lump. Four Steri-Strips. Might have a mild concussion."

Tony pulled out his phone and started texting.

I decided to let Gretchen know what was going on.

She answered on the first ring. "Let me guess: you want me to pick up your wet ass because you rode your scooter today."

"Why are you always such a smartass?"

"What's wrong?"

"You're asking that after the way you answered the phone?"

"Just tell me. Please. What happened? Are you okay?"

"Yes. I'm okay. Tony has a lump on his head." I turned to look at him. "Four Steri-Strips. And a shaved spot."

I summarized the last hour, including the news crew trying to identify us.

"Do you want me to come over? Anything I can do?"

"No. That news crew is hounding anyone they can corner. Probably love to get Bien on camera, too."

"I could have him bite the reporter."

If that was her attempt at humor, it failed miserably. "When they let us go, I'll text. What are you doing?"

"Studying for a final. I need to pass my courses to graduate."

"Yeah, I need to do that tonight or tomorrow. I have all my finals on Monday."

"Me, too."

Gage arrived at the same time a forensics team van pulled up. After he talked with Copeland, he texted to let me know they wouldn't let him talk to me. But they did let him take the two remaining deliveries after forensics had photographed them.

We sat there for another half-hour. The rain increased to a light shower. The drumming on the truck roof was putting me to sleep.

I must have dozed off because I jumped when Tony rolled down his window.

A voice from outside said, "How's the head?"

"Got a lump. It'll be fine."

"How'd he get you?"

Tony pointed to the picnic table. "I was sitting there. He came out of the hotel, walked over, sat down. Chatted a little. Seemed like a smoker. Had a new pack of cigarettes he opened. Got up to toss the wrapper in the trash can and clocked me from behind."

"Ouch."

I leaned forward to see who was talking to Tony outside the passenger side of the truck. It was a tall Black man in a black suit and black trench coat. He stood back out of my line of sight, so it was hard for me to see him. Like a cop does when he stops someone. Definitely law enforcement. I scanned my mirrors. No new vehicles.

The guy outside said, "I took care of the newsies. You stay out of trouble. Should have you out of here soon."

"Thanks," said Tony.

The guy walked away, crossed the yellow tape, and disappeared around the corner of the hotel.

"Who was that?"

"I called in a favor. Got us erased from the news people."

"Nice to have friends in the right places."

Tony glanced at me. "Yes." He touched the lump on his head. "I need to get some Tylenol or something. And we need to get out of here before our news immunity wears off."

Gonzalez was sitting in his patrol car. It looked like he was entering data into the mounted laptop.

"Let me see if Gonzalez can do anything." I popped the door and pulled the hood up on my jacket. Two guys in raincoats rolled a gurney into the room. An empty black body bag lay on it. Despite these guys following us, and probably one of them shooting at me, I felt bad for their families. Somewhere, a son or maybe a father wasn't coming home.

When I knocked on Gonzalez' window, he jumped.

He cranked open the window and said, "Jesus, kid, don't sneak up on me like that."

"Sorry. Just wanted to see how long we need to stay here. My uncle has a lump on his head, and I think I need to get him home."

He rolled his window up and climbed out. "Let me talk to the detective and I'll see what I can do."

"Thanks." I walked back to the truck and climbed in. "He needs to talk to the detective."

I had just closed the door when room 130 exploded. I saw the windows blow out before I heard the blast. The side walls were made of concrete block, but the wall facing us that used to have a door and two windows, was wood framed. And now it was mostly shredded pieces in the parking lot. OliveTree had a gaping hole where room 130 used to be. The second story balcony above the room was also shredded. The window air conditioner was lying on its side across the parking lot, twisted into two pieces where it had slammed into the picnic table. My scooter was a twisted mess wrapped around the picnic table legs.

The truck rocked, but no windows broke. My ears were ringing. I was lucky to have closed the door before the explosion.

Gonzalez sprawled on his side, halfway across the parking lot. Most of an ugly teal door lay on top of him, which probably saved him from more damage. He pushed the door off and sat up. I could see him working the radio microphone clipped to his shoulder.

Tony yelled, "We need to get out of here. Now. Past the TV van. Go through the tape."

"But Gonzalez is hurt. We need to help him."

"They've got paramedics here. They'll do more than you can. Just go, Buck. You can't help anyone here."

I started the truck and cut the wheel hard to the left. I gunned it and we drove through the police tape and out of the parking lot.

"Where to?"

"Left on Auburn."

I pulled onto Auburn and stopped immediately at a red light. "You sure we shouldn't help? We left the scene of a crime."

"I'm sure. Give me your phone."

"Why?"

"Just give it to me." His voice was stern and controlled, like he was in crisis mode. I handed him my phone. He rolled down the window and tossed it across the northbound ramp into the weeds. The light turned green. "Take the south ramp on the 217. How much gas do we have?"

I glanced at the dash. "Three-quarters. What about your phone? The truck?"

"The GPS in the truck was removed. My phone isn't traceable."

Even though Tony worked for the federal government, that didn't sound normal to me. A desk jockey in IT didn't need their vehicle and phone to be untraceable. Did they?

I made the left turn and merged onto the 217. "What's going on, Tony?"

"I don't know. But until we do know, I want to make sure we keep our distance and remain safe."

I ran through the scenario in my head. A bomb had gone off. What was the motivation? Surely not to kill innocents. There had to be something else.

Get rid of the bodies so they couldn't be identified? But why here in this hotel room? And why now, hours after the bodies are discovered? I thought about the guys with the gurney there to retrieve the bodies—innocent victims. The bomb went off when they rolled the body. It was a booby trap.

But for who? There was something else in play I didn't know or understand.

Gretchen came to mind. She could sort this out and come up with options I couldn't. But I didn't have a phone to call her.

"Can you call Gretchen? Make sure she's okay." My hands were sweating on the wheel. I wiped them on my pants.

"Take I-5 south. Get off at Nyberg. There's a Cabela's on the right. Pull into the parking lot and park away from the store. I'll call Gretchen."

When she answered, he said, "Scramble. Meet us in the parking lot of Cabela's on Nyberg." Tony hung up.

"You didn't ask her if she was okay."

"She wouldn't have answered if she wasn't."

I wanted to argue, but Tony's tone didn't invite questions.

We were silent for a few minutes until he shifted in his seat. I said, "What's going on?"

"I'm not sure, but better safe than sorry. The only person at the scene who knew us was Gonzalez. He knows we aren't involved. Leaving immediately keeps us out of it."

"What about the paramedics who treated your head?"

"I only gave them my first name."

There was silence again as I transitioned onto the 5 freeway.

"That explosion might have been meant for you, Buck."

"I'm thinking the boom sounded when the paramedics rolled a body. I wouldn't have moved a body. And he didn't kill you, so who was the intended?"

"Must be some missing puzzle piece."

"Wait, what about DJ? Maybe the killer didn't know she was arrested. Could she have been staying there? I wonder if she would have tried to move the bodies."

The order I was supposed to deliver was lying on the seat. I grabbed it and read the name. "Erin Powell" Another DJ alias? A chill went up my spine.

I showed it to Tony. "Not good."

He tapped on his phone for a few minutes. "DJ's not in custody now. At least not by the feds."

"Why place a delivery order? Or did she place it? Even if she didn't, why was it placed? And why did someone want me at the hotel room? The odds of me being there when it blew up were slim."

"Clearly, someone wanted to get rid of the guys who've been following you. For what reason, I don't know. But given there were two of them, I'm thinking they were the arsonists. Someone, probably the murderer, wanted them to go away and stop burning stuff down. It was probably the guy who cracked my head. He was a professional. Had no grudge with me. Just wanted to get my eyes off room 130."

"Why did we take off, then?"

"Precaution. In case I'm wrong."

* * *

At his instruction, I dropped Tony at Cabela's and drove across the freeway to Best Buy. He handed me $600 and told me to buy six burner phones. They only had five in stock. I took them all and got some raised eyebrows, but no questions.

It felt weird to not have my phone. I still owed more than $500 on it and Tony had just tossed it out the window. But I smiled. That was a ridiculous thought—we might be running for our lives and I'm worried about my phone debt.

I knew Tony was doing the right thing. It was kind of shocking, though, to see him kick into action so quickly. He was cool, knew what to do, and seemed to have an immediate plan, almost like he had a backup plan already in his head. Maybe that whack to the head had given him time to think about options and alternatives while he was tied up on the floor of this truck.

I drove back to Cabela's and parked at the outer edge of the cars. Tony had said not too far out, or we'll look conspicuous, but out as far as possible so we aren't noticed. That seemed like a good idea.

Gretchen arrived before Tony returned. She was driving the red Taurus. She pulled up, her driver's side facing my driver's side. She didn't get out but rolled down the window. I followed suit.

"Where's Tony?"

"In Cabela's."

She nodded and rolled up her window. Maybe Tony had talked to her again since I dropped him off. I was shocked that she'd show up on such short notice from Tony. And why was she driving the Taurus?

My head hurt. It might have been from the blast, but I was thinking it was from the craziness we'd encountered in the last few hours.

I spotted Tony walking our way. He was carrying a couple of what seemed to be heavy bags in one hand and a short shotgun in the other. I could feel the adrenaline kicking into my bloodstream. His purchases didn't frighten me, but the implication of buying them made my hands start to tremble. With no hesitation, I'd shot at someone just a few nights ago. But Tony looked like he had an arsenal, like he was ready for a shootout. This is where I wanted to drop in on a local police station and let them take over. I glanced out the window at Gretchen. I could tell from her face that she'd spotted Tony as well. And she'd recognized what he was carrying.

* * *

An hour later we turned off Interstate 5 towards Corvallis. Gretchen was in the back seat of the crew cab with Bien. We'd parked her car in the back of an apartment complex behind Cabela's where it would be both safe and unnoticed for at least a week.

Once we got on the road, I asked about her Taurus being tracked. She said, "It doesn't have GPS. And I left my phone at home." She held up a flip phone. "Got a burner."

I glanced at Tony. She seemed calm, compliant, and prepared. It occurred to me that Tony seemed to know more about Gretchen than I did. That frightened me. There seemed to be a lot of stuff going on lately that I didn't fully understand.

Tony said, "Follow Route 34 through Corvalis, then Route 20 out of town."

It was different driving without GPS talking to me. I had to watch for signs to make sure I stayed on the correct route.

About eight miles after Corvallis, Tony said, "Take a left on Woods Creek Road. Just up here on the left."

After a couple of miles, Tony said, "There's a driveway on the left up ahead. About a half-mile. I'll tell you when to turn."

It was a gravel turn-off in the wall of trees. A small house to the right hid behind a double row of trees.

"Go on around to the left."

I continued along the gravel drive, looping to the left. A quarter mile in, we came to another opening. A larger two-story house sat behind a steel gate.

Tony tapped his phone and the gate swung inward. A small barn huddled against the left side of the house. The ten-foot roll-up door began to rise. The barn was at least thirty feet wide with four bents on the left side. An old Volkswagen bug sat in the first bay. It was obviously a vintage model, probably from the 60s or 70s. The bright red paint had dulled, but it looked to be in good shape.

In the second bay was a small, twenty-foot Four Winds RV. It wasn't new, but it wasn't more than five years old, either. It was clean, like the Volkswagen.

The third bay was empty. Tony pointed. "Pull in there."

Gretchen got out and took Bien to do his business. Tony lowered the tailgate and pulled out three large backpacks.

"Where did those come from?"

"Gretchen stopped by our house and brought them. We transferred them from her car while you were getting the first burner working."

I got angry that there was a lot going on that I didn't know about. Not just with the Chester case, but with Gretchen. And Tony. Where were we? Who owned this place? We had to be in or near the Siuslaw National Forest.

Inside the house, Tony walked directly to the refrigerator and opened the door. It was filled with food. He fished a beer out of the door. "Help yourself. Let's sit in the living room. We have a lot to talk about.

He was right about that.

* * *

Although the house was timber frame construction, with tongue-and-groove high ceilings in the living and dining areas, it was remarkably light inside. A prow of windows made up most of the back wall. It overlooked a small lake and a gurgling stream that disappeared into the sea of green woods beyond. To the left was a five-foot hedge intended to screen what it enclosed—a three-meter satellite communications dish.

Heavy wooden furniture throughout blended with the timber style. In the center of the prow, a limestone fireplace went from floor to ceiling.

As soon as we sat down, I started with my questions. "What is this place?"

"It's my getaway place. My annual hunting trip—this is where I go."

"Why did you keep it a secret from me?"

"It's complicated."

I didn't say anything, a trick Tony himself had taught me. Sometimes silence encourages people to talk more than prodding them does.

"Although I work behind the scenes, it's often the evidence I dig up that convicts. Sometimes, though, the people I help put away are part of big, powerful organizations, organizations that have deep roots and deep pockets. And an appetite for revenge. So occasionally they come looking for who fingered them. They come looking for me.

"There's always the chance they might get to me. So FinCEN and I take precautions. Or maybe I should call it preparations." He pointed at the two camouflage backpacks sitting by the door. "Our go-bags from under our beds. In case you and I needed to leave in a hurry, we have what we need to survive. This house is our hidey-hole, a place no one knows about where we can hang out until the situation is resolved."

I pointed at the third dirt-colored bag, looking at Gretchen. "And you?"

"I have a go-bag, too."

"Why."

"You don't need to know."

"And the Taurus. You have a car with the GPS removed so it can't be tracked. Like Tony's truck. I mean, his makes sense. But you?"

"You don't need to know."

I'd never seen that look on her face. It was scary for a moment. Her eyes were on fire and bore right through me. But the longer she looked, the more her face softened. After a moment, I realized she was welling up. I looked away.

I wanted to get up and hug her, try to make her feel better, tell her she was safe with us. But she already knew that. That's why she was here. Safety. But she was scared, too.

"Buck," said Tony, "I want to explain why we ran. The folks behind the Chesters' murders may or may not know who we are or that we have boxes of secret evidence and an encrypted flash drive. But with a news crew already on scene and an investigation that was now going to become federal, our faces and names were likely to end up on the news. The conscientious investigative reporter has an almost religious zeal to unearth information. Most of them have no concern about the consequences of exposing that information.

"In our case, it could lead the murderers to our doorstep. As a completely unrelated side effect, it also might lead others to my doorstep. We don't want to meet any of these people, or their agents. So I chose for all of us to remain anonymous.

"In a few days, FinCEN will intervene in the investigation and erase us from the whole thing. The news guys won't even know we were there. And we can go back home."

"And Gretchen? Why is she here?"

"She's a loose end. The right reporter could tie us together. We don't know why DJ went to her, or even who DJ is. But if they pulled on that string enough, they might get to us. So could the murderer."

I looked at her. I wanted to say something spiteful like how does it feel to be a loose end. But my frustration with her didn't warrant hurting her. I trusted her. Tony trusted her. That said a lot. And she was here. With us. For her own reasons, as well as Tony's.

I looked at Bien lying at her feet. "I guess someone has to manage the dog."

Gretchen jumped to her feet. Bien sprang to attention and looked at us. "Bien, *bleib*. The cat. I forgot about him." She rushed towards the garage door. "He's in the truck." A minute later she came back carrying Chester. When she put him down, he sauntered over to Bien and began rubbing against his leg. Bien looked at him, then back at Gretchen. *"Platz."* Bien lay down and Chester curled up against his chest.

I said, "Bien looks like he might swallow Chester whole sometimes. But he puts up with him."

Gretchen said, "He's male."

She had that look on her face like she knew she'd just cracked a joke but she wasn't going to admit it by smiling. She struggled with it for a moment, then stood. "Anyone need another beer? What are we doing for dinner?"

Tony said, "I'll cook. We have lots of options. Let me see what's in the refrigerator."

"Tony, who takes care of this place?" I asked. "You're here maybe twice a year. How'd the food get in the refrigerator?"

"The couple at the little house near the driveway entrance."

I sighed. These two were alike in some ways. Secretive. Never sharing more than was necessary. I'd grown up in that world with Tony, but my friends had provided another, warmer side of life. With Tony, there always seemed to be the proverbial elephant in the room—the unspoken. Initially, I'd thought it was about my parents and their death. We didn't talk about that. But over the years I came to realize it wasn't that. There was a whole side of Tony that he never exposed. It encompassed his office, his work, and his lack of socialization. He'd come to my baseball games, nearly every one of them. But he never engaged with the other parents. Never drove my friends to a movie. He remained in the background, always there, always attentive. But never very visible.

At home, his love for me was evident though. We talked freely about life, relationships, and what troubled me. We hugged often. But he never talked about the details of his work. Current events, politics, and my friends were common household topics. I didn't know if Tony had any friends. I'd never met any. He never dated. At one point, I'd asked him if he was gay. He laughed and said no. For a few minutes he talked about his former love life, the two women he'd loved, and how they'd grown apart. He'd seemed wistful. I reminded him of his counseling to me—inaction never attains the goal. He clapped me on the shoulder and said he was glad

I'd learned some of his lessons. Then he walked away, went to his office, and closed the door.

Tony and Gretchen stood in front of the open refrigerator, assessing the meal options. I decided to explore outside. "Hey. I'm going to look around outside. Okay if Bien and Chester come?"

Gretchen pointed to me as she looked at Bien and said, *"Geh Draussen."* Bien stood and looked back and forth between her and me.

I walked over to the side door and opened it. Bien walked past me and down the steps to the pond. Chester trotted along behind him. I felt like the animal babysitter, like the guy who narrated those *Animal Planet* shows. I could be his sidekick.

The smell of the outdoors swept over me as I walked down the limestone steps to the pond's edge. Most of the trees around us were pine or something carnivorous. No, that wasn't the right word. That meant meat-eating, like the dinosaurs. Or a wild boar. I wondered if any of those were around. This area felt more like bobcat or lynx territory. Bien could take care of himself, but Chester could be their prey.

I recalled the right word: coniferous. Pines, spruces, and firs. That was the smell. Their needles. It reminded me of Irish Spring soap.

A rabbit ambled along the bank of the pond to the right. The movement caught Bien's attention. He turned his head and looked at me. I said, *"Nein,"* one of the few German words I knew. Bien stood still and watched the rabbit for a few minutes, then ambled over into the grass and relieved himself. Chester sat at the pond's edge, staring into the water.

The pond didn't seem big enough or deep enough to support many fish, but when I walked over to where Chester sat, a few small fish swam about. Apparently, they fascinated Chester. His tail flipped back and forth to a beat only he heard.

To the left, the hedge hid the satellite dish, but there was an opening towards the back. I could also see a generator perched on a concrete pad of its own. With all the trees, I would expect power service to get knocked out routinely. Now that I thought about it, I hadn't seen any power lines along the driveway. Apparently, that part was underground.

The wind shifted, and with it came the smell of something dead. Bien smelled it, too, his head in the air sampling the fetid odor. He looked at me and I shrugged. "Beats me, boy. We're in the country. Critters die out here. Then they rot and become fertilizer for the trees."

I glanced around at the trees. Stephen King trees, maybe. Not so friendly. Snagging critters and turning them to compost for their own digestion. Or amusement. They were starting to whip around as the wind picked up. I heard thunder in the distance. From the west. Maybe a storm was coming in from the coast. The dead animal odor had shifted to one of rain. It started to sprinkle.

"Let's go guys. Back in the house." I started up the steps. Bien and Chester scampered by me and stopped at the door. Maybe they were a little spooked, too. I chastised my city-kid mentality and vowed to "go hunting" with Tony on his next trip. I wondered if he ever met women here. Maybe he had a secret relationship, and his hunting trips were like a sabbatical from me so he could go have wild, drunken sex with a bevy of women. I shook my head, scolding myself. I sounded like a raging-hormone teenager. Tony might meet someone, but wild partying was not his style.

Inside, someone had started cooking. Steam rose from a pair of pans on the stove.

Gretchen turned toward me and hefted a goblet of red wine in my direction. "Want some wine? Tony opened the good stuff."

I didn't care for wine. It tasted like combinations of vinegar mixes to me. "Thanks. I'll stick to beer."

"Good. More of God's nectar for me." She had put on a white apron with a red Eiffel Tower in the middle. She raised her index finger from the wine glass and pointed to me. "Did you know the Olympian gods thought wine had magical properties that gave immortality to anyone who drank it?"

"Does that mean the Thunderbird drinkers on the streets of downtown are immortal, too."

"Don't ruin my mood." She stirred one of the pots and took a sip from her glass. "Do you or Tony have any allergies I should know about? I don't want to kill you unintentionally. At least, not yet."

"No." She seemed to be on some cooking cloud enjoying herself, so I decided not to ruin it. "Do we have food for the animals?"

"Check the pantry. If not, we can use people food."

"Where's Tony?"

"He took the backpacks upstairs to the bedrooms."

I found food for Bien and Chester in the pantry. When I set his bowl in front of him, Bien just stared at it, occasionally glancing at Gretchen.

"He won't eat unless you tell him to."

"Nimm Futter." I said.

He dove in like he hadn't had a meal in a week.

"What does that mean?"

"Eat food."

"Makes sense." I looked at Bien. "What are you going to do with him?"

"Give him back to DJ. She'll contact me when she gets released."

"She's already out. Tony checked on the way."

Gretchen frowned. "We'll have to keep him until this whole thing gets cleared up and we go home."

The doorbell rang. I went to the door and looked through the peep hole. Apparently, our disappearing act was not as thorough as we thought. DJ stood there with a suitcase in one hand and a large brown shopping bag in the other.

CHAPTER 19

Tony came down the stairs and slid up next to me.

"Come in. I'm Tony. I guess you're DJ?" He put his hand out and she handed him the shopping bag, then walked inside. A white Tesla sat in the driveway.

Bien poked his head around the corner. DJ set her suitcase on the floor and squatted, holding out both arms. *"Hier."* He rushed into her hug, nearly knocking her over, licking her face and hands. His stubby tail was wagging rapidly.

After a moment, she stood and said, *"So ist bray."*

"He's been a good dog," Tony said. "Except Gretchen has to command him to eat."

"He's amazingly intelligent." She looked at Tony. "Well, I expect we have a lot to discuss."

"Dinner's ready, I believe. Let's eat and then we can get into it."

When we walked into the living room, Gretchen gave DJ a hug. "Would you like a glass of wine?"

"Thank you, but no. I have a lot of work this evening. Just water for me."

I said, "You guys go ahead and sit down. I'll help Gretchen get dinner on the table."

Tony and DJ headed to the table. I followed Gretchen into the kitchen. "What can I do?"

"How about water for everyone? The fridge has a water dispenser."

"What are we having?"

"Chicken adobo, the quick and easy kind."

"Smells great. Thanks for cooking."

She tipped her wine glass towards me. "You're welcome. Thanks for inviting me here."

"Wasn't me. All Tony."

"Yes, but you started it. And I'm glad you did."

I was carrying two glasses of water to the dining room, but I stopped and looked at her. She had a big smile. It was so unlike her. I glanced at the wine bottle on the counter. It was less than half full. "Maybe you better slow down on the wine."

"Why? You don't like me when I'm relaxed?"

I moved to the table and set the glasses down.

The chicken adobo was amazing. It was savory and salty with a tang of soy sauce. I wanted to lick my plate, but Gretchen had made enough for seconds. When I'd finished that, I still wanted to lick my plate.

While I was stuffing myself, DJ and Tony chit-chatted about the war in Ukraine, the likelihood of Putin being ousted soon, and the polarized front-runners for U.S. president. Gretchen seemed to be paying attention to their conversation, but she drank two more glasses of wine during dinner.

I shooed everyone into the living room and cleared the dishes. Along the way, I snagged Gretchen's wine bottle and re-corked it. There was less than a glass left in this, her second bottle.

I got a glass of ice water and handed it to her. "Here you go."

"Are you cutting me off?" She scowled but exchanged it for her empty wine glass and retreated to the living room.

I grabbed a beer from the fridge and joined them.

Everyone was silent for a moment, glancing around and wondering where to start. I smiled because I was thinking of Tony's advice again: silence is a great prompt.

DJ said, "Why don't you fill me in on the last twenty-four hours. Then I'll tell you what I can, how I got here, and what we need to do next."

I said, "Why don't you tell us that first? I'm not sure we trust you just yet."

"I left Bien with you. That should tell you how much I trust you."

"You didn't have any choice."

She shrugged. "Your perception. Not mine."

Tony said, "I have a pretty good idea how you found us. And you got out of custody for suspected murder very quickly. I vote to fill her in first, hoping she can stitch together the loose ends, including those from earlier today."

Gretchen looked at me. Tony knew more than I did. If he was okay sharing our recent story, then I figured it would be okay. He hadn't failed me yet. I nodded at Gretchen. "I'll start with making my deliveries today."

We spent an hour going over today's events. DJ asked a lot of detailed questions about the hotel. I did notice that Tony left out that he owned this place, his hideaway.

We went silent, all eyes on DJ.

Tony said, "Maybe tell us how you knew where we were and why you came here."

She pursed her lips and nodded. "Okay. This is quite delicate. There's a lot going on you don't understand. If you don't mind, let's back up and start with the Chesters."

Tony leaned back in his chair and took a swig of beer.

"Ray and Kay Chester. Not their real names of course. Obviously under witness protection. Ray was a Chinese national. Brilliant electronics engineer. Kay was Chinese, too, but born and raised in Serbia, and an equally brilliant software programmer. She was recruited by a Russian hacker group right out of university. You've probably heard of their activities where they hack into a company's computers for a ransom payment. HyperBit is the most famous group and the one Kay worked for.

"A few years after Kay started working for them, the HyperBit leaders realized there were only so many companies they could ransom for large sums of money."

Tony interrupted. "There must be thousands. Was it the number of targets, or were there limits on which ones would pay?"

"Not sure, but these guys are long term thinkers. They started looking for other opportunities and approached the Chinese government. They wanted the Chinese to build them an electric submarine. There are hundreds of undersea communications cables around the world, with another fifty in planning or construction. They wanted to target them and extort the cable owner for huge sums of money."

I said, "How does the sub play into that?"

"It drops remote-controlled mines at each cable. They sever the cable if the owner doesn't pay. In the U.S., we mostly use land cables. But 98% of international internet traffic flows through one or more undersea cables. The Ukrainian war showed how important Internet access is not only for commercial traffic, but for command and control of military operations."

Tony said, "What an opportunity for the Chinese. They get immunity from these guys and probably maintain control of the mines. That's an enormous military advantage."

"Correct. As I said, these HyperBit people are very smart and long-term thinkers. But they're also arrogant to a fault.

"Anyhow, the Chinese sent Ray to Serbia to help design the communications and control systems for the submarine and the mines. He met Kay, and they had a daughter nearly fifteen years ago.

"Not long after the daughter was born, Kay started having second thoughts about HyperBit. She didn't mind extorting money from what she perceived as rich companies run by oligarchs. But the cable-cutting scheme bothered her for some reason we don't really know. Together, she and Ray began to plot their exit. Their first priority was the safety of their now-teenage daughter. They began collecting their own ransom information they could use to protect themselves from the Chinese and HyperBit."

Tony said, "They were going to blackmail the Chinese and HyperBit to ensure their safety?"

"That was their plan. But the Chinese got wind of it just before we extracted them. They grabbed the daughter. We got Ray and Kay out. They told us they had the identity and location of nearly all HyperBit's personnel and data servers. They also brought the submarine design information and a backdoor to their mine communications system."

"But no daughter," said Tony. "And they didn't turn anything over to you because you were supposed to extract the daughter."

I said, "The Chesters had this information they threatened to make public, but if they did, the Chinese would kill their daughter. So it was a stalemate?"

"Without the daughter, they wouldn't release anything except monthly information about the mines. It was their way of making sure we understood the increasing severity of the problem."

"And increasing pressure to free the daughter," said Gretchen.

That's why Ray went to Sand Island each month. He was sending the mine data somehow. And DJ was the one who picked it up. "Who is 'we,' DJ?"

"I don't think it's necessary to specifically identify organizations."

"Who do you work for?"

"I'm a professor emeritus at Oregon State. I run a research project on deep underwater waves using magno-induction detection based on the ampere swimming rule."

Most of that was mumbo jumbo, but I deciphered enough of it to see where it was going. "You're trying to detect the mines and subs."

"HyperBit's latest test was last year off the coast of Scotland. They severed two cables but made no ransom demands. We think it was a final live demonstration of their ability before they started the mine ransom operation. Right now, there are about fifty mines in place. They add four more per month with two operational submarines."

Tony said, "How do you communicate with a mine on the seafloor? VLF communications is the best for that, but it isn't good for anything that deep."

"Ray devised a tethered buoy that surfaces monthly. It transmits status data, receives commands and updates, and has solar arrays that recharge the mine's battery."

That was the monthly data Ray was sending. "How do we intercept that data?"

"Not important."

I said, "I thought you were here to cooperate and help us."

"Hmmm…you misunderstood. In any case, I'm not going to reveal classified details that have no bearing on the Chesters' murders just because you're curious."

I hadn't liked DJ from the start, but her condescension was starting to get under my skin. I glanced at Tony.

He said, "What's the status of your research? Is it operational?"

"We've been working with ACS Alaska-Oregon Network, AKORN for short. They're very cooperative and have a shore station near Florence so it's convenient to our work."

I said, "DJ, is it odd that Wayne Durbin's ID listed Florence as his residence? Or was it coincidence?" The hair on the back of my neck was standing up, but I knew she wasn't going to answer. I moved on. "Is there a mine on their cable?"

DJ smiled but didn't respond.

Gretchen said, "What about the daughter? Does she know her parents are dead?"

DJ looked at her folded hands in her lap for a moment. She frowned. "I don't know. I'm not even sure she's still alive."

Gretchen teared up. "Someone ought to find that poor girl. It's not her fault. She didn't get to choose where she was born or who her parents were."

Gretchen's question raised some kind of vague alarm in my head. I couldn't put my finger on it, but I could feel something elusive that I should recognize. I kept asking myself why *that* question, Gretchen.

"You're right, Gretchen," said Tony. "Let's not lose sight of that, but there are still lots of unanswered questions." He looked at DJ.

"I only have a few answers. HyperBit came after the Chesters. They hired some mercenaries from Mexico as soon as the Chesters disappeared from Serbia. I'm sure they figured the Chesters were in WITSEC, but they didn't have any way to find them. Until last month.

"WITSEC was always a target for penetration. There's big money in finding people the U.S. is hiding. Apparently, they finally bought off someone. The Mexicans torched any place where the Chesters could have hidden their blackmail information—the names and faces of HyperBit."

"HyperBit killed the Chesters?" I asked.

"We don't think so. We think the Chinese got the same information, or maybe they orchestrated the penetration and passed it on to HyperBit. In any case, the working theory is the Chinese poisoned the Chesters. Then they let HyperBit know where they were. The Mexicans started torching places, and that upset the Chinese, but they couldn't stop them. Until they did, by killing them."

"Why another cannabis order?" I asked. "Why blow up the OliveTree after they were dead?"

She glanced at Tony, then back to me. "Witnesses. You know they tried to pin the toxin on me. They probably knew Ray had visited my lab a few times. They figured out what I was doing and thought Ray was helping. They wanted to get me out of the way but killing me would bring too much investigation. There are too many three-letter agencies involved in my research.

"Yesterday, they wanted to dispose of the Mexican bodies and you, too, Buck. You had taken pictures of the hit man hired by the Chinese. You could identify him."

"He was sitting at the picnic table in the parking lot. Why didn't he just shoot me?"

"Had you gone inside, he would have blown the place up with a remote detonator. But you didn't go in. His fail-safe was the body booby trap to get rid of the Mexican bodies. You're still a problem for them."

Tony said, "I saw the guy, too. He could have shot me, but he just knocked me out."

"Just guessing, but he probably thought you were an innocent bystander. You were sitting in his seat, in his way. He just needed you to leave."

My head was reeling from the twisted story. But most importantly, the Chinese apparently still wanted to eliminate me. That didn't sound like a good place to be.

Tony said, "And how you found us and why you came here?"

She smiled. "I suspect you guessed right. You texted a mutual friend. A work contact, I think. He reached out to me. Asked me to brief you into this mess so you didn't get yourselves killed. Plus, I had to get Bien back."

"Why were you at Gretchen's place?"

"I knew you delivered the cannabis that killed the Chesters. I'd just learned you also delivered a cannabis order to my room at the OliveTree a week before. But I was too slow. Before you could explain how that happened, Massey showed up."

"And they let you go right away?"

"Yes. My arrest triggered some phone calls to Massey's boss."

I looked over at Gretchen. She'd curled her legs up under her and her eyes were almost closed. I looked at my watch. It was already 11:30 p.m. "Maybe it's time we get some sleep. It's been a long, stressful day. Tony, is there a bedroom for DJ?"

He nodded.

DJ said, "Give me a minute and I'll let Bien out before we go."

She walked to the slider and opened it. Bien jumped up and trotted outside. He was back in less than a minute.

Tony carried DJ's bag, and she and Bien followed him upstairs. I went over to Gretchen, who seemed to have dozed off. My first instinct was to tickle her ear with her hair. But I still had bruises from her. Who said corporal punishment wasn't effective?

I tapped her on the knee. "Gretchen. We're going to bed." She stirred a little bit. I tapped her on the knee again, standing back at arm's length. Her eyes fluttered open. She looked at me and smiled. "You're learning. And I don't even have to use German commands."

CHAPTER 20

Just after 2:00 a.m. a crack of lightning flashed, and thunder boomed immediately, rattling the windows. The room was almost pitch-black, except for a nightlight in the Jack-and-Jill bath. We were, after all, in the middle of a forest with no city lights.

I felt, more than heard, someone tiptoeing across the floor. My bed was queen-sized, opposite the bath, and I slept towards the left where there was a bedside stand next to it. I slid my hand out slowly and felt around for my gun on the stand top. After I found it, I picked it up and slid my arm back under the covers, flipping off the safety.

Another flash of lightning illuminated the room. By the time the thunder cracked, less than a second later, I had turned, and brought up my gun as the person jumped onto my bed. I rolled to the floor, switched on the lamp, and drew aim at the person in my bed.

It was Gretchen. She raised her arm to shield her eyes from the light. "Turn it off."

"What are you doing?"

She swept her hair back out of her face.

I turned off the light. A flash of lightning revealed tears streaming down her cheeks. I clicked the safety on and put the gun back on the nightstand.

She whispered, "I'm scared. Can I stay here?"

If she could have seen my mind at that moment, it would have convinced her that men can have more than one box open at a time. I had so many conflicting thoughts, but the one that won out was the friend box. "Sure."

We got under the covers, both on our backs. She was sniffing. I slid my arm under her neck and said, "Come here." She rolled into me with her head on my shoulder. She was trembling. I wrapped my other arm around her. "It's gonna be okay, Gretchen. And it will feel a lot better in the morning when it's daylight."

She jumped when the lightning flashed again. I rubbed her back. "It's okay. Just a storm."

We lay there like that for a while. Her breathing became more and more regular. After ten minutes, she started a shallow, quiet snore. So I lay still, Gretchen half-lying on me and me with my arms wrapped around her. I smiled and dozed off.

When I woke, it was just getting light outside. Neither Gretchen nor I had moved, but my left arm under her was completely numb. Her light snore continued, and I willed myself to lie still. I busied myself with running through DJ's information from last night. It tied a lot together, but still left a few holes. I still didn't know how the toxin-laced cannabis got into the shop. There had to be an insider there, which we hadn't identified. Gage was obvious because he had unfettered access to everything, including the video system. Because he was obvious, though, I thought he might be a red herring. Each of the three leads, Choice, Thomas, and Jennifer, had similar access. Any budtender could have switched the package, but they didn't have access to the video system—unless they or a helper hacked it.

And the guy at the hotel that cracked Tony's skull and got away on the freeway—where was he and was he still after me?

No one knew we'd snagged the submarine and mine design docs. The HyperBit information was probably what was on that flash drive. They didn't know we had that, either. At least, I didn't see how they could know that.

Maybe that was what would keep us all alive. It had kept the Chesters alive. For a while. But they were dead now. There had to be a way we could leverage that information to make them leave us alone. If we turned it over to the government, they might go away. Or they might kill us as retribution or punishment. On the other hand, letting them know we had the information could be a path to a sure death.

I needed to talk with Tony, but I was stuck. I looked at Gretchen's sleeping face six inches from mine.

There was a little freckle in her right eyebrow I'd never noticed before. As tall and pretty as she was, she could be a model. But she'd probably kick a photographer's ass if he got out of line or took a picture she didn't like.

Her eyes slid open like a viper. She didn't move. "Good morning."

"Good morning. Sleep well?"

"No. I hate storms. And you snore."

"So do you."

She raised her head and ran her hand over the center of my bare chest. "Where'd you get these bruises?"

"There's another one to the left of center." I winced when she poked at it.

"Are these from me?"

"Yes."

"I'm sorry. Didn't know you were so fragile."

"Sensitive, too."

She climbed out of bed and headed toward the bathroom.

At the doorway, she stopped and looked back. "Thanks for letting me stay with you last night."

CHAPTER 21

Friday, May 5

Gretchen poured herself a cup of coffee and walked around to the other side of the dining table. She was wearing jeans and a tank top today. I noticed that the back of the tank top was cut high enough to cover her scar. No accident. She was smart and avoided anything to attract attention.

I poured myself some coffee and sat down across from her. "Mind if I ask a personal question."

"Yes."

I frowned. Why did I start with that question? I knew what she'd say. There had to be a way I could get at this without making her feel like I was prying. Of course, I was prying. It was none of my business. I didn't need to know. I groaned internally at the use of that phrase—need to know. That had always been a part of my life with Tony.

But I was curious. It was natural. I wanted to know more about her, even at the risk of broken ribs. I tried a different tack.

"Did you know you have a freckle in your left eyebrow? I'd never noticed it until this morning."

She set the cup down. "I know the German word for bite."

I couldn't help myself—I laughed, long and hard.

"How'd you get that scar on your spine?"

She stared at me for a moment. "Maybe some other time."

DJ and Tony came in chatting like they were old friends. I wondered if Tony somehow knew DJ, or at least of her, before she showed up here. The fed maze had odd connections.

DJ said to Gretchen. "Did the storm bother you last night?"

"I slept very well. Quite comfortable beds."

"It freaked me out," said DJ. "I was awake for hours." She glanced at Tony.

He looked away. "Coffee, DJ?"

"Please."

I noticed Tony didn't ask if she wanted cream or sugar. Either everyone in government drank it black, or they had history.

I glanced at Gretchen to see if she was picking up these Tony/DJ vibes, but she was staring out the window towards the pond. She said, "I'm sorry if I dozed off last night. Probably drank too much wine. Did I miss anything at the end?"

"Not much," I said. "Except the OliveTree bomb was probably intended for me."

Her head snapped back to look at me. "At you? Why?"

DJ said, "Loose ends. When Buck delivered to room 130, he took the hit man's picture. Saw him up close. Talked with him. And could probably ID him."

Since she arrived, I hadn't seen DJ use her phone. None of the rest of us had, either, but either DJ was the ultimate professional and left her phone at home, or...I didn't have another explanation. But her Tesla was still a problem. I have wanted a Tesla since before I got my driver's license. We couldn't afford it, of course, but that didn't mean I couldn't read everything I could find out about it. One of the curious aspects was that Tesla, the company, tracked all their cars in near-real time. You could turn off the GPS from the control panel, but that only disabled GPS from the Apps. There were still ways to connect to the vehicle and retrieve its location. That was a major reason why no government agency ever considered Tesla vehicles.

When it came down to it, I didn't trust DJ. It was a gut feeling, and the gut was wrong as often as it was right. But we only heard about it when it was right because when it was wrong, you often died.

I wanted to talk to Tony. Alone. With no chance of bugs or other people around. "Tony, is it too early to walk up to the caretaker's house and introduce me?"

"Sure. Let's get that out of the way." He looked at DJ. "Any chance you could make breakfast for us? It will only take us ten minutes."

"Leave the girls to do the cooking? Kind of sexist." DJ turned to Gretchen. "What do you think?"

"Definitely sexist. I could use a good run."

"Bien could use the exercise, too. So you boys run along and when you get back, we'll have girl time. And you can fix your own breakfast."

I glanced at Gretchen. "Thanks. We won't be long."

Tony and I headed out the front door. As we walked by the Tesla, I said, "Doesn't that Tesla worry you?"

"I trust DJ. She wouldn't bring a car that can be tracked. Or maybe the car can't be linked to her."

"Why do you trust her?" Before I accused him of sleeping with her, I wanted to see if Tony would come clean or there was some other story I hadn't thought of.

"She seems deeply involved in government projects, so she's been cleared. And she came to us. The U.S. Marshals cleared her of murder in a couple of hours." He looked at me. "Why don't you don't trust her?"

I wasn't sure how to respond. "She sure knows a lot about the Chester case."

"Of course she does. She's in the middle of it."

We rounded a bend in the road so we could no longer be seen from the house. I stopped and faced Tony. "It's none of my business, but I have to ask: did you sleep with her last night?"

Tony's face went a little pale. Not the reaction I expected.

Before he could reply, I said, "Let me rephrase that. Why does it make you anxious that I ask that question?"

"Okay. I knew of her but had never met her before. Apparently, she also knew about me. Mutual friend has been trying to set us up for some time."

"You trust her, then?"

"Yes. Our mutual friend is vetted."

We walked on. "Are we really going to meet the people who take care of…this?" I waved my hand around.

"You inherit this if I die. A couple takes care of it. Jeff and Kristie Milligan. Mid-forties, no kids. Love living off the land as much as possible."

"You have an office here like at home?"

"Yes. I'll show you when we get back."

"Why have you kept this place a secret?"

"Couple of reasons. When you were younger, I couldn't always trust you to keep secrets. Sometimes young guys get in situations where they try to brag about what their parents, or in your case, uncle does or owns."

"And the other reason?"

We walked in silence for a minute. "Sometimes I needed a refuge. A place to get away. Be on my own."

"You mean without me?"

"Not like that. You know how much I love you. But the weight of being an all-parent gets heavy sometimes. A short break helps recharge."

Thinking back about the times he must have been here, it did seem he came home with renewed enthusiasm and a smile on his face. "I think I get it."

We approached the house. There was a fenced garden behind it three times the size of the house. Tony knocked on the door. It was opened at once by a middle-aged guy in a red plaid shirt and suspendered overalls.

"Hi, Tony. Everything okay?"

"Hi Jeff. Everything's fine. I wanted you to meet my nephew, Buck."

We shook and exchanged greetings. His hand was callused and rough.

"We're here for a few days with some friends. Kind of unplanned. I appreciate the quick supply run you made."

"No problem. That was some storm last night."

"At least we didn't lose power."

"Yeah. Doesn't happen so much since they buried the line along Woods Creek Road."

"Generator working okay?"

"Yep. Propane's full, too."

"Okay. I just wanted you to meet Buck. He might be up here on his own sometime and I wanted you to know his face. Say hello to Kristie for me."

"Will do." He closed the door, and we started the walk back.

When we rounded the bend in the road, the house and the Tesla came into view. Tony stopped walking. I stopped and looked at him.

"What?"

"Something's off. Jeff's knuckles on his right hand. He's been in a fight. Recently. Not even a day old. And we didn't see or hear Kristie. And what he said about power lines being buried on West Creek. They aren't. They're still on poles."

"You thinking someone is in there with him?"

A muffled triplet of barks came from our house. We began to run. Tony said, "Stop at the door. Go left. Pull your weapon."

We crouched on either side of the door, pulled our weapons, and on Tony's nod, burst through the doorway.

Bien met us with a growl. We froze. A burst of laughter rang out.

Tony called out, "DJ. Gretchen. It's Tony and Buck."

DJ said, "Bien, *Fuss.*" Bien turned and trotted over to DJ. She held a pen-like device in her hand.

She and Gretchen had huge grins on their faces. Gretchen said, "You've got to see this."

DJ turned and pointed the pen, which turned out to be a laser pointer, towards a timber brace eight feet above the floor. Chester was up there, and he started pawing at the red dot as DJ moved it around. He scampered around the brace and up the queen post and across a tie beam, following the dot. Bien watched attentively, but I wasn't sure if he was following the dot or the cat. The women howled.

Tony and I looked at each other. The behavior of the women was a lot funnier than the cat chasing a laser pointer.

Tony said, "I guess we're cooking our own breakfast." He leaned over to me and said into my ear. "I'll be right back to scan for bugs."

I went to the refrigerator and got out the eggs and a package of sausage links. Then I opened and closed drawers, searching for pans. When I found a skillet, I shuffled it with the other three several times to make pan noises. "Ladies, if you'll set the table, I'll have breakfast ready shortly."

They burst into laughter again. I decided to leave them alone because they were making plenty of noise that would entertain anyone listening.

Tony returned with a bug wand a moment later. He started walking a grid in the house, looking for bugs. The women noticed and grew somber. They looked at me.

I held my finger to my lips to shush them.

Gretchen gave a hands-upturned gesture. I pointed to my ear. She nodded. "I'll get the drinks.

DJ didn't say anything, but she gathered the plates and silverware and carried them to the table.

I started cooking.

Gretchen said, "Anyone for toast?"

Tony and DJ said, "Yes," in unison.

I nodded to her.

In fifteen minutes, the room had been swept clean. "No bugs," said Tony.

Tony disappeared into the garage for a minute and returned with guns from his truck. He laid them on the countertop alongside the ammo. We loaded the shotgun and handguns.

While we sat down and began eating, Tony fired up one of the burner phones. He made a call while I filled in the women on our trip to Jeff's house and our suspicions. The mood went from one of glee to a dark, foreboding tone.

Chester, who'd been up on the beam chasing the laser, inched down backwards on one of the posts.

Tony finished his call. "The local sheriff is going to make a call on Jeff's house. Should be within the hour. It will be about ninety minutes before the feds can get here. Let's hope we can just wait it out.

Everyone was quiet sitting around the dining table for a while. Chester meowed at the door. I got up and opened it so he could go out. Bien walked over to my side, then looked back over his shoulder at DJ. I never heard any official changeover from Gretchen to DJ, but he seemed to know that DJ was in charge of him now.

She said, *"Voraus."*

He walked outside and down the steps towards the pond. Chester was already over in the dirt next to the fence.

As Bien got to the bottom step, he turned west towards Jeff's house. He stood there with his head in the air, sniffing.

He suddenly yelped and jumped to the side, then took two or three running steps toward the fence before he fell over.

I stepped outside, intending to run to Bien. But my left shoulder suddenly slammed me back against the doorjamb and my head cracked into the door. Dazed, I stood there for a moment before I realized I'd been shot. By a silenced weapon. Just like Bien.

I staggered back inside the door as best I could by some combination of twisting, rolling, and falling.

I heard Tony shouting and the women's voices. Someone grabbed my shirt by the collar and began dragging me across the floor.

The dining table flipped over on its side. DJ and Gretchen, crouching behind it, shoved the table in front of the windows on the right side.

Gretchen was in my face, blocking everything else from view. "Just look at me, look at my eyes. I'm gonna work on your wound." She grabbed my shirt with one hand and ripped it open. I didn't feel any pain. I was numb, though everything was in slow motion.

I could hear DJ and Tony shouting, but I didn't know what they were saying. It seemed I was floating through the air, moving across the room. I wondered if I had died, and my spirit was now floating away up the stairs.

When I rolled my head to the left, I was kind of disappointed I hadn't died. But it was just Gretchen carrying me up the stairs. I remembered her shoulders and arms and the muscles she had. This woman was strong. And if she was carrying my 200-plus up the stairs, her legs were as jacked as her arms.

I heard some crashes and gunfire in the background. Tony shouted, "Grenade." A moment later there was a loud boom, some gunfire, and then I heard the burp of automatic gunfire. One short burst, a second short burst, then a longer burst. Followed by silence.

Gretchen set me on the bed. She ripped off a pillowcase, folded it, and got in my face again. "You've got an exit wound on the backside but I'm hoping the bed will staunch the blood there."

From the pressure, it felt like she was sitting on my shoulder. It was hard to breathe, too. I wondered if I'd been hit in the lung. Was it filling with blood? Collapsing? I tried to cough. It didn't sound right.

"Shit, Buck, you're bleeding from your head, too."

Her hand slid under my head. When she drew it back, it was slick with blood.

I said, "I'm sorry."

"Not now. You don't need to be sorry. Just stay with me."

She was such a strong woman. I wondered why she was afraid of storms. Tears ran down her cheeks. I wanted to stop them, roll them back up into her eyes. I focused on that eyebrow freckle as she worked. She pushed some hair back out of her face and left a red smudge on her cheek.

My vision started to go black like I was looking through a donut hole. The hole got smaller and smaller. I could see Gretchen's mouth moving like she was yelling, but I couldn't tell what she was saying. The hole shrank to a pinpoint, like a star. And then it went out.

CHAPTER 22

My shoulder was on fire. Someone was yelling my name. I managed to crack open one eye. Standing to the left of the bed was Wayne Durbin, the guy I delivered the cannabis to, the one who tried to blow me up.

He was shaking me by the shoulders.

"Wake up, asshole. Wake up so I can put a bullet in your brain."

I saw him glance at my face, saw my eyes were open. He stopped shaking me. My head cleared a little, but my left shoulder was screaming at me. And I had a giant headache.

"Hello, Buck. Welcome to the party. We've missed you."

"Missed you, too, Wayne. Or are you using a different name today?"

He smiled and waved a .45 pistol around. "Wayne works. You've been a real pain in the ass, and I don't have time to pay you back for all the trouble you've caused. If you'll just tell me what you did with the Chesters' blackmail files, I'll be on my way."

"I don't know what you're talking about."

"Thought you might say that." He reached down and grabbed a foot-long sliver of wood sticking out of my shoulder. He pulled it out slowly. I could hear me screaming, but it was coming from far away. Things went black again.

I don't know how long I was out, but he was shaking me again. The fire in my shoulder had spread to my entire left side, throbbing and burning like nothing I'd ever felt.

Wayne got back in my face. "Looks like you faint at the sight of a little blood. Particularly your own." He chuckled. "Now about those files."

"I don't know what you're talking about."

Wayne smiled.

"You're an ugly bastard, Wayne."

He waved his gun at me. "Glad you can see just fine." He pushed the gun into his belt and produced a switchblade knife. "I'm gonna start filling up that hole in your shoulder. We don't want you to bleed out. So, I'm gonna pack it with your girlfriend's fingers, one by one. And if that ain't enough, I'll finish with the toes."

I raised my head enough to see across the room. Gretchen was hanging by her feet from an overhead beam. The rope that held her was tied off to the foot of the bed. Her bound hands were a couple inches from the floor. She was gagged with a piece of gray duct tape, but her eyes were enormous and bloodshot. One eye was nearly swollen shut.

I was confused about the splinter of wood Wayne had pulled out of my shoulder. I wondered if he shoved it in there. Or maybe it was the wood that pierced my shoulder, a big sliver of the door frame blown out by his gunshot that missed me.

In any case, the adrenaline had been working in my body since I was shot. Given I hadn't died yet, I didn't think I was going to bleed out or suffocate from a collapsed lung. But just raising my head to look around the room brought darks spots and flashing lights in my vision. Still, Wayne's threat to cut off Gretchen's fingers must have caused my adrenal glands to kick into overtime.

Wayne had his back to me, grabbing Gretchen's hands. She was writhing and jumping, trying to elude him, but she couldn't get away.

"Stop it," he snarled. "You want another boot in the head? It's just like clipping your nails. Except it's a little shorter than usual."

He grabbed her arms and pinned them under one of his. With his other hand, he grabbed her hand and folded all her fingers except her pinkie. He held it straight out and raised his knife to slash it off.

I could hear Gretchen screaming behind the duct tape.

I was surprised to find my gun still in my ankle holster. And then Wayne's head exploded. A few pieces splattered blood and brain matter onto the wall behind him.

I struggled to keep my gun pointed at him. He now lay slumped on the floor, his headless body pumping his blood uselessly into a pool. I holstered my gun and picked up the wooden splinter he'd pulled out of my shoulder. Crawling over to his body, I shoved the splinter into one of the pumping arteries.

When I lowered Gretchen to the floor, she pushed and shoved with her hands to move away from Wayne as much as possible. As soon as her feet hit the floor, I crawled over and pulled the duct tape from her mouth. She said nothing. Wayne's knife lay nearby, so I used that to slice the duct tape off her hands. She took the knife and sliced the tape off her feet.

I said, "Go find Tony. Please."

She nodded and bounded down the stairs. I could hear her calling Tony's name. In a couple of minutes, I heard voices. Plural. Two voices. I couldn't understand what they were saying, but one was male. Tony was alive.

In another minute, Gretchen and Tony rushed into the room. He glanced at Wayne's body, then helped me get off the floor and sit on the side of the bed.

I said, "Some professional. He didn't even search me."

Gretchen swooped me up in her arms and carried me downstairs. She sat me in a living room chair and Tony sat down beside me. In a moment, Gretchen brought some water and helped me drink slowly.

Chester appeared from under the chair and started rubbing against my leg. I picked him up and sat him in my lap. He sniffed the blood all over me, then started purring.

"Where's DJ?"

Tony made a face. "When that guy came through the door, either DJ was an awful shot, or terribly unlucky. She had my 12-gauge shotgun and never touched him at thirty feet. He never once fired in her direction.

"I ran out of ammo. He had a clean shot at me. But just before he fired, Chester jumped down and landed on his head from the beams above. He missed. And then DJ yelled at him. Told him to just tie me up. The guy stood there for a moment or two, then told me to back up against the post. He wrapped me with a whole roll of duct tape."

Gretchen said, "Just his face was sticking out. It took some cutting."

"So DJ was in on it," I said. "We misjudged her. Your vetted friend was wrong."

Tony nodded. "We need to get you to the hospital first and then figure out how to proceed."

Gretchen said, "Bien's gone and so is her Tesla."

Tony said, "She was yelling at him about killing her dog. He said it was just tranquilized. She ran out the door towards the pond and never came back."

"Her untraceable Tesla."

Tony smiled. "Maybe not. I put a tracker on it."

We heard a car pull up outside. Gretchen looked out.

"Sheriff's car. Two uniforms getting out. With their guns drawn."

* * *

Before the paramedics took me to the hospital, Gretchen fired up another burner and took pictures of where I'd been standing when the wood sliver pierced my shoulder. She showed it to me. "The wood was a piece of doorjamb that blew off when the bullet hit it. You must have moved at just the right time. Missed you by a couple of inches."

"With that rifle he could shoot right through the wall, even if he didn't have a clean shot."

"I found the slug in the floor about ten feet back."

"I was lucky the round missed, and even luckier that the wood didn't hit me in the face or take out an eye."

At the hospital, the doctor said, "The wood spike missed everything important in your shoulder except a good-sized vein, which explains all the blood. You have a two-inch laceration on the back of your head, but no skull fracture. Just a mild concussion. We'll keep you here for a couple of days and you'll be good as new."

"I can't stay here."

"I can't dismiss you in this condition."

"Doesn't matter. I can't stay here. You can check with my friends or with the sheriffs."

I had to sign some papers releasing the hospital, and a couple hours later we were on our way home.

Gretchen sat in the passenger seat this time. I laid across the back seat, keeping my stitched-up shoulder elevated. They gave me back my jeans, but they'd cut my shirt off and now my arm was in a sling. I had a hospital blanket draped over my shoulder, covering the bandages on both sides. They'd given me some pain pills, but I wanted to hold off until I could hear their update.

Tony said, "I gave DJ's tracker information to the feds and they're following up. When I last looked, her car was parked in the Eugene airport long-term lot. I suspect she caught the first flight out."

"Maybe," I said. "Do they have international flights?"

"No. All domestic."

"I'd look at San Diego first, if they have a flight there. She'll go through Mexico. I bet she was the one who brought in the Mexican arsonists who ended up at the OliveTree."

Gretchen turned in her seat so she could see me behind Tony. "That's what Vikram said, too."

"He was there?"

"Yeah. Vikram is really CIA, right Tony?"

"Correct. So was DJ. There's been a leak in WITSEC for a while. Vikram's been trying to find it. Now they're trying to figure out if it was DJ."

I said, "How about Vikram? He vouched for DJ and look where that got us."

"He was duped, too. Along with several others up his chain of command."

Gretchen said, "I don't see how DJ could be their leak. She wasn't in the U.S. Marshal's office. But maybe she had access to their information."

"Buck, remember when Mendoza got upset at our house?" Tony said. "Wouldn't let us scan her? She was wearing a wire because they suspected Diaz. Mendoza didn't want us to blow their investigation."

"Makes sense," I said, "but it made her look guilty instead. Is Diaz still a suspect?"

"No," Tony said. "She's been cleared."

"What about Jeff and Kristie—they okay?"

"Yeah. Scuffed up a little. Wayne, or whatever his name was, had her tied up when Jeff talked to us. Threatened to kill her if Jeff tipped us off. He tied up Jeff before he came after us. The sheriffs found them."

"Did DJ tell Wayne where we were?" I asked Tony.

"It's the only plausible explanation, although there's a slim chance they also have a leak within the CIA."

"Are the feds always this convoluted?" I asked.

"Not in my experience. Maybe that's why DJ fooled everyone."

Gretchen said, "Did Vikram tell anyone else where we were?"

Tony said, "I don't think so, but I can't be certain. Remember, the arsonist burned down his place, too. Hard to imagine he's complicit."

Gretchen said, "They identified Wayne from his fingerprints. They didn't know his real name—apparently, he has many names— but he's a well-known assassin, formerly of the Wagner Group in Russia."

"What happens now?" I asked. "What do we do with the boxes I lifted from the Chesters?"

"Turn them over to Vikram," Tony said, "along with the flash drive and lamp. We've done what we can."

"Not completely. There's someone complicit, or at least implicated, in the dispensary. They had to get the toxin-laced cannabis into my deliveries."

"You need rest," Gretchen said. "Can Vikram chase that?"

"Maybe." My head was throbbing, and pain shot through my shoulder every time the truck hit a bump.

Tony exited the freeway and drove to the apartment complex where we'd parked Gretchen's car. She said, "I'm going to go by my place, trade cars, and grab some clothes. Then I'll be over to your place."

She climbed out, but I stayed in the back where I was mostly lying down. Chester snoozed by my feet. I thought about the pain pills, but I still needed my wits.

We arrived home just after 7:00 p.m.

Tony said, "I'll carry the stuff, Buck. You go on in."

I let Chester out of the car and slung my backpack over my good shoulder. Tony grabbed an armful of stuff and followed me to the door. I fished around in my pocket and found the key, then unlocked the door. The room was dim as I pushed the door back. Tony flicked on a light with his elbow.

Bien sat six feet away, staring at us.

CHAPTER 23

"Close the door, if you don't mind," said DJ.

Tony pushed the door closed with his foot and set his stuff down on the floor.

DJ sat at the table holding a silenced Beretta. It was pointed our way. She had short, blond hair now. I wasn't sure if it was a wig or if she'd cut and dyed her hair. It changed her appearance dramatically. She'd also changed into gray Nike warmups with pink Nike running shoes. "Where's your girlfriend, Buck?'

"She went home."

"Too bad. Another loose end I have to clean up."

"What do you want, DJ?" Tony asked.

She ignored his question. "Since you're here, I guess Motka underestimated you. I won't make that mistake. Besides, I already have what I wanted."

"The files," Tony said. "You traded the files for an offshore account and a one-way to someplace where you can spend it."

"Tenured professors don't make that much." She smiled. "Even ones like me who spent ten years inside HyperBit."

"You were a spy for the hackers."

"I've switched sides so many times I lost count. Now I get to be on my side."

"Forever looking over your shoulder."

She shook her head. "I'll pay someone to do that for me."

"If you got what you wanted, why are you still here?"

"My ride doesn't arrive for a while. You were so sociable and cordial, I thought I'd return the favor before I left." She slid a chair towards us with her foot. "Why don't you have a seat. Buck is looking a little pale. Don't want him passing out."

Tony pulled a chair over for me and I sat down. I felt a little light-headed, but between the Beretta and Bien, they had my full attention.

"You have a cozy little setup upstairs, Tony. Even have the room shielded. Very clever way to hide all that gear. You had a document scanner, too. And all those boxes of documents—they'd had their staples removed and were neatly organized. Thank you for that." She shrugged. "But destroying just the documents wouldn't be enough, would it? I had to fry your computers. I couldn't leave any scanned copies behind."

Tony glanced at the stairs.

"I'm sure the government would replace most of it," she said. "But your data, I'm glad to say, will be gone. As will you. My Mexican friends, may they rest in peace, had some excellent incendiary devices from their Chinese buddies. Quite a clever detonator, and they pass right through airport scanners."

Tony glanced at the stairs again.

"They left me a couple. My farewell gift to you, repaying your hospitality."

I said, "What about Bien?"

"How nice of you to ask, Buck. He can't go with me, so I'll leave him to you."

"You said he won't accept commands from men."

She shrugged. "He won't be accepting commands at all with a bullet in his head."

"You're going to shoot him? A dog like that?"

"Why not? I can buy a dozen like him where I'm going. Nothing against Bien. He's been good company. Loyal. Obedient. More than I can say about most of my colleagues."

"What about your project?"

"What project? You mean the detection device for the cable?" She waved her other hand. "They'll keep working on it without me. Might even get it to work. Who cares? HyperBit has so much money, they'll just find another way to ransom millions from the rich."

Chester jumped up on the counter. He knew he wasn't supposed to be up there, but he sat, looking at the dining table six feet away, his tail swishing back and forth.

DJ reached into a bag on the floor and pulled out a roll of duct tape. "Tony, would you please do the honors? Tape Buck to his chair. Arms first. Then each foot to a chair leg. Not too tight. We don't want to cut off the poor injured dear's circulation."

Tony began to tape me to my chair.

"Oh, come on, Tony. Not that loose or I'll have to put a bullet in him, too. I don't want to kill you two. I just want you to stay put until I get away. You boys have been neutered and can't touch me now. That girl, Gretchen, too."

Tony said, "What do you mean by 'neutered?'"

"Tony! For shame. Don't ruin my surprise. After all, I am a professor and I love teaching lessons to my students. It's so much fun."

He finished with my legs and stood looking at DJ. At first, I thought he might rush her. I guess she did, too.

"Bien, Gib Laut."

Bien barked.

"Reminder, Bien is still here. Set the tape on the table."

Tony set the tape on the table, then sat down in his chair.

"Bien, *wache.*"

He trotted over and stood staring at Tony from three feet away.

DJ laid her gun on the table and picked up the tape. "It won't be too hard to get loose. You should be able to kick over your chair quickly where there will be maximum oxygen and little smoke along the floor. But don't take too long. Those Chinese learned about fire from their fireworks ancestors. They know how to make it burn."

While she taped Tony to his chair, I was thinking about Ray's monthly data transfer. He got a new monthly encryption key from the phone call to the number DJ left in the restroom. He must have taken the key home and sent the data from there. Probably from his laptop. But we'd never worked out where the lamp fit in. It was still sitting right there on the counter.

I started to sweat. My head was pounding. It felt like my shoulder was on fire, too. I hoped that wasn't a hint of things to come.

DJ's phone dinged from her purse. She stepped back. "Well, boys, my work here is done. Time to go. It's been nice working with you. Bien, *pass auf.*"

Bien stood and growled.

"I don't think he'll chew off too much meat after the flames roll down those stairs. Enjoy." She picked up her gun and bag and walked out through the slider. Bien never took his eyes off us.

I said, "I'm getting pretty weak, Tony. Don't think I can rock the chair."

We heard a loud whoosh upstairs. In a moment, we could hear crackling as the accelerant caused things to burst into flames.

Bien turned his head to look at the slider, then back at us.

Tony said, "I think the dog is gonna get upset if I start moving. But we don't have much time. Let me see if I can walk the chair back to you and get a hand on your arm tape."

Using his toes, he was able to wobble the chair a little bit and started turning it to slide alongside me. Bien growled, then barked once. I was sure that was a warning to sit still. But Tony kept at it.

"Maybe he'll bite the duct tape off my leg."

"Probably wouldn't stop at the tape, though."

He got his chair next to mine and tried to reach the tape binding my arm. But his thumb was on the inside of his chair arm. He couldn't reach the tape.

Smoke began to drift down the stairs. It wasn't long before we could see flames burning the carpet on the steps. I was beginning to feel drowsy.

Bien danced around and whined, glancing from us to the smoke.

"Buck, we have to push our chairs over now. The fire is sucking the oxygen out of here. Use your toes and tip back as much as possible. I'll try to knock you over."

I leaned back. Pain shot through my shoulder. I thought my head might explode. If I went over backwards, my head would be the first to hit the floor. I tried to turn sideways to Tony, but he suddenly rammed me and pushed me over. The corner of the chair took most of the fall.

Bien didn't like that. He grabbed my left leg and began pulling, dragging me across the floor. Tony took the opportunity to tip himself over, but he landed on me. We were stacked together now with Tony on top. Too much for Bien to pull, so he started prancing around, chewing at clothes, shoes, arms, or legs. It wasn't clear if he was attacking us or trying to get us away from the fire. Right now, though, he was chewing on my calf, clearly not trying to save me.

From somewhere I heard a screech. Bien released my leg. I could see him through the legs of Tony's chair. Chester was clinging to Bien's face as Bien shook his head back and forth. He finally bent down, and pawed Chester off. Blood dripped down Bien's face where Chester's claws had dug in.

Chester let out a blood-curdling cat yell as if to tell Bien to back off. Bien stood there, looking at us, then back at Chester. After a few moments, he sat down and began panting.

The smoke was building. The stairs were fully engulfed and now the sofa began to burn. I wondered if there was anything toxic in Tony's office. Maybe the smoke would kill us before the fire burned us up.

My pains were starting to fade along with my vision. I figured I'd pass out soon.

Tony said, "Stay with me. I'm working on it. I looked down at his left hand. He was working the arm of the chair back and forth, trying to break it off. In my feeble brain, I tried to calculate how long it would take him versus how long we had to live. I didn't think the odds were in our favor.

I closed my eyes. The smoke was making them sting and water. There was another, small whoosh, and the flames on the couch shot to the ceiling. There were some other scraping noises and then I heard someone coughing.

Tony's chair suddenly lifted off me. A gray shadow worked at his arms, then his legs, cutting him free. The two of them stood my chair up and cut me loose. Something in my brain was yelling at me, telling me we needed the lamp. As Tony picked me up, I whispered. "Get the lamp. On the counter." I wasn't sure he heard me as he lifted me over his shoulder and carried me out the front door.

Gretchen opened the back door of his truck and Tony slid me inside. She and Tony climbed in, and we drove out onto the street. Three blocks down, we pulled into a fire station. In a couple of minutes, they had me on a gurney with oxygen.

Gretchen came over and took my hand. "Hey. They're gonna give you something for the pain. I'll be there when you wake up."

Something cold coursed up my good arm. I realized it was the drug as everything went black.

CHAPTER 24

Tuesday, May 9

The smell of antiseptic filled my nose. I forced my eyes open. It was dark outside. Something was beeping behind me, keeping time with my pulse.

It was a hospital room. Not unexpected. There was a tube of some kind stuck under my nose. I couldn't remember the medical term for that. Can of something?

I coughed. Someone jumped up from the chair in the corner. Gretchen walked over.

"Hi."

I smiled. "Hi yourself."

"How are you feeling?"

"Groggy." I glanced at my arm where a tube disappeared under a square of tape. "Drugs?"

"Yeah. They wanted you to keep still for a while."

"How long?"

She smiled.

I never noticed what perfect white teeth she had.

"A while. You're gonna be fine. Let me text Tony. He went to the cafeteria for coffee."

"Can I have some?"

"Coffee? Not yet. Just water

"Did you grow up a fighter?"

"Muy Thai since I was six. Protection from four older brothers."

"I don't have a chance."

"No, you don't." She laughed.

She was pretty when she laughed.

Tony came in. "Hey, champ, how you feeling?"

"Kinda high. Groggy. Must kinda be out of my mind."

"Why is that?"

"I was just thinking Gretchen is pretty."

Tony said, "She is."

Gretchen held up two fingers. "That's two."

I tried to shrug. My left shoulder wouldn't move.

Tony held my water cup, and I took a few sips. "Tastes good."

I looked at Gretchen. "I bet your lips taste good, too."

"What?"

Tony bent over laughing. Gretchen was laughing, too, but she was trying to pretend to be mad. It wasn't working, though.

The door flew open and a woman in bluish scrubs walked in. "What's going on in here? I see sleeping beauty has awakened."

"Sleeping beauty? I'm glad someone appreciates me."

She jerked a thumb towards Tony and Gretchen. "These two cranks sure aren't going to bestow any praise your way."

I looked at their surprised faces, and said, "They're lost without their leader."

"Yeah, that's been obvious." She put a stethoscope on my chest and told me to take a deep breath.

When she was done, she said, "You want some crackers? A little broth? Gotta go light today."

"Definitely hungry. I'll take whatever you have."

"I'll be back in a minute."

"I have to go to the bathroom."

"Go ahead. You've got a catheter hooked to a bag on your bed."

I glanced down but couldn't see the bag.

Gretchen was giggling.

"What?"

"Sorta takes away from that macho image, doesn't it."

The nurse came back, opened a package of crackers, and handed them to me. "I'll be back in ten minutes to check on you." She turned to Tony and Gretchen. "He needs to rest. You go home and get some sleep yourselves. Come back tomorrow. He'll be off the meds and not so saucy."

I put a cracker in my mouth and munched. The nurse handed me the water cup. After I swallowed, I took a sip of water.

Tony came over and took my hand. "Glad to see you're doing so well, Buck. I'll see you tomorrow."

Gretchen stepped in. She leaned over and kissed my forehead.

"You missed."

"What?"

I pointed to my lips.

"Pleasant dreams, Buck."

They walked out.

CHAPTER 25

Wednesday, May 10

Apparently, the hospital had stopped the drugs. My shoulder was painful, and there was no position where I could make it quit aching. It was annoying. My head was sore where they'd Steri-Stripped the gash together, but I awoke with only a moderate headache.

Before I could push the call button, a doctor came in with a resident and nurse in tow. They took out the catheter and asked that I try going to the bathroom. I was relieved to see everything still worked.

I was steadier on my feet than I expected. I walked back from the bathroom on my own and climbed back into the bed. "When can I go home?

"Probably tomorrow. We need to make sure you've fully flushed all the drugs from your system. That can take twenty-four hours or so."

"Could it be early tomorrow? I have finals at Portland State Monday, and I sure don't want to miss them. I graduate this term."

He glanced at the resident, then the nurse. "Buck, I think Portland State has already dismissed classes. You've been asleep for a few days."

"What? What day is it?"

"This is Wednesday. You've been under sedation since Friday."

"Wednesday? Are you kidding? I've been here five days? I missed my finals." As I said that, Tony and Gretchen walked in.

Tony said, "It's okay. All taken care of."

"What do you mean?"

He held up his hand. "Let's wait until the doc is finished."

The resident took my vitals, which seemed kind of silly since they were clearly displayed on the monitor behind me. Then he listened to my heart and lungs. I had to sit up while I took deep breaths and he listened from my back. It made me a little light-headed and I closed my eyes when I laid back down.

Apparently, I drifted asleep for a few minutes. When I woke, the doctor and his team were gone. Tony and Gretchen sat looking at their phones.

"I'm baaaack."

They both stood and came to my bedside.

"I guess that crack on my head made me weak."

Gretchen smiled. "You were already weak."

Tony said, "You two can bicker later. We have some things to discuss." He pulled their chairs over next to my bed and they sat down.

I raised my bed into a semi-sitting position and took a few sips of water.

Tony handed me a laminated menu. "You better order your breakfast before you miss it."

I scanned the menu items, read the instructions for ordering, and placed the order from the bedside phone. "You guys want anything?"

"Extra coffee," said Gretchen. "We ate at Elmer's."

When I hung up, Tony made a face with his lower lip up over his upper lip. I'd seen it a few times before when he was really stressed or had something important to discuss. Like when he told me my parents had been killed. It was always bad news. I felt my stomach lurch. "Okay. You have that face, Tony. Go ahead, I'm ready."

"Well, it's not all bad. But our house did burn down."

I stared at him. "I forgot it was on fire."

"Yeah. They saved the adjacent apartment building because they weren't connected. So just our place."

"Where are we going to live now?"

Gretchen said, "At my place. At least until you find something better."

I looked at Tony. He nodded. "I've been staying there since the fire. She's been really gracious. And she's a better cook than either of us."

I wanted to say something clever, but this was serious. We didn't have a home anymore. All my stuff was gone.

"What about the lamp? The one from the Chesters' house. Did you ever figure that out?"

Gretchen said, "It's in the back of Tony's truck. I grabbed it off the counter on the way out of the house."

"Why is it important?" asked Tony.

I waved my hand. "We'll get back to it. Tell me the rest."

"DJ got away. We think she was picked up at our place and driven to a dock in Florence."

"Good 'ole Florence. It's popped up a lot lately."

"Vikram tells me they think she was picked up by a boat. The Siuslaw River empties into the ocean there. Tons of private docks. She and her driver. Mendoza."

"Mendoza? She was the leak in the Marshal's office?"

"Apparently. Internal affairs read her in on their investigation and enlisted her help in vetting others. Perfect cover for her."

"Is there someone higher up in the CIA or other feds that is on the take, got her assigned to the investigation?"

"Unknown. But a question Vikram has already posed. And we probably identified the woman who bugged our house."

"Are we safe now? Will they send someone else?"

"I don't think so. They think they destroyed the documents you snagged from the Chesters', and that the HyperBit information was included. So DJ gets rewarded for doing her job. And there are no murder charges against her."

"I'm glad about that for our sakes. But won't there be espionage charges?"

Tony shrugged. "Those kinds of things are buried inside the government. We'll never know if they go after her. Or if they find her. But I think she's gone. For good."

Tony glanced at Gretchen.

I said, "There's more?"

Gretchen said. "We missed our finals."

"I know. What do we do about that?"

She glanced at Tony. He said, "Go ahead. It's your story."

"Well, I went to campus Monday. I had three finals scheduled. At least I thought I did. At the first one, the professor kicked me out. He said I'd somehow been attending his class all semester but wasn't really registered. He wouldn't let me sit for the exam.

"I marched over to the registrar's office, mad as hell. They'd erased me, Buck. I wasn't in their records. Never attended any classes. Was never admitted. Completely gone."

I stared at her for a minute, trying to comprehend what she was saying and how this could be. "HyperBit," I said. "They hacked Portland State's systems. Did you get it fixed?"

"No."

Tony said, "Even with Vikram's help, the records are gone."

"Backups?"

"They hacked those, too."

"So, what now?"

"I have to start over."

"That's crazy. You did all the work, attended all the classes. Don't you have some emails from them. Grade reports?"

"All gone. They cleaned my email of every trace. Texts, too."

"How can they do that? Tony?"

"It takes a lot of coordinated effort, but it's not really that hard. You just need know how."

"Can't you do something, Tony? Recover her data? You have to fix it."

"I'm sorry, Buck. I tried. Vikram tried. My boss tried. HyperBit was thorough and ruthless." He scrunched up his face and I realized he was holding back tears.

Gretchen reached over and took my hand. I looked at her, then at our hands. "That's not all. They erased you, too, Buck."

CHAPTER 26

Thursday, May 11

We arrived at Gretchen's place just before noon. She and
Tony had purchased some clothes for me. I sported a new gray
sweatshirt and a pair of black sweatpants with my black Hokas.

Gretchen's place had only two bedrooms, each with its own
bath. She'd made space in her bedroom for me. There were other
clothes for me in a small section of her closet. And she'd cleared two
drawers from her dresser. New t-shirts, underwear, and socks took
up most of one.

I looked at the other empty drawer for a while. It was a lot
like my life now. No college degree. No plans for the future. Part of
my life erased. I wanted to get back at HyperBit. Destroy them. But
meanwhile, I needed a job. Income. We needed to find a new house
or live in Tony's hideaway. Either way, we needed income.

From the door, Gretchen said, "Lost in your empty box?"

I sat down on the bed. My left shoulder, still in a sling, ached.
"I seem to have a lot of empty boxes these days."

"You're alive, Buck. Could have been much worse."

She was right. Still, this adventure had turned into a
nightmare. Tony had warned me about the risk. I was naive and
never seriously considered what the consequences could be. And as
for Gretchen, my cavalier attitude about risk and danger to myself
was bad enough. I'd erased years of her work and her degree. Those
were way more important to me than my own life. I'd let people

down who I cared about. Made selfish, childish decisions without recognizing how bad it could be.

"I'm sorry I dragged you into this, Gretchen."

She scoffed. "I came willingly. You know by now that I make my own decisions. It wasn't your fault."

"We were amateurs trying to play in the big league. And we got burned."

"Yes. Some."

"What about our degrees?"

"I'm not sure. First, we need to get you healed up. Then figure out a plan. See what comes next."

"What about Tony? He lost all his equipment, his office. What's he going to do?"

"He talked about working from your place in the woods, but he said the geography is a problem over the long haul. Not sure what he meant."

"The lamp?"

"In Tony's room."

Chester came into the room, jumped on the bed, and walked onto my lap. I petted him and he began to purr and rub against my hand.

"Thanks for saving him. And me. And Tony. What happened to…" I turned to look up at Gretchen in the doorway. A large black head next to her thigh was looking into the room. "Bien. You got him too."

"Of course." She patted him on the head. He looked up at her. She looked at the dog.

"Bien, *beh voraus.*" She waved an arm towards me. Bien walked over and stared at Chester, who was now lying in my lap. Bien glanced up at me and licked his lips.

I wondered if that meant Chester looked tasty, or it was a more general indication that he saw lots to eat.

He took a couple of steps and sniffed my leg where he had bitten down and dragged me across the floor. There were a few puncture marks, but he'd barely broken the skin.

I said, "Do you think he would be okay if I petted his head?"

"It's your hand."

I moved my hand toward Bien. Somewhere, I'd been told to let a dog smell your hand before you tried to pet it. Now, I thought that advice maybe meant it would give the dog a good target if they were going to bite you.

Bien raised his head and looked at my hand hovering in front of him. He glanced at me, then leaned towards it and licked his lips again.

I didn't need another wound. Maybe I should put my hand back on Chester. Or under Chester. Let him guard my hands. But it was too late.

Bien leaned forward and licked my hand. I felt myself tearing up. It was a weird moment. Chester stood and began rubbing against my arm. Bien looked up at me and held my stare for a few seconds before he looked away.

I slowly moved my hand over his head and patted him a couple of times. He started panting. I scratched a little behind one ear. He cocked his head to the side, leaning into my hand. I tried the other ear. He cocked his head to that side. A couple more pets and I put my hand back in my lap. Bien put his head down on my leg. Tears dribbled down my cheeks. I felt stupid and had no idea why I was crying.

Gretchen sat down on the bed behind me and wrapped her arms around me. Pain shot through my shoulder, but I gritted my teeth. I wasn't about to complain about a hug from her.

"It's okay, Buck. Everything's gonna be okay."

I put my good hand over hers. "Thanks, Gretchen. Thanks for being my friend."

"Remember that when you're sleeping in my bed."

"Friends with benefits?"

"Do you know the German word for bite?"

Tony stuck his head in the room. "Sorry for interrupting. I see Bien remembers his training from the hospital."

Gretchen stood up and moved away.

"What training?"

"Gretchen got permission to bring him in while you were out. She worked with him to accept you."

I looked at Gretchen. Her face had turned red. I said, "And here I thought I was just communing with his dog soul."

"Equals meet," she said.

Tony held up his phone. "I'm running to the grocery store. Anything I should add to my list?"

"Dog food," I said, and laughed.

His phone rang. He looked at it for a moment, then answered. After listening for thirty seconds, he said, "That's fine." He hung up. "Meeting here at 2:00 p.m. with Vikram." He looked at me. "Maybe you want to take a nap."

"Tony, did I say anything offensive while I was in the hospital?"

He laughed. "I guess it depends on your perspective. You were out of it for several days. Some gibberish and stuff we won't repeat. Just have to consider the drugs and their effect." He waved a hand towards Gretchen. "I think she gave you a pass."

* * *

Vikram was by himself. We sat around the table. He wore a white turban today. I thought his beard had been trimmed since I last saw him, but I couldn't be sure. That puzzled me because I didn't think Sikhs were allowed to cut their hair or beard. As I looked closer, his whole face seemed to be thinner. There were dark circles under his eyes.

I said, "Vikram, I apologize if this is too personal, but are you well? You look thinner."

He nodded. "Thank you for asking, Buck. At first, I was concerned that I had been poisoned, but it was just stomach flu. I am much better now."

"That's awful. I hope your family didn't get it."

"I believe it is they who gave it to me." He sighed and glanced around the room, his face growing sober. "In this line of work, we have many secrets. It is difficult to keep them all hidden. Sometimes, one may escape like smoke into the wind. We can never be sure who will notice it.

"In my case, someone within the U.S. Marshals figured out that I really worked for the CIA. We think it was Mendoza. It's not clear why the HyperBit assassins targeted my garage. They may have thought I had the Chesters' evidence, or they may have decided I was a threat to their mole. In any case, I survived, and their mole is gone."

Tony said, "I've been at this a while, you know. Although they burned my office and destroyed all my equipment, I have my data backup offsite on my own servers. They looked for cloud backup or storage, but all they found was my regular backup."

I said, "So you still have the documents?"

He nodded. "DJ was right. I scanned them. And she destroyed my backup. One of them. Once I get a new laptop, I'll retrieve them and send them to Vikram."

"That is excellent," said Vikram. "With those design documents, we hope to keep track of HyperBit's mines. We think the Chinese are the ones who really want the mines. They're using HyperBit as a cover, though HyperBit doesn't seem to know that."

"What about the flash drive with HyperBit personnel information," said Gretchen.

"Gone in the fire," said Tony.

I said, "That's too bad. We could have used it to take out most of HyperBit. If we could have decrypted it. But we still have the Chesters' lamp."

"What lamp?" Vikram asked.

"Gone in the fire," Tony said.

Gretchen said the lamp was in Tony's room. I looked at him, about to object. I looked over at Gretchen. Stonefaced. I kept quiet.

"There are a couple more 'secrets,'" Tony said making air quotes with his fingers.

Gretchen cleared her throat. She folded her hands on the table and stared at them. "Buck, Vikram and Tony already know this, but I've been in WITSEC since I was ten years old. Because of who my family was. Vikram, the CIA agent who doubles as a U.S. Marshal, was my contact."

I stared at Gretchen, completely dumbfounded. "How…" I didn't know what to say.

"I grew up in Germany until I was ten and was then relocated to California."

"That's why you speak German."

She laughed. "That's your first reaction?"

"I have a lot of questions. Like why?"

Tony said, "Let's hold those for the moment, please. There's another thing you need to know." He shifted in his chair and glanced at Vikram.

"Buck, you and I are in WITSEC, too. We have been since before you were born."

Maybe my ears failed me. He couldn't have said what I think I heard.

He nodded. "I know it's hard to believe. You probably think I should have told you earlier. But you had to be old enough to handle and understand the risks."

"Are you serious?"

"Yes."

"Mom and Dad. Did they know?"

"They're why we're in WITSEC."

Vikram said, "Your parents both worked for the CIA. In fact, they met there. When your mother got pregnant with you, it became too dangerous for them to continue. So, they were put in WITSEC."

"What, you're telling me they were spies or something?"

Tony said, "More or less. After WITSEC, your dad taught at the Naval Academy. Your mom worked part-time at a law office."

I nodded. "We lived in that little white house in the suburbs of Annapolis." I felt overwhelmed with the wave of new information. Who Tony was, who my parents were. Who I was.

"Why'd we move to Portland?"

Tony looked at Vikram. Vikram said, "Your parents' death might not have been accidental."

"You mean, it might have been a hit?"

"We could never determine any link to be sure. But it's possible. So you were moved to Portland as a precaution."

I looked at Tony. "Did you really retire when we moved here?"

"No. I continued to work for FinCEN. But I retired four years ago. Occasionally do contract work for them."

Talking about my parents made me miss them even more. Tony was my only remaining link to them. And he…"Did you work with Mom and Dad? I mean as spies, or whatever they did?"

"Let me answer a different question. I went into WITSEC when they retired because I was your dad's brother. I was the only living family they had before you came along. It seemed the retaliation risk to me was high enough to warrant the WITSEC route. Not because of my work, but because of theirs, and I was related to them."

Vikram said, "There is an orientation program you could attend. It will answer many questions about WITSEC."

"Waste of time," said Gretchen. "Plus, it's dangerous. Somebody gets the attendance list, and you're compromised." She looked at me. "I'll teach you what you need to know. Besides, you've already been in the program your whole life."

I said, "Did DJ or Mendoza know?"

"No," said Vikram.

I looked around at the people sitting at the table. Everyone had secrets. Even me. Secrets I hadn't known about. "Any more? I'm not sure how much I can absorb." My headache wasn't just from my shoulder now.

Tony and Gretchen shook their heads. Vikram said, "I've looked into the data wipe they did on your education records. We could probably get the university to confer degrees anyhow, but there is a considerable risk. If some overzealous reporter got hold of the story about wiping your records, it could be big news. News you don't want. Attention you don't want. I think your only viable alternative is to move on."

Gretchen said, "I need to go to the gym so I can punch some stuff." She glanced at me.

"Great idea…about the gym."

Vikram said, "I almost forgot. The manager at the cannabis dispensary was the link to how the toxin-laced cannabis got into the deliveries. He vanished the day DJ disappeared. We investigated his background. It was all fabricated, probably by HyperBit. He started work there a month after the Chesters moved here."

"Gage was a spy? I thought he was just high all the time."

"He chartered a seaplane, but we haven't been able to track that down yet."

"Did he get on the boat with DJ?"

"No, he was still at the dispensary. He didn't leave until an hour later."

"Maybe he's dead. Job completed. Don't need him. Don't want him to talk."

"You watch too many movies, Buck," Tony said.

* * *

In bed that night, I closed my eyes and thought about all the new realities from today.

On the one hand, nothing much had changed. Tony and I would go on living like we had been. On the other hand, I had to find a job, figure out what to do, decide what, if anything, I could do about my degree. My first reaction was revenge on HyperBit for taking away my degree. But Gretchen had pointed out that college was supposed to be about learning. We'd certainly done that. And we'd proved we could use a lot of what we'd learned, too.

Gretchen had similar issues, and I wasn't sure what our relationship was now. We certainly weren't going to be lab partners anymore. They say surviving life-threatening situations together forms a bond of camaraderie, like soldiers fighting together in battle. As a WITSEC person, I could see why she would be reticent to develop personal relationships. She couldn't risk sharing her secret because they might let it slip, accidentally, or even on purpose if the relationship ended badly. But if she kept it a secret, then the relationship already had some built-in lies that could rot the relationship from within.

It occurred to me that the same applied to me. Always had. I just hadn't known before.

The bed shifted. I had nearly drifted off, but I opened my eyes to see Gretchen sitting on the edge of the bed with her back towards me.

"Buck, I want to show you something." She lifted her black T-shirt above her shoulders. That red scar I'd glimpsed ran most of the way down her back. It was more than a foot long.

She let her shirt fall back down, then turned out the lights and slid into bed next to me.

"You ever see the TV show *American Ninja Warrior?*"

"Yeah."

"I used to compete. Hit the buzzer five times in qualifying rounds. Once in semifinals. But never made it to the finals."

I figured anything I said might interrupt her confession in the dark, so I stayed quiet.

"I fell. Instead of falling straight down into water, I went off the side. Landed on my back, along a metal strut sticking out from the equipment. They had to fuse my back. All twelve thoracic vertebrae."

"Did you sue them?"

"No. Signed a waiver beforehand. But they paid all my medical bills."

"I'm sorry, Gretchen."

"Ended my ability to compete. Ended Muay Thai for me, too."

We were quiet for a long moment.

"Do you miss it?"

"Yes."

"I'm sorry."

"Thanks."

"Accidents change a lot of lives," she said.

"Yeah. Chance. Risk. Timing. Life's like a roller coaster in a dark building—you never know when a twist or turn is coming. Look at us. A couple of WITSEC kids were put together in a project group. Complete random chance."

"Nearly got us both killed, too."

She was silent again. This time she waited me out.

I said, "What are you thinking about?"

"What now? I mean, they took away my life direction. And I was already on a re-route."

"I'm so sorry I got you into this, Gretchen."

"Stop saying that. I make my choices." She was quiet for another moment, then said, "I have an idea.

"This investigation thing we did about the Chesters' getting poisoned—we made a lot of mistakes, but we stayed alive, and we solved the case. Pretty good for amateurs."

"True. Some credit goes to Tony, too," I said.

"Agreed. I was thinking maybe we could do that again. But get paid."

"You mean like private investigators?"

"Yeah. We've got a reference now. Might even get some leads from the fed friends we've made."

I thought about Copeland and Gonzalez, the Beaverton police guys I'd first met at the Chesters'. And Vikram. And the guys at the sheriff's office where I used to intern. It wasn't a bad idea. Tony could be our silent partner and back-office hacker. "Interesting idea," I said. "Would I have to get shot again?"

"You didn't get shot. You got a splinter."

"A foot-long splinter that went clear through my shoulder. Compares better to 'shot' than to 'splinter.'"

I thought about her broken back. "How long were you in the hospital?"

"In and out for a year. Five surgeries. Despite the waivers I had to sign, Akbar, one of the American Ninja Warrior show hosts, went to bat for me. He was the first by my side when I fell and wouldn't let anyone move me until the paramedics put me on a backboard. He held my head in place during that move. Probably saved my life. Certainly kept me from being paralyzed."

She turned on the lamp next to the bed and snapped the bracelet on her left wrist. "He came to the hospital. Gave me this. Knew I'd be angry. It's supposed to help release my anger instead of hitting something." She held up her wrist so I could see the bracelet. It had an engraved plate that said Fearless.

"Does it work?"

"Sometimes." She smiled.

She'd been through a lot. Still, I knew very little about her. I wondered why she'd chosen now to tell me about her back. Was it because we were both in WITSEC?

"Did you tell me about your back now to soften me up for the private investigator thing?"

"Maybe."

"Let's say you did. Using your back injury to get me to agree with you—I think that's called manipulation. I'm seeing the real Gretchen now."

"You think you're clever. Even amused by your own cleverness. But that's a cover so you don't have to put yourself out there and be honest or vulnerable."

"I see a pattern. You tease me, then when I react, you punch me, verbally or physically. Do I want to go into business with that kind of relationship?"

"It's the best relationship you've ever had. Besides, I'm already sleeping with you."

I laughed. "Not really. Maybe physically, but not like that implies."

"You mean we're not having sex."

"Yes."

"You're right. We're not. Can you put it back in your pants so we can talk business?"

I was confused. Surely there was logic in her comments, even though they bounced around like a pinball. Okay, I admit, I keep throwing in jokes and innuendos and that probably clouds things for both of us. I blamed testosterone and a near-naked girl lying next to me.

I sighed. "Okay. I'm interested in the private investigator thing. Let's talk about it with Tony."

"Good. Thank you."

I shifted over to my right side and propped my head on my right hand looking at Gretchen.

She said, "What are you doing?"

"I'm looking at you."

"Well stop it. I don't like people staring at me." She turned out the lamp.

"But I can't see you. I keep trying, but you won't let me."

"Buck, the lights are off."

"I'm being metaphorical. Or philosophical. Maybe both."

"Just say it."

"You shut me out, Gretchen. From the day we started working on our first project, you made it clear that it was business only. You've reminded me many times since then. I still know almost nothing about you."

She was silent for a moment. "I just showed you my back. I don't do that. I've been a loner for a long time. It's natural to me now. Until you and Tony came along, I didn't know anyone else in WITSEC."

"Makes sense. You didn't know who you could trust."

"No. I knew I couldn't trust anyone. Ever."

"Now?"

"I'm working on it."

ACKNOWLEDGMENTS

When I write a story, I like to make the location and setting as accurate as feasible. I hope that most of my Portland, Oregon information is consistent with the real world. Of course, there are some creative elements required. It is, after all, a work of fiction.

Buck originally delivered cannabis on a bicycle, but that is illegal in Oregon. The electric scooter is likely questionable, but it gets closer to the legal definition of a motorized vehicle and met the needs of the fictional story.

Thanks to my beta readers, Druanne Kendrick, Ashley Dorros, and Catherine Pfeffer. Special thanks to Hannah Anderson for her deep read and scrub that cleaned up so much.

Thanks to my son, Brandon Cooper, who provided the insight into the cannabis business in Portland, Oregon. You didn't think I knew decarboxylation converts inert THCA to psychoactive THC, did you?

Thanks to Cathy Hull for her usual superb editing, feedback, and comments.

You can find more information about my writing on my website at www.terryrcooper.com. Look for a new novel in summer, 2024.

Thanks to my wife for allowing me the time to write, edit, and publish my novels. She is forever supportive of my writing endeavor.

ABOUT THE AUTHOR

Terry Cooper grew up on a dairy farm in southern Ohio where he gazed at the stars and dreamed of being an astronaut. Not far from that dream, he became an aerospace engineer and information technology manager whose forty-year career included multiple black projects for the U. S. federal government. He holds Bachelor's and Master's degrees in Computer and Information Science from The Ohio State University, and a Master's in Business Administration from Loyola Marymount University (Los Angeles). He studied under Raymond Obstfeld through classes at Orange Coast College, seminars, writing retreats, and personal coaching. He currently lives in Cincinnati with his wife and boasts four adult children and nine grandchildren. His self-built, soundproof music room is home to his guitars and writing cave. His webpage can be found at www.terryrcooper.com.